ZANE’S CHC

The Doms of Club Mystique 4

Mardi Maxwell

EROTIC ROMANCE

Siren Publishing, Inc.
www.SirenPublishing.com

A SIREN PUBLISHING BOOK
IMPRINT: Erotic Romance

ZANE'S CHOICE

ISBN: 978-1-63258-467-0

First Printing: December 2014

Cover design by Harris Channing

Printed in the U.S.A.

PUBLISHER
Siren Publishing, Inc.
www.SirenPublishing.com

DEDICATION

For the dreamers who choose love.

ZANE'S CHOICE

The Doms of Club Mystique 4

MARDI MAXWELL

Prologue

Sunday, September 15

Ravyn Dolman reminded herself that she was Ravyn Templeton since the divorce, then gave herself a pep talk and followed Addison Ramsey into her husband's den. A few steps ahead of her, Addison waved her hand in a conjuring motion, then laughed and said, "Cade, guess who's here? Zane's friend, Ravyn!"

Ravyn could almost hear the silent "ta da," at the end of that statement and she wondered once again if she was being played by the tiny Irish beauty. While pondering that possibility, she managed to keep a smile on her face as she took note of the people gathered in the room. When Addison grabbed her hand, she flinched then let her pull her toward a desk to their left.

Addison sent her a small grin then stepped away from her. "The press is giving her a really hard time, so I invited her to hide out with us for a few weeks. Isn't that right, Ravyn?"

"Yes, and I appreciate the invitation." Ravyn smiled as a large man, who looked remarkably like Zane Ramsey, stood up and stepped around the desk.

"Ravyn, this is my husband, Cade."

Ravyn watched the exchange between the couple closely. Addison slid her arm around Cade's waist and smiled up at him but he sent her a little frown before he suddenly looked amused then extended his hand toward her. "You're welcome to stay as long as you like, Mrs. Dolman."

She couldn't prevent the small shudder of distaste that swept through her at the mention of her ex-husband's name. "Templeton now, Mr. Ramsey. I've taken my mother's maiden name since my divorce, but please call me Ravyn."

Addison laughed. "If you're going to call them all Mr. Ramsey, it's going to get confusing quicker than usual around here."

"Addison has a good point, Ravyn, so I insist you call me Cade."

His voice sounded friendly but the look in his eyes was intense, as if he was seeing into her and discovering her secrets. Ravyn tried to meet his eyes, failed, and instead pretended to do a quick survey of the room. There were three other men present who looked like Zane, and then a huge man with long blond hair who reminded her of a Viking, and two other men, one with dark-brown hair and blue eyes, and one with sun-bleached blond hair and brown eyes. "Zane told me he had a large family."

Addison laughed. "Oh, yes, very large, and I have to warn you—we're all meddlers."

A woman with chin-length platinum hair stood up and joined them. "Speak for yourself, Addison. I'm Jenna Parnelle, and I'm definitely not a meddler." She waved her hand toward the dark-haired man whose lap she had just vacated. "This is my fiancé, Jackson Ramsey."

Ravyn smiled. She'd wondered about these women ever since Zane had told her about them, and they were exactly as she'd imagined them. "It's a pleasure to meet you, Jenna." She looked up at Jackson as he moved behind Jenna and cupped her slender shoulders with large hands. "Zane has mentioned all of you so often I feel I know you."

To her left, the last of Zane's brothers, the twins in the family, stood up. The small, golden blonde between them stepped toward her with a challenging look on her face. "I'm Cassie Edwards." She pointed to the man on her left. "This is my fiancé Luc Ramsey"—then she pointed to the man on her right—"and my fiancé Logan Ramsey."

"Congratulations on your engagement," Ravyn said, then smiled and received a smile in return from the three of them. She looked toward the last three men in the room. The huge blond approached her and held out his hand.

"Ravyn, I'm Thor Larkin. Cade and I are partners in The Larkin Agency," he said in a deep voice that resonated through her. He flicked his thumb at the last two men in the room. "These two jokers are Mac Malone and Ben Harrington. They work for Cade and me when they aren't gambling and drinking."

"Hey, boss, don't forget the 'chasing women' part," the tall, sable-haired man with blue eyes said as he stepped forward and smiled down at her. "In case you didn't catch my name, I'm Mac. I know how hard it can be to get back in the dating scene after a divorce and I'd like to help you with that, darlin'. How do you feel about spankings?"

Before she could answer him, the sandy-haired man with brown eyes shouldered him away. "You don't ask that yet, Mac. You wait until after the first date." He smiled down at her. "I'm Ben Harrington. Do you like to dance, honey?"

Ravyn laughed, but before she could say yes or no, the sound of the front door slamming followed by heavy footsteps hurrying toward the den drew everyone's attention to the open doorway. A moment later, Zane Ramsey appeared. His black hair was mussed as if he'd shoved his hands through it a dozen times, and his black suit jacket was rumpled and hung open. His leaf-green eyes blazed with rage and she wanted to slip behind Thor or Mac, or even Ben for protection. Instead, she lifted her chin and dared him to do his worst. He took one step into the room before his eyes zeroed in on her.

"You can't be here, Ravyn. This puts me in an impossible position."

Ravyn rested a graceful hand on her hip. "Well, hello to you, too, lover."

Zane cursed, then stalked toward her. Without pausing, he clenched his fist in the hair at her nape, then curved her into him until their noses were almost touching.

The heat from his body sent a shiver of arousal through her. "Let go, Zane."

"You need to leave, Ravyn. Now."

"No. I'm hiding from the press and everyone else who wants to put me behind bars—people like you."

"Dammit, Ravyn. I told you I would protect you."

"No, you didn't. You said you would get me the best deal you could if I would turn state's evidence." She tried to move away, but he tightened his hand and pulled her head farther back while curving her pelvis against his. His erection pressed into her belly and she breathed a swift sigh of relief at the proof that he still wanted her.

"I told you from the beginning if you were guilty, I wouldn't lie for you," Zane said, the words gritted out between clenched teeth.

"Then you shouldn't have fucked me." Ravyn reached up and tried to pry his fingers from her hair. "Let go, Zane."

"This time you've gone too far. Be still or I'll beat your ass."

"You can't. You're the one who set the limits of our relationship." She gave up trying to pry his hand loose then lowered her voice. "You said fucking only. Nothing else."

"Tell me the truth, then—tell me what you know and I'll help you."

"Nothing. I don't know anything."

"You lie to me and then you question why I won't—" He pulled her head back until the tendons in her neck stood out. "Just don't lie to me again. It really pisses me off."

Ravyn glanced to her right and saw that everyone's attention was focused on them. "Zane, let go. Everyone's watching."

"Don't mind us," Cade said. "You'd be surprised how often something like this happens around here lately."

Zane shot a dirty look toward the room's occupants, then focused on her again. "Everyone out."

Cade picked Addison up, then settled in the chair behind his desk and smiled. Addison grinned at Zane, then snuggled into Cade, letting him know they were staying.

"We may have some information you might be interested in knowing, little brother." Cade smoothed his hand down the length of Addison's braid.

Ravyn glanced at the wall behind Cade's desk and saw a large portrait of him and Addison. In it, Addison was over Cade's shoulder. One of her hands grasped the waistband of his leather pants as she looked down at the camera with a huge smile on her beautiful face. Cade's large hand nearly covered her entire bottom as he held her in place and looked over his shoulder at someone below them. The dark look of passion on their faces was mesmerizing.

That was the way she wanted to be loved. Passionately, as if her death would totally destroy the man who loved her. She glanced at Zane and wondered what he would do if something happened to her. Would he grieve, or would he just move on? Before she could come to a conclusion, the sound of Thor's voice drew her attention away from the portrait and back to the present.

"Better get comfortable, Ravyn." Thor pointed to the chair he'd just vacated. "This is going to take a while."

A soft growl of anger emanated from Zane as he released her hair. She smiled and heard him growl again. Knowing he was as pissed off as she was worried made her feel better about their situation.

Ravyn slid into the chair, then crossed her long, slender legs. The skirt of her wrap dress slid apart and she saw Zane's eyes trace up her legs. He shrugged out of his suit jacket, then loosened his tie and jerked it away. A second later, he dropped his clothing on the seat next to her, then settled onto the arm of her chair and unbuttoned the top two buttons of his white dress shirt. She saw him glance at her lap again and without thinking, she wiggled and the gap in the dress fell farther apart. He sent her a sardonic smile and a blush of unexpected shame heated her cheeks. She adjusted the skirt then rolled his tie into a tight coil. She fussed with it for a moment, then tucked it into one of the jacket pockets before she smoothed her hand over the expensive fabric. When she looked up, the eyes of the room's occupants were on her and Zane, waiting to see what his next move would be. Next to her, he shifted and then squeezed her shoulder. "Are you with us here, princess, or are you off in your rich little world where everything is sunshine and roses?"

Ravyn sat up straighter and crossed her hands on his jacket. "I'm listening, of course, Zane."

He nodded, then looked at Cade. "Okay, let's hear what you have to say."

Cade's sigh of annoyance hissed across the room as he leaned back in his chair. "You're aware that eight years ago Cassie was abducted by three men and held at a house for two days—when I contacted you about going to that house, Zane, we believed it belonged to Ravyn's ex-husband, Charles Dolman."

Ravyn tensed as Cade sent a gentle smile her way. "We know now that the house is actually your family home, Ravyn."

"What the hell are you talking about?" Zane stood up, his stance aggressive as Ravyn cried out, then collapsed back in the chair.

Cade held up his hand. "Just calm down and listen."

Zane cursed then settled back onto the arm of Ravyn's chair. "Go on then, spit it out, but please keep in mind I'm the prosecuting attorney on Dolman's case."

"Cassie was held in a room on the third floor, but she managed to escape once and make it to the first floor. She hid in the den and while she was in there she took a flash drive from the computer. She jammed it in a decorative gold-and-enamel dragon that was on the mantel. A week ago, the drive was retrieved and the room on the third floor was entered."

"Dammit, you promised you wouldn't do that without a search warrant." Zane ran his hands through his hair again, making even more of a mess of it. "Don't tell me anything else."

"I wouldn't have to do shit like this if I'd killed Mendez when I had the chance, or if they'd kept him locked up the way they should have. What kind of judge releases the head of a drug cartel who was caught red-handed, Zane? Tell me that." Cade slammed his fist down on the desk and glared at his youngest brother while he waited for an answer.

When he didn't get one, he reached over and activated the large monitor on the wall, and a recording began to play. "This is a video of the room on the third floor. The pictures on the walls are of the women who were abducted and held in this room over the past fifteen years. The three men in the pictures are Larry Tyson, Leroy Taylor, and Dale Miller. We believe Miller is one of the enforcers for Carlos Mendez's drug cartel and that Mendez ordered him to kill Tyler and Taylor, as well as Cassie's father, Ryan Edwards."

"Go on," Zane said.

"This girl"—Cade pointed to a picture of a young girl with short, curly hair—"is Shelly Kyle. She was the daughter of John Kyle, the president of the Long Valley Bank. She disappeared fifteen years ago."

"I remember when she disappeared," Zane said. "Wasn't she best friends with Earl Baume's cousin?"

Cade nodded. "We have evidence that her father and Earl Baume were laundering money for Carlos Mendez at the time. Shelly was never found and her father died in an accident a few months after her disappearance. Earl Baume was the police officer who investigated John Kyle's death."

Zane nodded. "He was also the first officer on the scene when our parents died in that car wreck right outside of Long Valley."

"That's right, but what you don't know is that we now have evidence that Earl Baume deliberately ran our parents off the road. Of all these men, only Miller, Charles Dolman, and Mendez are still alive. Dolman is in jail, Mendez is in Colombia, and Miller was apprehended last week when he tried to kidnap Cassie again. He's being interrogated by Thor's people at this time."

Ravyn glanced at Cassie then leaned toward Cade and Thor. "Did my ex-husband kidnap Cassie eight years ago?" She asked the question even though she was afraid she already knew the answer.

Thor joined Cade by the monitor. "We think either your father or ex-husband kidnapped Cassie. They both match the description she's given us. Medium height, slightly overweight, Boston accent."

Zane grasped Ravyn's shoulder and shook it to get her attention. "Don't say anything in front of me, Ravyn. Not one word. Do you understand?"

Ravyn nodded, then clenched her hands on her lap.

Cade turned off the video. "We believe either your father or Dolman began moving drugs and laundering money for Carlos Mendez around fifteen years ago, Ravyn. After your father's death seven years ago, the activity continued. We're trying to prove now that your father wasn't involved and that it was Dolman who had the agreement with Mendez."

"Dolman claims Ravyn's father began the partnership and Ravyn continued it," Zane said. "Can you prove she wasn't involved?"

Cade shook his head. "No. The flash drive has information on it going back nine years. Names of contacts and women who were taken and held, dates of drug deliveries, and bank accounts, but it doesn't indicate who kept the records. We think Dolman began keeping the records as insurance in case Mendez turned on him."

"Or, Ravyn's father began keeping the records for the same reason," Zane said. "Dolman claims that seven years ago, after

Benson's death, Ravyn took over her father's illegal activities. Eight months ago, he realized she was trying to frame him and had already made arrangements for him to be killed. He claims the reason he didn't go to the police is because she has friends in the local, state, and federal agencies. He claims his only choice was to try to kill her first."

Ravyn jumped up and turned to Zane, her hands on her hips. "You damn bastard. You want to believe I'm guilty so you don't have to deal with our relationship." She swiveled on her four-inch stilettos and walked toward the door. "Sorry, Addison. I appreciate the invitation, but I can't stay here."

"Ravyn, if you walk through that door, you'll be sorry," Zane said.

Ravyn turned around and smiled as she backed toward the door, then sent him a one-finger wave as she disappeared into the hall.

Feminine giggles swept around the room as the men cleared their throats and sent him what-are-you-going-to-do-now looks.

Zane began rolling up his sleeves as he stood up and walked toward the door. "We'll be right back."

Ravyn heard his footsteps behind her as she hurried toward the front door. When he grabbed her arm and pulled her around, she shoved him back and then ran for the front door. He caught up to her and wrapped his right arm around her waist, then hoisted her onto his hip and carried her, kicking and screaming, into the dining room. He hooked a chair with his foot, pulled it out, then sat down and pulled her over his lap.

"Don't you dare, you bastard." Ravyn reached back and tried to cover her butt.

In seconds, he had her skirt shoved up around her waist. "You've been begging for this for months." Zane ran his hand over her plump ass, then snapped the strap of the thong that separated her rounded cheeks and laughed when she screamed with rage.

"I have not." She kicked her legs and felt him shove her shoes from her feet before he swept her panties down her legs.

"Yes, you have, and I'm going to give you a taste of what you think you want." He tangled her panties around her ankles, then stroked his hand up the back of her legs to her butt.

Ravyn grabbed the leg of the chair and lifted her torso. Zane hooked one leg over hers, then held her in place by pressing his hand against the small of her back. He stroked his hand over her ass, then squeezed each cheek.

"Be still, pet."

"I'm supposed to have a safe word and a list of limits."

"Pick a safe word, then. Something you wouldn't normally say."

"Guilty." Ravyn screeched when he swatted her ass, hard. "Let me up, damn you."

"You said you wanted to be my sub. Well, I've got news for you, princess. In this house, there are rules for subs and you've just broken several of them." He swatted her rounded ass five times as he talked. "And, you don't air our personal business in front of my family and friends." Zane swatted her another five times, each swat harder than the last while he ignored her screams. "Subs don't cuss in this house." He swatted her five more times. "No disrespecting a Dom in this house, and that goes double for me." Five more swats landed on her ass.

Ravyn sniffled as her tears mixed with her mascara and burned her eyes. She screamed at him to let her up, then blinked her eyes rapidly to clear the sting from them. Zane ignored her as he squeezed her stinging bottom. "Subs don't speak without permission in this house, and they don't give orders. Ever. When they're given permission to speak, they use the correct title to the Dom." He swatted her ass five more times, then ran his fingers over her pussy and pinched her labial lips together before wiggling his finger between them and pressing on her clit. He stroked it a couple times then ran his fingers over her mound. "Subs have bare mounds in this house, and you already listed your limits three weeks ago when I was in your bed fucking you silly."

Ravyn shivered then moaned and couldn't keep her hips from wiggling. "I hate you." She felt him lift his hand and quickly added, "Sir."

Zane laughed. "You hate that you can't control me." He rubbed her ass again, then moved his fingers back to her pussy and her swollen clit. He teased her until she shivered again. "Now, apologize and I'll let you up."

Ravyn thought about it for a moment. "No. You apologize for believing I did all those horrible things." She heard Zane's sigh, then felt his hand slide between her hip and his hard belly. A second later, she realized he was unbuckling his belt. "What are you doing?"

"This is what you said you wanted. Remember? You said you wanted me to take control." He rubbed her ass again. "This is me taking control."

Ravyn moaned as she decided she was beginning to regret the night they'd spoken about a D/s relationship and she'd confessed her fantasies to him. She'd been very explicit, even though they shouldn't have been together at the time. He was right about their affair compromising his position as the Assistant District Attorney in charge of the case against her ex-husband. A feeling of hopelessness swamped her and she slumped over his lap. "I'm sorry, Sir."

"What are you sorry for?" Zane continued to run his hands over her ass cheeks.

"For coming here. For involving your family. For everything." She dried her tears with her free hand and felt Zane pull her panties off her feet and smooth the skirt of her dress over her sore bottom. "What are you doing with my panties?"

"Subs don't wear panties in this house."

"I'm leaving. We shouldn't be seeing each other. I've put you in danger of losing your job."

Zane patted her bottom. "First, I'm going to see what else my brothers and Thor know." He lifted her until she was sitting up on his lap.

"That hurts, Zane," she said, and he chuckled.

"It's supposed to hurt." He slid his hand under her skirt and swiped his finger over her pussy. "It also aroused you." He slid his lips over hers then smiled into her eyes. "You're wet and hot, so don't even try to tell me you don't want me. Right now, I'd love to bend you over this table and fuck you until you scream my name and come all over my cock."

Ravyn shivered with longing then leaned against him and hid her face against his neck. She was so tired of keeping secrets and worrying about what was going to happen. Tired of hiding her tears and being alone. "What I want and what I can have are two different things."

Zane slid his fingers beneath her chin and lifted her face to his before he threaded his fingers into her long mass of raven hair. "Damn you. Even with a red nose, smeared lipstick, and raccoon eyes you're still beautiful." He used his thumb to rub the dark trails of mascara from her cheeks, then surrounded her face with his hands and forced her to look at him. "Tell me one of your secrets."

Ravyn hesitated for a moment as he watched her. If she didn't speak up now, she would lose him forever, but what could she tell him? She knew her ex-husband had laundered money for Mendez. But she hadn't known she was living in a house where he'd held and abused women, although she had no doubts that he was capable of doing something like that. Her attention was drawn back to Zane when he sighed and began to lift her from his lap. She panicked and rushed into speech. "I think Charles had my father killed."

Zane narrowed his eyes at her. "Why would he do that when you claim your father made you marry him?"

"Charles had me but my father wanted my son to inherit the company. He made Charles promise to name our first son Benson after him."

"You were married for eight years. I don't see any kids hanging around."

Ravyn shivered, then buried her face against Zane's neck. "Charles liked it rough. The more I fought him, the better he liked it." She looked up at him. "He left me alone when I quit fighting him." A muscle in Zane's jaw began to pulse and she reached up and ran her finger over it. "Are you mad at me?"

"No." Zane slid her off his lap, then patted her sore bottom, and chuckled when she squeaked with pain. "We better get back in there and see what else they know."

Ravyn stepped into him and wrapped her arms around his waist. "Does this mean we're in a D/s relationship?"

Zane cupped her shoulders, then moved her back a couple inches. "It means you're going to go home and I'm going to have Thor arrange security for you. You were right—I never should have seduced you."

"I think we seduced each other." Ravyn tightened her arms around him and rubbed her cheek against his chest. "You're leaving me?"

"I can't see you and do my job at the same time."

"Because you think I'm guilty?"

"Because I don't know. Because you're keeping secrets. Because it's a conflict of interest for me. Pick one, princess."

Ravyn held onto him. He rubbed soothing circles on her back, comforting her, even as he told her he was leaving her. She blinked her eyes but couldn't stop the tears from sliding down her cheeks. "I'll never be sorry I met you."

Zane nuzzled her neck and tightened his arms around her, but didn't say anything.

Ravyn pulled his scent into her lungs, then forced herself to let him go. “I need to wash my face.” She stepped back but kept her eyes lowered.

Zane picked her up and pulled her close to his chest as he carried her from the dining room.

“I can walk.”

“I know, but I want to carry you, so be quiet and let me.”

Ravyn wrapped her arms around his neck, then rested her head on his shoulder. She wanted to say something, but she didn’t know what. All the important words had been spoken. Zane slid her to her feet and waved her into the half bath.

“The den is through that hall and to the right.” He slid a kiss over her lips. “Take your time.”

She nodded, then stepped into the room and closed the door behind her. There was a stack of washcloths in a large basket on the counter, so she grabbed one and dampened it, then forced herself to face the image in the mirror. She stared at herself for a moment, then scrubbed the black streaks and lipstick from her face. Her eyes were bloodshot, so she rinsed the cloth in cold water and held it over her eyes for a moment while she blanked her expression. When she looked into the mirror again, her eyes were empty. She swallowed, then ran her fingers through her long, wavy hair before she braced herself and returned to the den.

Zane waved her into the chair she’d left earlier and Ravyn settled into it, then blushed when she saw the other occupants of the room staring at her. She looked down and saw her shoes on the floor in front of her, but she also saw the lacy edge of her panties sticking out of Zane’s pocket. She tucked it into his pocket, then smiled at him when he looked down at her. When he didn’t smile back, she lowered her eyes and concentrated on slipping her feet into her shoes.

“What else is on the flash drive that I need to know?” Zane asked. “And keep in mind that I’m the prosecutor on this case and I shouldn’t have access to inside information. You’ve already told me more than I should know." He turned to Thor. "I want you to put a security team together for Ravyn. Twenty-four-seven. I'll pay."

"No, you won't." Ravyn stood up and brushed down her skirt. "That would compromise your position as well. Besides, I'm rich. Remember?"

"Rich on blood money," Zane said.

Without thinking, Ravyn slapped him. Her hand stung from the force of the blow. "My blood." She pushed against his chest, trying to move him back from her as he stood. "My blood, too, damn you."

Zane grabbed her by her shoulders and jerked her up against him. A nerve by his lips was pulsing with anger. For a moment, she thought he was going to whip his belt off and take it to her ass. Instead, he gently squeezed her shoulders, then calmly moved her back away from him and released her. "Is there anything else you need to tell me, Cade?" His eyes remained on her the entire time.

"Nothing I can tell you at this point without compromising your position further."

"Then, I'm going back to Dallas." Zane picked up his jacket and shrugged into it before he stepped around her.

She grabbed his wrist and held onto him, then shivered at the hard, cold look in his eyes. Her lips moved, but no sound came out. The red mark on his cheek drew her attention and she reached up to touch it. Zane blocked her hand, then pried her fingers loose from his wrist. She nodded, then let him go and stepped back. No help there, she thought, as she watched him leave the den through dry eyes.

A few moments later, she heard the sound of his car starting, then driving away. She composed herself then looked up. "I need to get back to Dallas as well." Her lips trembled as she forced them into a smile. "Thank you for the invitation, Addison, but I think under the circumstances I should leave." She looked at Cade, then Thor. "Perhaps we could talk about security on Monday. I could meet you at your Dallas office."

"No, we'll discuss your needs after dinner." Thor glanced at Addison. "You did say something about dinner, didn't you, Addison?"

Addison jumped up from Cade's lap. "Yes. Right now, actually."

"I'm starving, baby," Cade said as he grabbed her hand, then led her toward Ravyn. "It's late for a woman to be on the road by herself. I suggest you have dinner with us, then spend the night. By tomorrow, we'll have a team together for you."

Mac glanced at Thor, then moved toward Ravyn. "Can I be team leader, boss? Please? I promise to sleep in Ravyn's room and make sure she's safe at all times."

Thor tried to bump him out of the way, but Mac held his ground.

"We'll see, Mac." Thor smiled at Ravyn as he passed her. "Everything will look better in the morning. It always does."

The sound of the front door slamming again gave Ravyn a moment of hope as she thought Zane had changed his mind and returned. Her hopes were proven wrong when a furious woman appeared in the doorway.

"Marisol," Thor said. "What the hell are you doing here?"

"Thor, the driver. He is *un idiota*!" She brushed the dust from her skirt, then held out her boot-covered foot. "I walk—in boots." She shuddered, then glared at him. "Snakes. The noisy kind." She shuddered again.

Addison, Jenna, and Cassie surrounded the newest addition to what Ravyn was coming to believe was a three-ring circus, or maybe a four-ring circus, if there was such a thing. She remained where she was with Thor and Mac until Addison reached out and snagged her wrist and pulled her into the giggling circle of noisy feminine chatter.

Addison waved at the newcomer. "This is Thor's—"

"Prisoner," the dark-haired beauty said with a heavy Spanish accent.

"You are not my prisoner, Marisol," Thor said, his voice exasperated, as if they had been over this subject many times in the past.

Marisol sent the blond giant a dirty look, then looked back at Ravyn with a little smile and a wink, letting her know she was screwing with the big guy. Ravyn noted that Addison, Jenna, and Cassie hid their smiles by suddenly finding something on the floor fascinating. She felt an unexpected camaraderie with them and let her stiff shoulders relax. Maybe she was in safe company and could drop her guard for a few hours.

Thor grasped Marisol's arm and tugged her to his side. "Be good, or there will be consequences."

Marisol snorted, then laughed in his face and said something in Spanish that was apparently very rude as the men in the room frowned, then sent Thor another one of those Dom looks.

Addison giggled then tugged on Ravyn's hand. "If you're going to be one of us you have to side with us at all times."

"But, I'm not one of you," Ravyn said as Addison led her from the den and toward the dining room.

Jenna and Cassie laughed.

"Any woman who gets spanked in this house by a Ramsey is one of us," Jenna said.

Ravyn looked back at Marisol, worried that Zane had been involved with the voluptuous beauty. "Who spanked you, Marisol?"

"Nobody, yet," Thor said as he followed behind them. Marisol pulled away from him and hurried to Ravyn's side, chattering about snakes the entire time.

Before Ravyn could respond, they entered the dining room and Addison pointed to a chair at the large dining table. "Welcome to the family, Ravyn."

Chapter One

Three days later, Ravyn was still trying to leave the Ramsey ranch. She looked around the pool area and smiled at the noisy chatter of Marisol, Addison, Jenna, and Cassie. Marisol had just finished telling them a story about several young girls she and her group had rescued from a brothel. They'd captured the kidnappers and then had tied them to a pole in the village square, naked as the day they'd been born. The story was funny, but the fact she was telling it in perfect English was the really hilarious part. Before Ravyn could control herself, a small giggle left her lips, drawing their eyes to her. She shrugged, then said, "Sorry, I just think it's so funny how you switch to Spanish and broken English whenever Thor shows up."

Marisol laughed. "You should see him when I pretend I don't understand his Spanish. It really frustrates him."

"But, Thor speaks perfect Spanish," Addison said.

Marisol gave a throaty laugh. "Yes, and that's what frustrates him. I just keep telling him his accent is horrible. The other day, I caught him practicing rolling his r's."

Ravyn laughed, took another sip of her iced tea, then pushed her sunhat to the back of her head and raised her face to the sun. The last three nights had been the first time in years that she'd slept for more than a few hours. Just knowing she was safe had relieved the tremendous amount of stress she'd been under for the last eight years. She knew it wouldn't last and soon she would have to get back to her real life, but she was determined to enjoy it for as long as she could.

Thinking about the last three days, she had to smile. The first day after she'd spent the night, Thor had been called back to Dallas and had made her promise to stay until he could return. She was pretty sure it was a made-up story. Then, the second day, she'd remembered that Cade was Thor's partner. She'd approached him about putting together a security team for her, but he'd claimed that it was Thor's job and if he encroached, Thor would take him out. She wasn't sure what he meant by that but she thought he was trying to say Thor would kill him. Something she found highly unlikely. Today Cade had disappeared and she knew he was avoiding her.

Thinking about her need to get back to Dallas, she took a sip of ice tea while she listened to her companions bicker about what they should call themselves. Addison had decided she was tired of saying all their names when she made plans for them. She'd decided they needed a group name and had suggested that they call themselves "the deck."

Jenna shaded her eyes as she looked at Addison. "Being pregnant is making you lazy."

"She has a point, though." Cassie rubbed a glop of sunscreen into her leg. "It does get tedious."

Marisol nodded. "If we do that, then we could designate a card for each one of the men. I want the Joker for Thor."

"That's mean," Cassie said, then giggled.

"No, it's not," Addison said. "In poker, the joker is the wild card. It suits Thor. I want the Ace for Cade."

"Then, Jackson gets the King," Jenna said.

"That leaves the Queen for Luc and Logan," Cassie said.

"No," Addison said. "In an Italian deck the Queen is replaced by a knight. They can be the Knight, and Zane can be the Jack. That should confuse them when we talk about them."

"Calling ourselves the deck sounds boring," Jenna said.

"We can call ourselves the Royals," Addison said. "The royal flush is the best hand in poker. It's the ace, king, knight, jack and ten."

"Of hearts?" Marisol asked.

"No, spades is the strongest hand, then hearts," Addison said.

"We're women. We should be the hearts," Jenna said.

Addison rolled her eyes. "Okay, we can pretend to be hearts."

"You're being a bitch, Addison," Jenna said. "When did you last eat?"

Addison hushed Jenna, then placed her hands on her baby bump as if she was covering the baby's ears. "Don't talk like that in front of Limo."

Marisol and Cassie laughed but Ravyn said, "I don't get the joke."

"Cade and Addison call their baby Limo because he, or she, was conceived in the back of Thor's limousine. Addison had been kidnapped by Carlos Mendez and when she was returned to Cade by my father, they celebrated on their way home." Marisol winked, then made a rude gesture by making a circle with her fingers then thrusting the index finger of her other hand through it.

Ravyn laughed, then glanced at Addison. "Okay, now I get it." She waited a moment, then smiled at Marisol. "Zane said your father is Juan Rios."

Marisol smiled. "Yes, he is and yes, he's the head of a drug cartel. He sort of inherited it from my grandfather. It was him or his uncle, who is really, really bad. A real killer."

Ravyn nodded. "That's what Zane told me. You must be really worried about your father."

Marisol nodded. "Yes. For him and for my younger sister, Valentina. She's safe right now though as long as she stays at the convent and my father can take care of himself."

Jenna lightened the moment when she leaned over and spoke directly to Addison's belly. "Limo, your mom's nuts." She laughed then sat back. "If Limo's a boy he's coming out with a scowl on his face and a paddle in his hand. If it's a girl, she'll pick out some poor 'baby boy somebody' in the nursery and chase him until he marries her. The same way Addison chased his daddy."

"Jenna, that's mean," Addison said. "Cade's not as bad as he used to be and he says we are not having a daughter. Ever."

"Notice she doesn't deny that any daughter of hers would chase some poor guy until he gave in," Jenna said.

Addison laughed then stuck her nose in the air. "The women in my family know from an early age who they want to marry."

Jenna threw a towel at Addison. "I hope you have twin girls. That would teach Cade a lesson."

Ravyn laughed, then picked up her cell phone when it buzzed. She didn't recognize the name of the messenger and felt herself tighten with nerves. She opened the text and her hand shook, spilling ice-cold tea on her sun-warmed leg. Without looking, she reached out to set the plastic cup down and missed the table. It crashed to the ground as she looked at the picture that had been sent to her. She fought the tears in her eyes and bit her lip until she tasted blood, then closed the text. "I have to get back to Dallas," she said, relieved that her sunglasses hid the devastation in her eyes as she stood up, tried to smile, and failed.

Addison stood as well. "Can't you stay until Cade returns?"

Ravyn shook her head. "No. I have to go now." She lowered her eyes even though she knew they couldn't see them. "It's important."

"Royal group hug," Addison said, and Jenna, Cassie, and Marisol stood up and surrounded Ravyn.

Ravyn fought back the tears that were threatening to fall as they hugged her. She couldn't say anything without losing control, so she just hugged them back and squeezed her eyes shut as tightly as she could.

"We'll help you pack," Jenna said as they released her and then began walking with her toward the house.

"You don't have to do that. I didn't bring that much."

Marisol shook her head. "Nonsense. This is what friends are for, and we are your friends, Ravyn. If you ever need help, for any reason, we're all just a phone call away."

Ravyn nodded, then hurried into the house and up the stairs to her room. The ladies were one step behind her. She removed her hat and tossed it onto the bed, but kept hold of her phone.

"You can jump in the shower and wash the sunscreen off while we start packing your bag," Addison said.

"Okay." Ravyn looked around, trying to remember what she was supposed to be doing, then remembered the picture. "My bag is in the closet and I can pack my cosmetics when I get out of the shower." She sent them a little smile. "I really appreciate your help. The last three days have been wonderful."

"You're welcome to come back anytime you like," Addison said.

Ravyn stepped toward the bathroom, then shook her head and turned toward the closet and disappeared for a moment before she appeared again with some clothes over her arm. She closed the bathroom door and stared at herself in the mirror. Her hands hurt from clutching the phone so tightly. She looked at it then dropped it on the counter and made herself turn on the shower before she slipped out of her swimsuit and stepped beneath the warm spray.

She'd thought she was being watched, but she didn't know if whoever was tracking her knew she was at the Ramsey Ranch. Maybe they were just sending her another warning to remind her to keep her mouth shut. In any case, it was time she left. She shouldn't let herself get used to dropping her guard like this.

The one thing that surprised her the most was that Mendez hadn't yet ordered her to confess to the crimes Charles had committed. Somehow, though, she knew the demand was only a few days away. She'd spent hours wondering why the message hadn't already arrived and had come to the conclusion that Mendez was teaching Charles a lesson by letting him sweat it out in jail.

That thought led to the memory of Cade saying they had the flash drive Charles had kept as insurance against Mendez. She knew part of what was on it. Charles had made her an accomplice by forcing her to type in the information concerning the drug deliveries and money laundering. *He* had probably typed in the information concerning the women they'd abducted and abused. Although, his lover might have been included in that part of his criminal activities. If he'd included the unknown woman, she'd be surprised, though, as Charles was a paranoid bastard and a cold-blooded killer who didn't trust anyone.

She watched the suds swirl down the drain as the old feeling of hopelessness overwhelmed her again. She wanted to give up but no matter how she felt, she had to continue doing as she was ordered. If she didn't, Mendez might think she was ignoring his warnings and carry out his threat.

* * * *

Addison, Jenna, Cassie, and Marisol heard the shower running and looked at each other.

"Dammit, she took her phone with her," Cassie said.

"We've given her three days to open up to us. Whatever she's protecting, it's important enough that we couldn't crack her," Jenna said. "I know that look in her eyes because I've seen it in the eyes of trauma patients in the emergency room. Ravyn needs our help."

Addison nodded. "Jenna, you and Marisol start packing her things."

Jenna and Marisol disappeared into the closet as Addison settled into the chair by the window and planted her chin in the palm of her hand.

"How are we going to get her to trust us if she leaves?" Cassie asked.

Addison grinned. "I suddenly feel the need to shop for maternity clothes coming on."

Cassie smiled. "I need new, uh, stuff too."

Marisol and Jenna walked back into the room carrying an armload of clothes and a large suitcase. "Did I hear someone say something about shopping?" Jenna asked.

"I think we should go home with Ravyn and go shopping tomorrow," Addison said.

"There's no way we're getting off this ranch," Marisol said.

"Sure there is," Addison said. "The guys are in a meeting at Club Mystique so that gives us time to escape."

"Since we're going shopping all we have to do is grab some clothes for tonight and tomorrow, and our cosmetic bags, and put them in Ravyn's suitcase," Cassie said. "Then, we walk her out to her car, tell her we can't in good conscious let her go home alone and jump in her car, and off we go." She smiled at Marisol. "You might just get that spanking you've been wanting Thor to give you."

"We're all going to get a spanking if we do this," Jenna said.

"Won't be the first time," Addison replied.

"That's easy for you to say." Cassie frowned. "You're pregnant, so Cade's going easy on you."

Addison grinned and rubbed her baby bump. "You, too, can be in my condition—all you have to do is spread 'em and get 'em."

Marisol laughed then sobered. "That's oddly funny, Addison, but if we're going to do this let's get busy. Addison and Jenna, go grab what you'll need, and while you're at it could you grab my clothes from the spare room? My other things are at the club so I'll just have to make do with what I have here."

"Ravyn probably has something you can wear, Marisol," Jenna said. "And Addison can grab something for Cassie." Jenna looked at Cassie. "I'll grab your clothes from the spare room along with Marisol's."

They heard the sound of the shower being turned off and Addison and Jenna hurried from the room while Marisol and Cassie finished packing Ravyn's case. The blow dryer switched on as they put the last of Ravyn's things in the case.

"They better hurry or Ravyn will catch us," Marisol said.

"If she does and tries to stop us, we'll just follow her."

"You know, I think we should take Thor's vehicle. It has dark windows and security will just think he's leaving," Marisol said. "They'll just wave us through like they always do when they see his vehicle."

"Good idea," Cassie said as she walked around the room, gathering weapons from the places she'd hidden them during a previous visit with Cade and Addison. By the time she was finished, she had several guns, knives, zip ties, flashlights, and loops of cording piled on the bed.

"Do you have weapons hidden in every room in this house, Cassie?"

"Yes," Cassie said as she dropped to her knees and reached under the bed, and pulled out a backpack and several loaded magazines. She stood up and stuffed the items into the backpack.

"Do you have a weapon I can borrow?"

"Sure. You can take your pick." Cassie pointed to the backpack on the bed. "I'll be right back."

Marisol chose a 9mm with two fourteen-round magazines before she chose a knife and grabbed a couple zip ties.

The bedroom door opened and Addison and Jenna walked in, followed by a dressed Cassie with her hands full of weapons. Addison and Jenna stuffed their clothes in Ravyn's suitcase while Cassie shoved the weapons in the backpack.

"Look," Addison said, holding up a gun. "I'm armed, and so are Jenna and Cassie. We're loaded for bear."

Marisol squeaked in alarm and stepped back. Behind Addison, Cassie held up a magazine, then pointed toward Addison's gun. Marisol laughed then grabbed her dress from Addison and slipped it over her head before she stepped into her sandals. A moment later, she grabbed the weapons she'd chosen and shoved them in the skirt's deep pockets. "I'm ready. Did Cassie tell you about taking Thor's vehicle?"

"Yes, but who can drive it?" Addison asked. "I know I won't be able to reach the pedals."

"I think I can drive it," Marisol said as the bathroom door opened behind them and Ravyn walked out.

"I've got my cosmetic bag and I'm ready to go," Ravyn said.

"Wonderful," Jenna said. "I'm almost finished with your bag." She held out her hand. "Here, give me that and I'll add it to your suitcase."

Addison distracted Ravyn by walking closer to her. "Did you get everything from the bathroom?" She took the cosmetic bag from Ravyn and handed it to Jenna.

Ravyn looked around, but held onto her cell phone. "I'm sure I did." She picked up her purse, then dropped the phone into it. She looked around one last time, then reached for her case.

Cassie grabbed it and lowered it to the floor. "I've got it." She walked through the door, rolling the case behind her, then bumped it down the stairs. "You sure pack light, Ravyn."

"Well, I only planned to stay a week or so when I accepted Addison's invitation."

Addison walked down the steps beside Ravyn. Marisol tucked her purse beneath her arm, then stepped around them. "I'll meet you out on the front drive."

Ravyn stepped off the bottom step and forced a smile to her lips before she turned to face them. "I've really enjoyed the past three days," she said, then the memory of her father's stern voice demanding she play the social butterfly forced her to add, "Perhaps you can visit me sometime." She cleared her throat, then laughed nervously. "In prison, probably, but you'd be welcome. I mean, if you wanted to see me." She trailed off, feeling foolish. "You probably wouldn't want to, though."

Addison smiled and took her arm, then guided her onto the front porch. "Funny you should say that, Ravyn." She led her off the porch and down the sidewalk to a huge, black vehicle. "Because we've decided to go home with you and go shopping tomorrow."

Cassie stepped around them and the suitcase rumbled down the sidewalk and onto the drive before she opened the back hatch and dropped the case into the empty space, then jumped into the backseat. A second later, her hand appeared and she grabbed Ravyn, then pulled her into the vehicle. Jenna pushed on her bottom, then took a seat next to her. Addison jumped into the front seat and laughed as Ravyn realized she was trapped.

"Okay, here we go," Marisol said as she engaged the gears and they jerked forward and a grinding sound came from the engine before it died. "Oops! Sorry. I swear I'll get the hang of it before we reach Dallas." She started the engine again and they jerked forward a few more feet, then took off, leaving a screech of tires behind them. When they reached the new guard shack at the end of the mile-long drive, she didn't even try to slow down as the gates swept open and she sped through them. They took the turn on two wheels, then raced toward the interstate.

"Addison?" Ravyn asked. "What are you doing? My car is still at the ranch."

Addison knelt on the seat and tried to look over the large headrest. When she couldn't see over it, she leaned to the side and smiled. "We didn't think it would be okay for you to go home alone, so we're going with you. We can go shopping."

"Addison needs maternity clothes and I need shoes," Jenna said from her right.

"I need lingerie," Cassie said from her left, "or material so I can sew some. Luc and Logan are really hard on silk and lace."

"Yeah, they're barbarians." Addison giggled. "So is Cade. It's a good thing we're going shopping, because I don't have a bra left and I need bigger ones." She pushed out her chest and laughed.

Jenna rolled her eyes. “You were big enough before Cade knocked you up. Now, your nipples enter a room about five seconds before you do.”

Ravyn giggled, then covered her mouth. She couldn’t remember the last time she’d giggled so often. Maybe never, but certainly not since her mother had died.

“We need snacks,” Addison said. “Stop at Harry’s Truck Stop, Marisol.”

“I can’t,” Marisol said. “If we stop, we might get penned in and I won’t be able to get this tank out of there.” She glanced at Addison. “Turn around and get your seatbelt on.”

Ravyn waited until Addison was secure, then glanced around at their determined faces and said, “I can drive it.”

A second later, the vehicle came to a screeching, jerking halt in a cloud of dust as Marisol crammed on the brake without using the clutch and the vehicle jerked and then died. Four smiling faces looked her way.

“Really?” Marisol asked.

“Yes, really.” Ravyn looked down. “But you really can’t come home with me.”

“Because somebody is after you?” Addison asked.

“And you don’t want us to get hurt?” Cassie asked.

Ravyn nodded, then looked away. “I think I’m being watched. I don’t know by who, but I do know my ex-husband is probably part of it.” She stopped for a moment, then added, “And Mendez.”

Marisol laughed. “My father is keeping Mendez busy in Colombia.” She opened the driver’s door, stepped out and then leaned down and caught Ravyn’s eye. “You’re driving.”

Cassie opened her door and hopped out so Ravyn could slide out. Marisol high-fived Ravyn as she passed her and Ravyn slid into the driver’s seat. As soon as their seatbelts were fastened, she put the vehicle in gear and smoothly took off.

“Where’s this truck stop?” Ravyn asked.

"Just follow this road," Cassie said. "It ends at the truck stop and then merges onto the interstate."

They drove for a few minutes, then ahead of them Ravyn saw the large sign declaring they had arrived at Harry's Truck Stop. She pulled into the parking lot in front of the building. "I think I should stay in the car and someone should stay with me while the other three go in and grab some snacks."

Addison opened her door and slid off the side of her seat until her feet hit the ground. "I'm going in. I have to use the bathroom and I want to pick out my own snacks. Jenna always buys me healthy stuff."

Jenna slid out on her side of the vehicle. "I'm going in to control Addison. She eats way too much salt."

Cassie groaned, then said, "I'll go with them and keep them out of trouble. Marisol, you stay with Ravyn. If anything happens, call my cell and we'll be right out."

"Okay," Marisol said.

Ravyn craned her neck so she could see them go into the store. "Do you think they'll be okay in there?"

"Cassie will keep them out of trouble. You know she doesn't blame you for what happened to her, right?"

"I know, but I still feel responsible." Ravyn met Marisol's eyes in the rearview mirror. "I don't want anyone getting hurt because of me."

"Ravyn, you know when I tell you my father is keeping Mendez busy in Colombia, you can believe me." She paused for a moment. "I know Mendez. I know how he works, and if I had to take a guess about what's going on, I'd say your ex-husband decided to have you killed without getting Mendez's approval first. If Mendez had made the decision to kill you then you'd be dead right now."

Ravyn nodded. "I've been thinking the same thing, but by now Mendez knows what's happened. It won't be long before he takes action. When he does, everyone who knows me will be in danger."

Ravyn frowned then cursed. “Dammit, you’re good at getting me to drop my guard.”

“It’s a gift.” Marisol smiled. “Whatever you tell me will stay between us, but whatever you say in front of them”—she nodded toward the store—“they’ll have to tell their Doms or get punished for keeping secrets. I don’t have to tell Thor anything. He’s not my lover or my Dom.”

“I don’t think it’s safe for you to be at my house. I’m afraid some of the men who worked for Charles might know how to get past the security system. Cade said his people were in my house a week ago. I’ve been home every night and didn’t know anyone else had been in the house with me.” She trembled while she wondered how many nights she’d thought she was home alone and wasn’t.

“Tell me what was in the text you got that sent you into a panic.”

Ravyn shook her head. “No. Please don’t ask me to do that. I can’t.”

Marisol scooted to the center of the backseat and leaned forward. “Listen to me. This is big. Too big for you to fight on your own. You need help, and I can help you. My father can help you.”

Ravyn fought back the tears. “You don’t understand. I can’t risk it. I just can’t.”

Marisol laid her hand on Ravyn’s shoulder. “I understand, but remember, when it comes down to the life-or-death moment, my father and I are here to help you.”

The door being opened ended the conversation, but Ravyn nodded, then started the engine. As soon as everyone was buckled up, she drove onto the interstate and headed west toward Dallas.

Addison handed her a piece of beef jerky and an open water. “Jenna refused to let me buy soda, so everyone gets water.”

“Water is good for you and besides I let you have the jerky,” Jenna said, then added, “I think we should go to Thor’s house instead of Ravyn’s. It gives me the creeps to think those men held Cassie at your house, Ravyn. No offense.”

"None taken," Ravyn said. "Considering what Thor does for a living, I'd think he'd have good security at his house."

"He does," Marisol said. "And I've become friends with his housekeeper, Anna, and she won't tell him we're there. She loves messing with his head as much as I do."

"Why doesn't he fire her?" Jenna asked.

"She saved his sorry life in Colombia, so he brought her and her children back to the States with him." Marisol laughed. "Something about Viking honor and debts."

Jenna laughed. "That's what I call Thor—the Viking."

"He's a barbarian," Marisol said, then laughed.

"And you wish he'd pillage you," Addison said.

"Perhaps," Marisol said, "but right now, I still have him convinced I live at a convent."

"What?" Ravyn asked as giggles filled the air.

Addison turned toward Ravyn. "One night at dinner, Marisol asked Jenna what you called a place where a lot of women lived and worked. Instead of saying a brothel, Jenna said it was called a convent. Ever since then, Marisol has been trying to convince Thor that she lives at a convent."

"I wish I'd been there to see that," Ravyn said.

"You'll be present to join in the fun in the future," Marisol said, then added, "So we're going to Thor's house, right?"

"Yes," Ravyn said, "if you'll direct me."

"His turnoff is coming up in about fifteen miles," Marisol said. "He lives on a big acreage in the middle of nowhere. I know the security code to the gate."

"He must have a long commute into Dallas," Jenna said.

"Not really. He's just a few miles off the interstate, and if he's in a hurry, he calls a friend who owns a helicopter service and they fly him."

Ravyn took the turnoff Marisol indicated and a few minutes later, they arrived at a pair of gates that looked as if a tank couldn't break through them. She pulled up to the security pad and rolled down the passenger window then waited while Marisol leaned over Jenna and keyed in the code. The gates swung open and she drove through them, then followed the paved driveway to a large, two-story house. "Where should I park?"

"Just leave it on the driveway," Marisol said. "We'll need it in the morning when we go shopping."

Ravyn parked, then turned off the engine. "I can't believe we made it." She shoved open the door and stepped out.

As they walked toward the front door, it opened and a small woman with short, black hair stepped out onto the porch and smiled.

"Señor Thor has already called and said I was to call him if you came here," she said with a laugh.

"Hi, Anna. Are you going to call him?" Marisol asked.

"Yes, as soon as I find the phone. It has gone missing again," Anna said.

Marisol laughed, then hugged Anna. "These are my friends," she said, then introduced Addison, Jenna, Cassie, and Ravyn. "We're spending the night, then going shopping tomorrow. Do you want to come along?"

"I will stay here and hold down the house," Anna said, mangling one of Thor's quotes. "If Señor Thor shows up, I can call and warn you."

"Fort," Addison corrected, then added, "I thought the phone was missing."

"It is sure to show up like a bad man," Anna said.

"Penny," Jenna said. "Like a bad penny."

"Thor likes to play games, so he says a quote and Anna messes it up. It makes him laugh." Marisol smiled, then frowned. "Sometimes he broods. I don't like it."

"Me either," Anna said, then held the door open so they could enter the house. "I will get rooms ready for you."

Addison shook her head. "No. We'll get the rooms ready for ourselves and Jenna can help you fix our dinner. She's a great cook, and I'm in the mood for something hot and spicy."

Jenna groaned. "I'll cook it for you, but I'm not sharing a room with you, and you know why."

* * * *

The next day, Ravyn walked by her new friends, swiveled around on the stilettos she was modeling for them. Addison, Jenna, Cassie, and Marisol gave her four thumbs-up. She reminded herself to call them the royals then turned again when Cassie twirled her finger in the air, silently asking her to show the back of the shoes again.

"Very sexy," Cassie said. "Luc and Logan will approve."

"I think we should each buy a pair and then get matching outfits and go to that club you were talking about at lunch." Ravyn glanced at the shoes on her feet in the mirror. They really were sexy in a barely there kind of way. "I mean, if you want to go."

Addison clapped her hands together and laughed as she motioned for the clerk. "It's called Club Elysium, and I think it's a great idea. Wait until you meet the owner, Clint McCabe."

"Yes, he's absolutely gorgeous. Like a male model," Marisol said. "He has sable-brown hair with gold streaks and his eyes are so dark brown they're almost black. Like a vampire's. So sexy."

"He's a mystery I haven't been able to solve yet," Addison said, then added, "But his eyes are blue, Marisol."

Cassie laughed. "You're both wrong. They're green, and you might as well give up, Addison. Nobody knows anything about him."

Jenna placed her hand on Addison's arm. "Uh, I don't think Cade or any of our men would approve of us going there without them."

"Oh, pooh, they won't even know," Addison said.

"Oh, really? Have you ever gotten anything past Cade? If so, when?" Jenna asked.

Addison sighed, then pouted. “Never.”

Marisol leaned forward. “Well, I say we still get matching outfits and wear them at home tonight. It’ll be fun. We can have a BDSM-themed girls’ night party.”

Jenna pointed to Addison. “She knows where to get the most amazing corsets.”

Addison smiled. “The best place is only a few blocks from here. We’ll go there as soon as we each have a pair of those shoes.” She held out her bare foot and wiggled it. “I think we need to get pedicures and manicures before we go to Thor’s.”

Jenna pulled her phone out and made a call to her spa as the clerk slipped a pair of the stilettos on her feet. She smiled, then nodded at the clerk before she stood up and walked across the room. She sat down and slipped the shoes off, then hung up her phone. “They can work us in at four. That gives us two hours to pick out an outfit and drive to the salon.”

After paying for their shoes, they got back into Thor’s vehicle and Addison gave Ravyn directions to the shop Jenna had mentioned.

A tiny frown caused a wrinkle between Jenna’s eyes. “I can’t believe Jackson hasn’t caught up to us yet. It has me worried.”

Cassie nodded. “Me, too. Luc is usually sharper than this. Even Logan should be on our trail by now.”

“You don’t think something has happened to them?” Marisol asked.

“Oh, no. Do you think that’s why they haven’t shown up?” Ravyn’s hands jerked on the steering wheel and the vehicle swerved to the side before she corrected it. “You should call them.”

Cassie snorted. “There’s no way anyone would get the jump on all of them. They’re probably just pissed off at us and cooling off before they come after us.”

“They were meeting to go over the information they’ve gathered on Earl Baume and Mendez,” Jenna said. “Jackson thinks Earl’s cousin, Barbie Johnson, has taken over the drug trafficking in our area now that Earl is dead."

The vehicle swerved again. "Cade said her name the other day but I've heard that woman's name before," Ravyn said. "Who is she?"

Jenna met Ravyn's eyes in the rearview mirror. "She and Earl Baume are cousins. Earl had a grudge against Jackson's dad when he was a cop in Long Valley. Then he became the chief of police in Rendezvous a few years back. He came after me and Jackson a few weeks ago and Jackson killed him. We found out that Baume's been running the drug trafficking in our area for years. Now that he's dead we think Barbie is in charge of the drug supply."

"Pull in here," Addison said, pointing to a small parking lot next to a plain building.

Ravyn followed her directions, parked the SUV, then swiveled around and looked at them. "So, let's see—Addison was kidnapped by Mendez, and Jenna was hunted down by an enemy of Jackson's who used to be in charge of the drug trafficking in your area. Cassie was kidnapped by my ex-husband and he's involved with Mendez. What about you, Marisol? Anybody tried to kill you lately?"

"Not lately, but Thor might try when he catches up to us." Marisol laughed, then said, "Okay, everyone out. I'm going to talk to Ravyn for a moment and you can't hear what she has to say."

Addison, Cassie, and Jenna jumped out and walked a few feet away. Marisol leaned forward as Ravyn turned in her seat until their eyes met.

"Okay, tell me how you know Barbie's name," Marisol said.

"Charles said it," Ravyn said, leaving out that he had made her type the name on the flash drive.

"Did he say anything more about her?"

Ravyn nodded, stalling for time as she decided how much she could say without incriminating herself. "He said Earl was cheating him, and he was going to go after Barbie Johnson unless Earl gave him the money he owed him."

"Anything else?"

Ravyn shook her head, then stopped and said, "I know Charles had another woman in the Rendezvous area who was keeping an eye on things for him. She was, or is, his lover, but I don't know anything about her."

"No name or anything?" Marisol asked.

Ravyn shook her head. "Charles played in the clubs with other women, but I think his lover has long, blonde hair because I found it on his jacket several times." Realizing how much she'd told Marisol, she bit her lip, then said, "Please don't tell anyone what I've told you."

Marisol patted her shoulder. "This is between you and me. I promise. Now, let's go shopping and forget about all this for a while."

* * * *

Later that evening, they were dressed in their matching outfits, drinking non-alcoholic wine in Thor's large family room. A tearjerker chick flick was playing on the wall-sized flat-screen when Ravyn saw Thor, Cade, Jackson, Logan and Luc appear in the archway leading into the room. They looked seriously pissed and she was thankful she didn't belong to one of them. A moment later she watched as one-by-one, Addison, Jenna, Cassie and Marisol realized they were no longer alone. The expressions on their faces were a mix of fear and anticipation.

Addison stood up and said, "It was my idea, but don't worry." She reached down and picked up her gun from the table where she'd placed it earlier and held it up. "We're all armed."

The men scattered, hitting the floor and scooting behind the nearest solid object they could find.

"Ramsey," Thor yelled from behind the couch, "get that damn thing away from your wife."

"Addison, baby, put the gun down." Cade peeked over the back of the chair he'd ducked behind. "You know how accident prone you are."

"It's not loaded." Cassie moved in front of Addison, took the gun, and laid it on the table with a sharp click. "Okay, the weapon has been secured and you can come out now."

Cade stalked toward Addison. "You are racking up the punishments. You're not going to be able to sit for months after Limo is born."

Jackson moved in front of Jenna. "What do you have to say for yourself, angel?"

"Guilty as charged, Sir, but please keep in mind we took Thor's vehicle and we came to his house. The only way we'd been safer is if you'd come with us."

Jackson pulled her up against him. "That's not going to save your ass."

Jenna shrugged. "It was worth a try."

Ravyn sat still as a statue as Luc and Logan stood over Cassie who looked up, then quickly lowered her eyes again. Ravyn thought about all the things they'd told her about BDSM and shivered with a tiny bit of fear, but mostly with yearning.

Logan reached down and pinched Cassie's chin between two fingers then raised her face to his. "Sugar, I'm going to do the talking, because Luc is so angry he can't right now. You broke your promise to never leave us."

Cassie kept her eyes lowered. "I'm sorry, Sirs."

A rumble came from Logan. "Did we ask you a question?"

"No, Sirs."

"Do you have a bedroom by yourself?" Logan asked.

"Yes, Sirs"

Logan lifted her to her feet. "Lead the way." He swept his hand out in front of her, indicating she should get moving.

Cade stopped him. "Wait a minute. I want all five of them to line up first."

"Why?" Jackson asked.

"I want a picture of this. Five subs dressed in the same outfit. What are the odds?"

"I'm not a sub," Ravyn said.

The men laughed, then Cade gave her a fierce frown. "Do you want me to call Zane and tell him to get his ass over here to prove you wrong?"

Deciding to play it smart, Ravyn shook her head. "No, Sir."

"Right answer," Cade said before he told Addison to stand in front of the television.

On the screen, a lady in tears was driving in the rain in an effort to get to her critically ill best friend. Ravyn watched the scene for a moment, then thought about her friends. From the frowns on the men's faces, she knew her friends would be in tears before the night ended. "I would just like to say that this is all my fault. I insisted on leaving the ranch, and they didn't want me to go alone."

"They know the rules." Jackson led Jenna over to stand next to Addison.

Logan clicked his fingers, then pointed to the space next to Jenna. Cassie took her place in line.

Thor stood over Marisol. "You're no nun, damn you. Not dressed like that. Now get in line before I take my belt off."

Marisol leaned back on the couch, then examined her newly painted nails. "You're not my Dom or my lover, so you can't make me."

"You stole my vehicle," Thor said. "How long do you think it would take the feds to pick you up if I pressed charges and you went to jail?"

"You wouldn't dare," Marisol said.

"What have you given me besides trouble, *skjebne*?" Thor asked.

Marisol frowned. "What does that mean—shebna? It better not be something mean."

Thor laughed. "Maybe someday I'll tell you, but in the meantime, get in line."

Marisol's sigh echoed around the room, then she stood up as if she was only humoring him and took her place next to Cassie.

"Ravyn, get in line next to Marisol," Cade said.

Ravyn jumped to her feet and nearly ran to comply, all the while asking herself why she was cooperating.

"See, told you. Sub," Cade said, and the other men grunted their agreement, then pulled out their cell phones and began snapping pictures.

"Where did you find the clothes?" Jackson examined the red velvet corset with black embroidery the women wore, along with sheer red thongs and four-inch, red-and-black stilettos.

"At a store Addison knows," Jenna said.

Cade snapped a picture. "Okay, turn around, spread those legs, and grab your ankles. Addison, hands on knees. If you barf, you're cleaning it up."

The women hesitated until the men reached for their belt buckles, then, in unison, they twirled around, looked at each other, and then bent over and grabbed their ankles. Behind them, the soft whirring sound of pictures being taken filled the room.

"You know, there's something wrong with this picture," Logan said.

"Yup, you're right about that," Jackson said. "Those pale ass cheeks need some color."

Ravyn held her breath as she heard the men talking. When Logan asked about her punishment, she strained to hear what was said. She heard Logan say, "Zane wouldn't want her to go unpunished," then she heard Luc talking, but couldn't hear what he said until he said, "Zane said he was on his way to the ranch and he's just about at Thor's turnoff. He'll be here in about five minutes." She only had a moment to wonder why he was coming to Thor's house before Thor called for their attention.

"Okay, ladies, I want you to move to the rug in front of the fireplace and pile up like a bunch of sweet little puppies."

Ravyn breathed a sigh of relief as they moved to the rug. This punishment business wasn't so bad after all, she thought, as Jenna and Cassie sat down then leaned back against each other with their bodies in profile to Thor. Marisol knelt behind them, then surrounded their waists with her arms and looked at the men. Addison arranged herself over Jenna's legs while she positioned herself over Cassie's legs.

Luc frowned. "No. Jenna and Cassie, spread your legs. Addison and Ravyn, lie down on your sides between their legs and rest your heads on their laps."

Ravyn and Addison hesitated, then quickly moved into position when Luc took a threatening step toward them.

Several pictures later, the front door slammed and Ravyn's head came up. Zane appeared in the archway. He was dressed in a leather vest, old jeans, and a pair of expensive boots, but it was the belt in his hand that really caught her attention.

"Ah, oh," Addison said. "You were right, Jenna. Everybody's getting a spanking."

Chapter Two

Ravyn perched on the edge of the chair with her hands crossed on her lap. Zane paced from one side of the room to the other. The belt in his hand swung by his side as he moved by her. Luc slouched on a couch across from her, his body relaxed as he read text messages on his phone. Finally, Zane stopped in front of her. She looked at him, then lowered her eyes. The expression in his eyes didn't bode well for her.

"By leaving the ranch without a security team, you endangered not only your own life but the lives of Addison, Jenna, Cassie, and Marisol." Zane doubled the belt, then snapped it against his leg. "And, Cade and Addison's baby. Are you aware of that?"

"Yes, and I'm sorry, Sir." Ravyn kept her eyes on the belt in his hand. She'd enjoyed the spanking Zane had given her at the ranch. She wasn't sure she would ever want to be spanked with a leather belt, though. She peered up at him.

A dark brow flicked up over narrowed eyes before he said, "They've been sharing things with you—BDSM things."

Ravyn nodded but didn't speak. She was a quick study and he hadn't asked her a question.

"Do you know what is happening to them right now?"

"I think they're probably being spanked, Sir."

Zane nodded. "Do you think it's fair that they're being punished but you're not?"

"No, Sir."

"Do you know why I'm here?"

"To punish me, Sir."

Zane crossed his arms over his chest. He released one end of the belt and it hung down his side. "In what way do you think you should be punished?"

"I think I should be spanked, too, Sir."

Zane moved to the fireplace and leaned against the mantel. "What's your safe word, princess?"

Ravyn knew she didn't dare choose guilty again. She thought quickly, then said, "Spades, Sir."

Zane's left brow went up then his lips tightened. "I'm giving Luc permission to spank you. Do you understand?"

Ravyn shook her head. "I want you to do it. Please, Sir."

"You know that isn't possible. Now, you have a choice. You can use your safe word or you can get yourself over Luc's lap."

Ravyn felt the heat of a blush cover her face as she stood, then awkwardly lowered herself over Luc's lap. He chuckled, then adjusted her until the upper half of her body was lying half on the couch. Her toes were barely touching the floor and she had to grab the edge of the couch to keep from falling. Luc slid his hand beneath her belly and lifted her until her ass was sticking up, then his hands slid over her butt cheeks.

From his place at the fireplace, Zane said, "Luc, that's enough touching. Just get on with it."

Ravyn raised her head and twisted her neck as far as she could to see Zane. He glared at her, then nodded at Luc. "Twenty swats, Luc. Make them memorable."

As the last word left Zane's lips, Luc swatted her, hard.

"Ow, dam—dang." Before she could catch her breath, another swat landed, then Luc began giving her two slaps on each butt cheek while he worked his way down her butt to the backs of her thighs. Each swat was followed by a howled litany of ows and eventually sobs, as tears covered her cheeks. Luc stopped for a moment and rubbed her ass, and the heat on her butt increased, but not in a good way.

"I can't stand anymore." Ravyn sobbed, then wiggled and tried to get away.

"You have a safe word," Zane said. "Use it."

Ravyn sealed her lips, determined that if her new friends were being punished like this, then she would be, too.

Zane crouched down by her head and turned her to face him. "Be still, or I'll have Luc double your punishment."

She froze, her eyes zeroed in on Zane's, and Luc began swatting her again. His hand moved back and forth across the back of her thighs before moving back up to her bottom where he landed the last one right across the crack of her ass. She bit her lip to keep from screaming, but couldn't prevent the tears from running down her cheeks. Zane lifted her and set her on the couch next to Luc.

"Hurts," she sobbed as her hot, stinging bottom came into contact with the cool leather of the couch.

"It's supposed to hurt," Zane said, his voice stern.

Ravyn rubbed her eyes, then sniffled.

Zane stood up, then pinched her chin between his fingers and raised her face to his. "You're a beautiful mess."

Ravyn wanted to scream curses at him. How did the brute expect her to look after he let Luc beat her ass raw?

He pulled her up, then patted her bottom, and chuckled when she squealed with pain and jumped away from him. "There's a half bath at the end of the hall. You have one minute to wash your face and get back here."

Ravyn hurried away. As soon as she found the bathroom, she closed the door, then turned the faucet on and twisted around so she could see her bottom in the mirror. She gently ran her hands over her ass and grimaced with pain. Her ass was red and on fire, but surprisingly she wasn't aroused the way she'd been when Zane had spanked her. Puzzled, she wet a washcloth and scrubbed her face, then patted it dry. She opened the door and found Zane waiting in the hallway. Before she could step around him, he slid his hand behind her neck and held her still. A second later, his fingers slid beneath the dry crotch of her thong. He raised them, smiled, and then kept his hand curved around the back of her neck while he urged her toward the family room. "Let's go. They're waiting for us."

Addison, Jenna, Cassie, and Marisol were lined up facing the large TV again. Three bottoms were as red as hers but Addison's was only slightly pink. All of their faces were covered with tear tracks.

"Take your place with them." Zane gave her a little shove toward the line of sniffling women.

Ravyn stepped up next to a really pissed-off Marisol.

"Good," Cade said. "Now, spread those legs and grab those ankles."

Ravyn was the first one to obey him. To her left, she heard Marisol sigh, then mumble something under her breath in Spanish before she bent and circled her ankles with slender fingers. She glanced at Ravyn, winked, and then looked down.

"Now that's a beautiful sight," Jackson said.

"It sure is, and it deserves a better camera than this one." Thor left the room then returned a minute later and began snapping pictures. He took several close-up photos of Marisol's ass before he handed the camera to Cade who also began snapping pictures of Addison's butt.

Cade chuckled, then handed the camera to Logan. Logan snapped pictures of Cassie then handed the camera to Zane.

Ravyn started to protest, then bit her lip and let him photograph her.

Zane caught her eyes and smiled. "Don't worry. I'm only taking close-ups of your beautiful, red ass." He placed his hand on a blazing red cheek, then snapped a couple more photos. He held out the camera so she could see the screen, then chuckled and turned it upside down so the image would be right.

Ravyn knew her face was red from being upside down for so long, but when she looked at the picture on the screen, she gasped, then felt her face blaze with heat.

Zane slid his fingers beneath the crotch of her thong and she felt a rush of cream gush from her pussy onto his fingers. "Zane."

His eyes met hers for a moment, then returned to his fingers. "One touch," he said, his voice soft. "That's all it takes. I touch you and you're ready for me. Aren't you?"

"Yes," Ravyn answered. "Always."

Zane slid another finger between her labial lips, then spread the cream he found there over her clit. "That's it. Your clit's come out to play now," he said, his words increasing her arousal. "If I had spanked you"—he slid a finger into her and moved it around—"you'd have cream running down your thighs. Wouldn't you?"

"Yes, Sir." Ravyn wiggled her hips a little, silently asking him to slide another finger into her. He smiled, then granted her unspoken request. He pushed into her, then twisted his fingers and she moaned.

"Oh, god, Zane, please." Ravyn pushed back against him, forgetting where they were and that other people were not only watching but listening.

Zane swatted her ass. "Okay, stand up, princess." He helped her stand then held onto her until she was steady on her feet.

Addison, Jenna, Cassie, and Marisol were standing, too. Ravyn could hear their heavy breathing and knew it was because of what had just happened between her and Zane.

"I'm done here," Zane said. "Thor, get that security detail on Ravyn and get her back in her own home where she belongs. Tonight."

"I don't have the men to cover her," Thor said.

"Bullshit. Ben and Mac have been trailing them since they left the ranch," Zane said.

Ravyn heard Cade growl with anger before Luc said, "I'm going to kick your ass."

"Take your women home." Zane strung his belt through the loops on his jeans. As he pulled the buckle tight, he turned to Thor. "Send Ravyn home with Ben and Mac to watch over her."

Before he could walk through the archway, Ravyn ran after him, grabbed his arm, and pulled him around to face her. "Is that it? You show up, watch Luc punish me, get me all hot and bothered, and then you just walk away?"

"Yes." Zane pulled his arm away, then cruelly added, "Did you really think they'd let you leave the ranch with their women without having you trailed? You're an unknown element, and I'm not the only one who thinks you can't be trusted."

"You bastard." Logan fisted his hands and stepped toward Zane, but Luc pulled him back and let Cade and Thor take control.

"That's enough, Zane," Cade said.

Zane laughed, the sound cynical and weary. "She deserves to know that you're using her to find out what she knows about the situation in Rendezvous." He looked at them, his lips thin with anger. "How are you going to keep her out of prison when so many people, including federal agents, have died? Tell me that, big brother?" When neither Cade nor Thor answered him, he looked at Ravyn. "You need to know these guys like to bug things—things like cars." He put special emphasis on the last word. "And purses, clothes, houses. You name it, they bug it. Be careful what you say. I'd hate to see you get the death penalty."

Ravyn moved closer to him. He was angry. Was he angry because she'd put herself in danger? Had he been on his way to the ranch to see her? "Zane." She held out her hand to him, hoping he would take it. Needing him to care about her. "Would you protect me if you found out things I could explain but someone else might not believe?"

Zane stepped back, putting himself out of her reach. "Careful. If I find out you were involved with Mendez, I'll prosecute you and I won't care when you go to prison."

Ravyn dropped her hand, then stood still, her eyes focused on the floor as she listened to his footsteps fade away. Someone walked up behind her. For a moment, she let her shoulders drop with despair, then she imagined a rod of steel sliding down her spine and she straightened her posture, then smiled and turned around. "Well, that was interesting." She licked her lips, then swallowed. "In fact, the entire evening has been interesting, but it really is time I went home." Marisol reached out to her, but she shook her head and apparently, Marisol understood that she was barely holding it together. Ravyn breathed a silent sigh as Marisol dropped her hand and then sent her a small, encouraging smile in return.

Ravyn kept the smile on her face as she flicked a glance around the room, but avoided making eye contact until Thor stepped forward and trapped her focus.

"It isn't what Zane said," Thor said.

"It never is." Ravyn hugged her arms around herself as the air conditioning kicked on. She told herself it was for warmth, but knew she was trying to protect herself. She stood in a stranger's home, surrounded by people she didn't really know, and dressed in the scantiest outfit she'd ever worn. Funny, but she hadn't felt vulnerable until now. She swallowed, then looked at Thor. "So, is your car bugged, Mr. Larkin?" she asked, then paled as she remembered how much she'd told Marisol in Thor's car. That thought led her to wonder whose idea it had been to take his car. She looked at the dark-haired beauty and wondered if she'd been set up. Again. Past experience told her the answer was probably yes. Thank god, she'd kept her most important secret. "I'm going to get dressed and call a cab to take me home. Unless the police are on their way to arrest me?" She glanced at Cade and saw him shake his head.

"Dammit, Ravyn, you can't go home," Thor said. "You won't be safe there. Any of your ex-husband's friends could show up."

Ravyn felt a wave of sadness roll over her. "You're the ones who are in danger. They need me alive, at least for now." A cynical smiled curved her lips before she left the room. Once upstairs, she removed her phone from its hiding place. She called for a cab, then dressed and repacked her suitcase. After thinking about it, she knew that Marisol hadn't betrayed her, but it was better for the royals if she stayed away from them.

Behind her, the door opened and her friends trooped in. Addison lowered herself to the bed, then leaned back, sighed, and wiggled her bare toes. "Those shoes were killing me."

Jenna walked over, grabbed several pillows, and shoved them beneath Addison's feet. "Lie down. Your ankles are swelling." She folded her arms over her ample breasts. "You've been sneaking salt."

"She's always eating chips," Cassie said as she flung herself down on the bed next to Addison, then kicked her shoes off and sighed.

"Tattletale," Addison said, then sighed.

Ravyn watched the interaction from her place at the window seat. Her room overlooked the front drive, so she listened to them argue about chips and salt and water consumption while she watched for the taxi. Marisol sat down next to her as Jenna slid onto the ornate chair and crossed her legs, then ran her hands over her thighs.

"If Jackson keeps feeding me all the time, I'm going to gain back all the weight I lost," Jenna said.

Addison lifted her head and smiled. "You were too thin. You look better now."

Before they could say anything more, Ravyn took charge. "I don't think any of you betrayed me, but Zane was right. I need to go home. I should have gone home yesterday." She smiled. "I've had a good time, though. Well, except for the spanking." She sent Cassie a sympathetic grimace. "Luc spanks really hard."

"I know." Cassie giggled. "Actually, Logan can be a lot meaner, but I have to really piss him off before he gets serious."

"Nobody is worse than Jackson," Jenna said. "I swear that man's hands are made of leather. Old, rough leather."

Marisol snorted. "Thor's hands are like great big clubs." She make a spanking gesture and said, "Thump, thump, thump," then laughed.

All eyes turned to Addison, but all she did was lift her head and smile before relaxing again. "I'm so tired I could go to sleep right here. You could spend the night, Ravyn, and we could take you home in the morning."

"No thanks, Addison. Besides, my taxi is here now." Ravyn grabbed her purse and the handle of her suitcase and began rolling it toward the door. They followed her down the hall to the stairway.

At the bottom, she smiled at Cade and Thor. "I'll be okay. Don't send anyone to protect me. I was telling the truth when I said they need me alive." She hugged her friends, then left the house. She didn't look back.

* * * *

Zane took another long swig of whiskey, then slammed the bottle down on his desk and cursed. "I'm a bastard," he said to the room. "A big, fucking uncaring bastard." He threw his head back and laughed, the sound grating. "A big, fucking bastard who's in love with the wrong woman." He took another swig, then capped the bottle and threw it at the man who stepped into his den.

Jackson caught it, then read the label. "Ah, the cheap stuff." He looked at Cade as he dropped into a chair. "You can always tell when a man's in love. He always tries to drown his sorrows in cheap whiskey."

"Fuck you," Zane said, his words slurred.

Cade took the chair next to Jackson, then shook his head when Jackson offered him the bottle. "We thought we'd come and tell you that your woman is at her own home, all alone."

Thor sauntered into the room, eating a sandwich while holding a second one is his left hand. He slung himself into a chair, then shrugged. "I'm a big guy. I get hungry." He took another bite and chewed it.

Zane stood up, weaved for a moment, and then fell back into his chair. It rocked back and almost tipped over, but he managed to catch the edge of the desk and steady himself. "Where's Luc and Logan? Where's Ben and Mac?" He held up a hand. "Never mind, I don't want to know." He looked around, then said, "I need a drink."

"You've had enough," Cade said.

"Not yet, I haven't. I can still see her beautiful ass and smell her and want her." He ran his hands through his hair, then smelled his fingers. "God." He rested his head against the back of the chair. "I'm not in love with her. I just want to fuck her. Damned, beautiful temptation." He snorted, then slumped, and his chin hit his chest. A moment later, a soft snore rumbled from his throat.

"A lie which is half a truth is ever the blackest of lies," Thor said, then took a bite, and chewed it while looking expectantly at first Cade, then Jackson.

Cade shook his head. "This one's yours."

"Oh, hell," Jackson removed his hat, tapped it on his knee, then gave Thor the evil eye. "Nietzsche."

Thor swallowed, smiled, and held out his hand. "Alfred Lord Tennyson."

Jackson grunted and threw a twenty at him. "I'm going broke because of you and your fucking quotes. Why don't you just take a check for your youth center like any sane man would?"

"Where would be the fun for me in that?" Thor took a bite out of the second sandwich. "At the rate everyone's losing, we'll have a thousand dollars in the jar to send to the youth center this week. School has started and those kids need supplies."

"Oh, hell." Jackson and Cade reached for their wallets and tossed a couple bundles of cash at Thor. "Just get it over with."

Thor smiled. "I never did like being the only kid to show up without paper and pencils on the first day of school."

"Cade always made sure we had what we needed." Jackson glanced at Cade, then laughed. "Do you remember when we first moved to Long Valley and we barely had food to eat? You talked Old Man Muldoon into letting you work for him in exchange for school supplies? Damn, I think you're the only person in history to ever get that old man to open his wallet."

Cade grunted. "He worked my ass off."

"I'm rich because I hated being poor," Thor said.

Jackson smirked at Cade. "Your turn to guess, bro."

Cade showed Thor his empty wallet. "I already gave you all my cash—will you take an I.O.U?"

Thor laughed, then tossed the last bite of his sandwich into his mouth. "That wasn't a quote—it was just me talking." He stood up and hauled Zane over his shoulder. "I'll put this idiot to bed."

The movement woke Zane. "Hey, I'm busy. Don't you know I'm the fucking A.T? A–A."

"A.S.S." Thor spelled then laughed and carried him out of the room.

"So, little brother's in love," Jackson said. "Think we should torture him?"

"I think he's doing enough of that on his own." Cade ran his hands over the back of his neck. "What a fucking mess."

Jackson leaned forward, his elbows on his knees and his hands intertwined between them. "He may be right to worry. Ravyn knows a lot—maybe too much."

Cade nodded.

"You know, Cade, talking to you is like trying to pull teeth."

"I talk when I have something to say."

"Well, see if you have anything to say about this. How do you think she knows so much?"

"If she's like Addison, she might have overheard a lot of things."

Jackson rested his ankle on his knee, then tapped his boot. "I don't believe that's it. Addison's one of a kind."

"My gut tells me Ravyn's innocent. It's never let me down."

"So, let's say she's innocent, but she knows what been going on. Why wouldn't she go to the police?"

"Dolman accused her of having connections with law enforcement." Cade's stared at the wall behind Zane's desk. "Liars always twist the truth with the lie. Sounds to me like he's the one with the connections."

"You'd think she would tell us, then. She opened up to Marisol a little bit."

Cade stretched back in his chair and crossed his booted feet. "Those females are thick as thieves. If Thor hadn't had his Hummer bugged, we wouldn't have a second witness that knows there's a connection between Earl Baume and either Benson or Dolman, or both. We also wouldn't be sure Barbie was in business with Baume. Chances are she probably is running the drug supply in our area now that he's dead."

"Good thing we put a tail on Barbie, then. We'll have a better understanding of how they work once Dania finishes matching up the drug deliveries with the money transfers."

Thor walked back into the room, smiling. "He's sleeping like a baby." He laughed, then sat down in Zane's desk chair and began flipping through the open file lying on the desk. "Dolman's pretty confident he can testify against Ravyn and get her sent to prison. So, why's she willing to let him? That's the question we need to be asking her."

"She's not going to tell us," Cade said, "or our women."

Thor closed the file. "She might tell Marisol."

Jackson shook his head. "I could hear the 'no' in her voice when she told Marisol she wouldn't tell her. That's one secret Ravyn's never giving up."

Thor dialed his phone, then Cade and Jackson heard him tell whoever was on the other end that he wanted a detailed report on Ravyn Marie Benson Dolman—schools, activities, friends, everything. Thor hung up. "We've got a report on Dolman, but maybe what we really need is to take a closer look at Ravyn."

"He's been framing her," Cade said.

Thor nodded. "The information on the flash drive is the truth, but the information Dolman's giving the police is slightly twisted. Once we compare the two, then we can begin untangling his lies and prove her innocence." Thor stood up and stretched. His back cracked and he groaned with relief. "Damn chairs are too small. I'm going home. You coming?"

Cade and Jackson followed him into the hallway.

"I'll turn on the alarm system." Jackson waited for Cade and Thor to pass through the front door. "Think Zane will be okay on his own?"

Cade laughed. "He'll be okay, but he's going to have one hell of a hangover. Good thing tomorrow is Sunday."

* * * *

Zane squinted to block the pesky line of sunshine that insisted on stabbing into his eyes, then rolled onto his stomach and groaned. Damn, his head felt like someone had moved into it and was pounding on his skull, demanding to be let out. He pulled the pillow out from beneath his head, then wrapped it around his skull and sighed as the cool linen eased his headache.

The previous night was beginning to come back to him and he groaned again. Had Cade and Jackson really been here, and that damn Thor? "Fuckers," he said, then froze when the chair in the corner of his room squeaked. Who the hell was in his room, he wondered, as his feet hit the floor and he opened the nightstand drawer and groped for his gun. Before he could grab it he heard Ravyn say, "It's just me," followed by a muffled giggle.

Zane slammed the drawer shut then followed the direction of her eyes and cursed. "Those fuckers," he said as he looked down and saw that, instead of his usual boxers, he had on what appeared to be a diaper. Ravyn giggled again, then looked away and bit her lip.

Zane stalked into the bathroom, slammed the door behind him, and grimaced as the sound echoed through his aching head. He jerked on the knot on his belly where one or all of his late-night visitors had tied some kind of cloth around him. It came loose and he held it up, then cursed again when he saw that they'd cut up one of his favorite T-shirts. He dropped it in the trash, then turned on the shower and stepped in and just stood beneath the spray. What the hell was Ravyn doing in his house, and how had she gotten in? Had those fuckers let her in so she could torture him?

He gave himself a few moments to recover, then stepped out and dried off, brushed his teeth, decided not to shave, and opened the bathroom door. He expected to find Ravyn waiting for him. Instead, the room was empty, but the scent of frying bacon and coffee filled the air. He grabbed a pair of jeans and slipped into them, then headed toward the kitchen. Ravyn glanced over her shoulder as he entered, then turned back to the stove and moved several strips of bacon to a platter.

"I see you helped yourself to one of my shirts." He studied her for a moment, then against his will he asked, "Are you wearing panties?"

Ravyn flipped the tail of his shirt up, showing him her bare bottom. She expected him to smile. Instead, he looked even more remote. "I needed something to wear after I showered. You were sleeping and I didn't think you'd mind." When he didn't say anything more, she shrugged. "I'm making omelets and toast to go with the bacon." She glanced at him again, seeking his approval. "The coffee just finished brewing." She hesitated for a moment, then said, "I could serve you, if you like."

Zane grunted, then moved by her and poured himself a cup of coffee. He added a splash of cream, and stirred it as he sat down at the breakfast bar. "What are you doing here, Ravyn?"

"When I got home last night, my housekeeper was missing and my house had been trashed." She broke several eggs into a bowl. "I heard men's voices upstairs, so I took off." She began stirring the eggs. "I didn't have anywhere else to go."

"There are hotels all over Dallas."

"Well, you see, when I went to get some money, I discovered my ATM card no longer works and my credit cards have been cancelled. Would you know anything about that?"

"I'll check into it, but you were safe at the ranch. You should have stayed there."

"You told me to leave. You said my presence put your family in danger." Ravyn poured the eggs into the hot skillet.

"So, what do you want from me? Protection? Money? Or maybe you're ready to tell me the truth?"

"I don't know," she said, the tears in her throat making her voice husky. "I just couldn't think of anywhere else to go and I was scared, so I came here. I saw your brothers and Thor arrive, so I snuck in behind them and hid until they left. Nobody knows I'm here, so your job is safe." She moved the skillet away from the heat and turned around. "I just wanted to see you."

"You mean I left you hot and wet and aroused and you need me to fuck you?"

"Zane," Ravyn said, not sure if she was asking him to stop or continue.

Zane pushed his coffee away. "What do you want?"

"I want you to hold me for a little while until I feel safe again," Ravyn said. "I want you to make love to me."

Zane crossed his arms over his chest and shook his head. "We don't make love, princess, we fuck. Now, tell me what you want."

Ravyn couldn't make herself meet his eyes. He was killing her. Killing any hope she had left that they could somehow be together. She wanted to tell him to go to hell, then walk away, but she couldn't make herself leave him. She wanted one last time with him. One last memory, because no matter what Zane said, even when he fucked her, it somehow felt like he was making love to her. She licked her lips. "I want you to fuck me, Sir."

"You know what I want. Show me what they taught you."

Ravyn understood he was asking her about the girls' night in she had spent at Thor's home. She unbuttoned the shirt she wore and let it fall from her shoulders. She caught it then folded it and left it on the central island before she moved closer to him and dropped to her knees. She spread them, then laid her hands palms-up on her thighs and looked down.

"Knees a little farther apart."

She obeyed him, then waited.

Zane got up and walked around her. "That must have been some party the five of you had, pet. Did you practice this position?"

"Yes, Sir."

Zane ran his hand over her head, then grasped her hair and pulled her head back. "Look at me."

Ravyn obeyed him.

"I wanted you to be my slave. Do you understand what that means?"

"Yes, Sir. I want to serve you. Only you."

Zane lifted her to her feet. He clenched his hand at her nape, then pulled her mouth to his. He brushed his lips over hers, once, then again. Slowly, he stroked his tongue over the seam of her lips and when she opened to him, he teasingly slid away, then began again. She loved the way he kissed her, slowly building up to the moment when he slid his tongue into her mouth and tasted her. She moaned into his mouth and he deepened the kiss as his arms tightened around her and lifted her against him.

"God, you taste so fucking good."

Ravyn slid her arms around his shoulders and held onto him, never wanting to let him go. The kiss went on and on, one moment soft and teasing, then the next deep and devouring. She was panting for breath and her heart was pounding when she felt him reach between them and unbutton his jeans. A moment later, his fingers slid between her legs and he thrust them into her. She gasped into his mouth and he chuckled.

"I always tell myself I'm going to take you slowly and savor every moment, but we both know this is going to be fast and hard." Zane picked her up then turned and trapped her against the wall. "Don't we?"

She slid her hands down his back and pushed at the waistband of his jeans until they slid off his hips. His cock pressed between her legs. He stopped, then looked at her as he thrust into her. Ravyn saw what he was feeling as he became a part of her. He wasn't indifferent. He was as lost in her as she was in him. "Zane." She kissed him, then said his name again, softly, then kissed him again.

He pressed his forehead against hers as he thrust into her. His chest rose and fell with every breath as he thrust harder and deeper. He kissed her again and slid his hand between them and over her clit.

"Come for me, Ravyn."

"Oh, Zan—Sir," she breathed, then moaned and flew apart in his arms. She pressed her breasts into his chest and pressed her mouth against his shoulder, then bit him. He grunted, then continued to pump into her, every now and then stopping, then continuing again, and she knew he was holding back his own pleasure.

He leaned back so they could see where his cock disappeared into her. "I want to see you touch yourself."

His slick cock disappeared into her a couple more times, then she reached down and stroked her fingers over her clit. She made sure to keep her hand flat and to the side so he could see what she was doing.

"Does that feel good, pet?"

"Oh, yes, so good." She stroked herself, then let her fingers run over Zane's cock as he drew out of her before she raised her fingers to her mouth and licked them.

She looked into his eyes and saw a wave of heat flare in them as he groaned and began to pump into her. "Fuck, fuck. Come now, Ravyn." He pushed her hand aside then pinched her clit and thrust into her, deep and hard, again and then again.

Ravyn felt his hand cup her ass and hold her against him as he pressed into her, then paused and shuddered. He yelled her name and his hot cum flooded into her, filling her. She surrounded him with her arms as he rested against her. After a few moments, when their hearts slowed and their breathing returned to normal, he pulled out of her and set her on her feet. He buttoned his jeans but held her gaze and a rush of joy swept through her. He was going to let her stay. She smiled and he looked away from her.

"I'll call Thor and tell him to get a security team together. You can stay here until they pick you up."

Ravyn blinked, then stood, frozen, as he left the kitchen. A moment later, she jumped when his study door slammed shut. She slumped against the counter, then decided he wasn't the only one who could walk away. In the spare room, she dressed, then grabbed her purse. As she left his home, she told herself it had been foolish to turn to him anyway. Nothing good could come of it.

She passed a park, and it appeared so peaceful with its shady trees and empty spaces that she couldn't resist entering it. Apparently, it was too early in the day for people to be out and about, so she walked across a grassy area and sat down on a bench that faced a small pond. Several ducks quacked at her, then turned away when she didn't throw any food their way.

As she stared at the water, she went over everything she knew. It wouldn't be long until Mendez got tired of letting Charles sit in jail and he would be in touch with her. She would have to do it if she wanted to continue to protect Harper and the other men and women Mendez was holding hostage in Colombia. Confessing meant she would be going to jail for a very long time, and Zane had said she might even get the death penalty. In either case, with her out of the picture, there wouldn't be anyone left to save them. It was time to take Marisol up on her offer. Maybe with her help, she just might be able to beat Mendez at his own game. She opened her purse and dug around until she found her phone.

* * * *

Zane brooded in his study until he decided what to do with Ravyn. Cade and Jackson were already protecting Addison and Jenna at the ranch. He figured by now Luc and Logan had moved back to the ranch with Cassie. Next, Thor would add Marisol to the mix, so he might as well let them protect Ravyn as well. Having made his decision, he went to find Ravyn, only to discover she'd left.

Chapter Three

Ravyn watched Marisol step from a small, red car, then walk into the coffee shop. As soon as she was sure she'd seen her, she got up and went to the ladies' room. A few seconds later, the door opened and Marisol strolled in.

Ravyn lifted her hand in greeting. "Thanks for coming. How'd you get away from Thor?"

"He's at his office. I borrowed Anna's car, and I left my purse in the car, so as far as I know, I'm not bugged." She held out her arms, then turned her head. "No jewelry either."

"That's good." Ravyn looked around. "Sorry about the meeting place but I'm not sure if I was followed or not."

"You can't go back to your house. I think you should go home with me. Thor wouldn't mind." Marisol pushed a door open to one of the stalls and waved Ravyn in. "Just in case someone comes in."

Once the door was closed, Ravyn got her phone from her purse, then pulled up the text message she had received at the ranch. She held it out and showed it to Marisol.

Marisol looked at it and her brows drew down. "Who is he?"

"His name is Harper. The picture was taken three days ago by one of Mendez's men."

"Mendez is blackmailing you?"

"Yes. Soon he'll contact me and if I don't do what he tells me to do, he's going to kill him."

"What's Mendez going to tell you to do?"

"Confess to the crimes Charles has committed. But if I do that, I'll go to jail and there won't be anyone left to help Harper and the others Mendez is holding hostage. I need you to help me rescue them."

"Do you know where they're being held?"

"The house in the background belongs to Mendez. It's located a few miles outside of Turbaco in Colombia. He and Charles have kept a lot of prisoners there over the years." She handed Marisol a small notebook. "I've written down everything I know about it. Directions to the house, its layout, and the surrounding area as well as how many people lived there when Charles and I were there. Mendez lives elsewhere, so the security isn't as tight as it is at his home."

"You could tell Thor all this and he would help you."

Ravyn shook her head. "I went to the police once and Charles found out. He was really angry and taught me to keep my mouth shut. Besides, they said Dale Miller was the traitor in Thor's office. Is he the only one?"

Marisol shook her head. "There's another, but even my father doesn't know their identity. I promised my father I wouldn't give Thor the real flash drive until he gave me permission, or if Mendez kills him."

Tears glazed Ravyn's eyes. "I'm sorry, Marisol. This must be really hard for you."

Marisol hugged Ravyn. "As hard as it is for you. I know the kind of man my father is, but he's my father and I love him." She smiled, even though her lips trembled.

They held onto each other for a moment longer. "If we don't stop, I'm going to cry." Ravyn stepped back. "How have you managed to keep the second flash drive from Thor? I imagine he's searched your belongings many times."

Marisol grinned. "I snuck it into Addison's jewelry box."

Ravyn laughed, then sobered. "We've been in here long enough. I'm going to go home and wait for Mendez to contact me. Once he does, I'll confess to the police. I think I can testify for the state and that might buy you and your father more time to rescue Harper."

"Wait a minute. I was just thinking. You said on the phone that your house has been vandalized and you heard men's voices upstairs. Has anyone contacted you today?"

"No, but I called the police and told them the house had been broken into and the men were still there. I said I was a neighbor."

"Did you use your phone?"

"Yes, but it's one of those prepaid phones. Charles gave it to me." She smiled. "It's sort of ironic that I used their phone to call the police on them. Isn't it?"

Marisol nodded, then laughed. "Well, I think that means they either aren't watching you or they don't care where you're staying. If they cared, they would've contacted you by now."

Ravyn pulled up the texts on her phone. "They don't ever mention my location, so you're probably right about that."

"I want you to come with me." When Ravyn began to protest, Marisol held up her hand. "You can't go home and be safe. I know you don't have any money because Zane called the house looking for you. You can't go to a hotel." She paused and shook her head. "And, before you ask, I won't loan you any money because I'm trying to protect you in the only way I know how. Besides, we left a lot of your clothes at Addison's house. We can get someone to bring them to Thor's."

Ravyn frowned. "Okay, I'll come with you, but if they contact me and tell me to go home, I'll have to leave."

"If that happens, I'll drive you," Marisol said. "Let's get a coffee, and some pastries. I'm starving."

* * * *

Thor was standing on the porch when they drove up. He looked seriously pissed, and scary, with his arms crossed over his chest. The afternoon sun made his light-blue eyes look nearly translucent. Ravyn groaned and Marisol laughed, then parked the car behind Thor's SUV.

"Come on, Ravyn. I love fighting with the farmer."

"Farmer?"

"He says he's still sowing his wild oats, so I call him a farmer." Marisol threw the door open, then slammed it behind her. Ravyn followed her toward the house. When they reached the porch, Thor growled and Marisol laughed.

"Where the hell have you been?" Thor asked.

Ravyn stepped in front of Marisol. "I asked her to come and get me."

When he focused on her, Ravyn wished she'd kept quiet. "Was I talking to you, Ravyn?"

Ravyn lowered her eyes and stepped back. "Uh, no, Sir. Sorry, Sir."

Marisol stepped around her. "Don't be the bull to my friend."

Ravyn giggled, then scooted behind Marisol when he looked at her.

"Cut it out, Marisol. I heard everything you said when you stole my SUV, and I know you speak perfect English."

"Sorry"—Marisol shrugged—"habit." She grabbed Ravyn's hand and pulled her up the steps, around Thor, and into the house. Over her shoulder, she said, "Ravyn's staying with us for a few days, maybe weeks or months."

"Zane has half my men out looking for her." Thor followed them. "He's decided to send her back to the ranch."

"He doesn't get a say in where I go," Ravyn said, "and you said you didn't have any men who could protect me at my house. Did you lie to me?" She gasped when he looked in her direction. His eyes blazed with rage.

"Zane's going to use a crop on your ass. I'll have him add five for what you just said to me. Now, stand there"—he pointed to a spot on the floor—"and be quiet." He didn't wait for her response as he crowded Marisol against the wall. "I've decided to send you to the ranch as well. You have ten minutes to pack, and then we're leaving."

Ravyn saw the stubborn expression on Marisol's face and stepped back, waiting for Marisol's temper to explode. Instead of getting mad, Marisol smiled, then ran her finger down Thor's chest until she reached his belt. "Are you going to stay with me, farmer?"

Thor frowned then caught her hand. "I'm staying at the hotel at Club Mystique."

Marisol cursed, then shoved him away. "Come on, Ravyn. You can talk to me while I pack."

"No," Thor said. "She's going to talk to me while you pack. Get going." Then without waiting for Marisol's reaction, he grabbed Ravyn's arm and pulled her toward his family room.

"I don't have anything to say," Ravyn said, thinking he was taking her in there to punish her for endangering Marisol. "I have a safe word."

Thor squinted at her. "You have plenty to say, so don't give me that sh—crap. When the five of you stole my SUV, I heard you refuse to tell Marisol what was in the text you received at the ranch. It sent you into a panic, and I want to know what it said."

Ravyn sealed her lips, then shook her head. She could have told him the truth—that the message hadn't *said* anything, as it had only been a picture of Harper.

Thor sighed, then sat down next to her and gave her an understanding look. He grasped her hand and gave it a reassuring pat. "I can help you, but you've got to tell me the truth, little one."

"I can't. Not yet." Ravyn recognized the expression on his face as the one men got when they had to deal with an "unreasonable woman," so she held up her hand. Thor stared at her palm as if he'd never seen one before, and she smiled, because he probably hadn't ever had a woman put her hand up to stop him.

"Zane thinks you're in love with another man. I'm just trying to help you."

Ravyn snorted. "I lived with a father who controlled me and then a husband who bullied me. Intimidation, coercion, and sweet talking don't work on me. So don't even try it."

"You're going to be a bad influence on Marisol."

"I don't need anyone's help to misbehave." Marisol leaned against the open doorframe. "My suitcases are too heavy. I left them at the top of the stairs. You can get them."

Thor stood up. "Say 'please, Sir.'"

Marisol smiled. "Make me."

"Someday I just might, *skjebne*."

Marisol frowned. "How do you spell that? I want to look it up."

Thor laughed. "You're so clever, figure it out."

"Just tell me so I can torture you."

Thor moved until he stood over her. "I'd much rather torture you, *skjebne*."

Marisol pushed him away, then beckoned to Ravyn. "We'll wait for you in the car."

"You'll wait in the hallway until I put your cases in the SUV. Then, I'll come and get you and escort you to the vehicle. Do you understand?"

Marisol rolled her eyes, then said, "Yes, Sir."

Thor slapped her bottom as he brushed by her. "Don't roll your eyes at me."

Ravyn looked away so he wouldn't see her grin. Once he'd left, she joined Marisol and they moved into the hallway and watched as Thor carried four large suitcases down the stairs. Ravyn opened the door, then stepped aside.

Marisol laughed. "Addison has talked Cade into remodeling their house. They've moved their playroom to the attic so they can enlarge Jackson and Jenna's room into a second master suite. They're also soundproofing the nursery." Marisol winked at Ravyn. "She and Jenna want us to help them decorate the new rooms. It'll be fun."

"They might not have room for all of us," Ravyn said.

"Addison is putting you in Zane's room, since he's not going to be there. Jackson and Jenna have moved into the spare room next to you. Cassie, Luc, and Logan are in Luc's room, so Thor is going to use Logan's, and I'm in the spare room across from him."

"Addison seems to have everything worked out. What's she going to do if Zane shows up?"

"She'll work it out." Marisol slid the strap of her purse over her shoulder. "Here comes Thor. Are you ready?"

Ravyn held up her only possession, her purse. "As ready as I'll ever be."

* * * *

Ravyn checked her text messages again as she listened to Marisol chatter about anything that popped into her head. Every now and then, Thor would growl and threaten to gag her if she didn't shut up. Marisol would laugh, stay quiet for a moment, then begin talking again.

When the ranch came into view, Ravyn sighed with relief, then jumped out of the car as soon as it stopped on the circular driveway. She was pretty sure Thor had a few things he wanted to say to Marisol and she didn't want to witness their conversation. As she climbed the steps to the house, the front door opened and Addison appeared.

"Ravyn! Come on in." Addison glanced at the SUV in the driveway and laughed. "Are they arguing?"

"Marisol chattered the entire trip and Thor's growling."

"Then we'll leave them to it." Addison laughed, then hugged her. "Come on in. Did Marisol tell you we're remodeling the house?"

"Yes. Are you sure you have enough room? I could stay at the hotel at Club Mystique."

"No need for that. We have plenty of room." Addison winked at her, then said, "Now that you and Marisol are here, we're back to a royal flush." She laughed. "We're going to have so much fun." Addison led the way up the stairs. At the top, she turned right, then opened the last door on the right. "This is Zane's room."

Ravyn hugged Addison, then stepped back. "Thanks, Addison. This means a lot to me."

"You're welcome. We're here for you. Whatever you need, just ask." Addison pointed to a door on the far side of the room. "Your clothes are in there. Dinner is in an hour, but come down whenever you're ready."

After Addison left, Ravyn took a few minutes to admire Zane's room. She'd expected to find a modern design with clean, sharp lines. Instead, the room was gothic and done in black and silver. An ornately carved four-poster with a beautiful, wrought iron canopy took up most of the wall to her left. A small seating area was to the right with the door to the closet and bathroom beyond it. The only touch of color in the room was a faded red in the drapes, linens, and pillows.

Ravyn hid her purse then hurried into the bathroom. It was as ornate as the bedroom, with a huge shower and a tub that was made for a long, relaxing soak. A large basket with a red bow sat on the long two-sink vanity. It was piled with her favorite brands of shampoo, bath gels, and lotions. It even held her favorite makeup in her favorite shades. For a moment, she wondered how Addison had known which brands to buy, then, with a grin, she reminded herself who she was dealing with here. Addison seemed to know just about everything there was to know about everybody.

An hour later, showered and dressed in clean clothes, she entered the dining room.

Zane looked up and frowned at her. "You left my home without permission, Ravyn."

"I don't need your permission. Besides, you told me you didn't want me there, so I left."

"I didn't say I didn't want you there. I said I would have Thor send a team to get you and take you home."

"It's the same thing." Ravyn moved toward the last empty chair by Cade and Addison. Thor jumped up and pulled the chair out for her, then sat back down once she was seated. She looked across the table at Zane. "What are you doing here?"

"I came to check on you."

"Well, you've seen me. You can leave now."

"Are you telling me what to do, pet?"

"Are you airing our business in front of everyone? You spanked me for doing that. Maybe someone should take a paddle to you." She glanced at their audience. "Anyone want to help a girl out?"

The royals giggled and Ravyn smiled at them.

"You're pushing your luck," Zane said. "Better remember where you're at and the rules I listed for you."

"You going to have Luc spank me again?"

Cassie drew their attention to her when she leaned forward. "He can't. I didn't like him spanking someone else's bottom. He and Logan have promised to spank only my bottom from now on."

"That's right, sugar." Luc slung his arm around Cassie and gave her a hug. Logan nodded and elbowed Zane. "Looks like you'll have to do it yourself, unless you can get Cade, Jackson, or Thor to do it."

Ravyn smiled when the three men shook their heads.

Mac leaned forward and caught Ravyn's eye. "I'll do it."

"Fuck off, Mac," Zane said before he turned back to Ravyn. "Don't push me. You won't like the consequences."

Ravyn ignored his warning. "You can't be sure about that. I might."

Before Zane could snap back at her, the door leading into the kitchen swung open. A wheel squeaked as a cart laden with dishes and platters was pushed into the room by a woman with bright aqua hair.

"Who are you, and where's Jane?" Cade asked, his voice deadly as he stood up and pushed Addison behind him.

Addison slid around and smiled up at him, even though he fought to keep her behind him. "Cade, it's okay. Maggie sprained her ankle so I sent Jane to take care of her. Isabella is Luc and Logan's housekeeper. She volunteered to help us out."

"Damn it, Addison, how many times have I told you to keep me informed when you change things?" Cade picked her up until they were eye-to-eye. "Answer me."

"Sorry, Master, I thought I'd told you." Addison kissed him, then wrapped her arms around his neck. "Do I get a spanking?"

Cade sat down and arranged her on his lap. "No."

"Not even a teeny, tiny little one?"

"No, but you might spend some time in the corner while you think about the rules."

Isabella snorted, then began placing the dishes of food on the table.

Cassie smiled at Isabella. "I thought you had decided not to cook for any more sorry bas—men."

"I'm cooking for you and your misguided friends. These two yahoos"—Isabella nodded toward Luc and Logan—"would let you starve if I didn't keep an eye on them. When they had you locked up, I had to remind them to feed you." She placed the last dish on the table, then moved the cart with the dessert and two more pitchers of ice tea to the side.

"We didn't forget," Luc said. "Really, sugar. We just didn't feel like eating so we forgot that you might be hungry."

"I forgive you," Cassie said, then laughed when Isabella frowned at her.

"Too easy. Make them work for it, Cassie." Isabella adjusted the apron she wore as if it bothered her to be wearing it. "Nate and I are eating in the kitchen. You can get your own dessert. I'll clear up after you're gone."

Luc leaned forward and a silent message passed between him and Logan. Logan shook his head, then gave in to Luc's silent demand and asked, "Nate from Harry's Truck Stop?"

Isabella planted her hands on her hips. "You have a problem with that?"

"No, ma'am." Logan held up his hands and shook his head. "No problem here."

Cassie giggled. "Thanks, Isabella. We appreciate your help."

Isabella snorted as the kitchen door swung shut behind her.

"Damn, she scares the shit out of me when she gets that look on her face." Logan sniffed the bowl of corn, then looked at Cassie.

Cassie sighed then ate a spoonful. She chewed, swallowed, then grabbed her throat and acted like she'd been poisoned.

Luc frowned. "That's not funny, Cassandra. You just earned five swats."

"Who the hell is Nate?" Zane asked.

"Logan and I met him when we were hunting Cassie. He's the cook at Harry's Truck Stop, and he's one scary dude." Luc served himself and Cassie some sweet potatoes, then handed the bowl to Logan.

Logan placed a small spoonful of potatoes on his plate. "He's ex-military for sure. As tall as me and Luc. He shaves his head. Probably late forties, but in good condition. Scars on the right side of his face and his right hand." Logan hesitated for a moment, then added another large serving of potatoes to his plate.

Cassie patted Logan's arm. "That's my brave hero. You love sweet potatoes."

Logan stared at her until she took a bite of her potatoes, then he took a bite and made her laugh when he said, "Sugar, I've dodged bullets all over the world. I'm not getting taken out by a women's libber with a bad attitude."

Zane placed a huge pile of potatoes on his plate, then snorted. "Sounds like Nate's seen some hard combat."

Cassie took a sip of tea, then set the glass down while Luc and Logan nodded. "Isabella said she met Nate when he was in the hospital in Austin. He was injured in an explosion and had to have a lot of reconstructive surgery."

"She wasn't the cook, was she?" Logan asked.

Addison laughed. "No, Isabella was visiting a friend and Nate was in the same room with him. She said Nate never had visitors so she took things to him and they got to know each other."

"You women talk to each other too much," Thor said.

"Jealous?" Addison asked, and Cade gave her a light slap on her hip. She rolled her eyes and said, "Ouch, make me suffer, Master."

Jenna, Marisol, and Ravyn giggled. A second later, Jackson had Jenna over his lap with her skirt flipped up. He gave her five hard swats on her bottom before he sat her up again. "Don't encourage Addison to misbehave, angel."

Cassie looked at Logan then Luc. Logan winked at her and Luc said, "Later, sugar. We'll each give you five, followed by a nice reward."

Cassie giggled. "Thank you, Sirs."

Marisol grabbed onto the edge of the table, then glared at Thor when he reached for her. "Don't even think about it, farmer."

"'Dispute not with her, she is lunatic,'" Thor quoted.

Addison leaned toward Thor. "Shakespeare." She smiled. "'There are no good girls gone wrong—just bad girls found out.'"

"Mae West," Marisol said. "'Women have always been spies.'"

"Harriet Rubin." Ravyn shrugged, then smiled when all eyes turned her way. "Zane won't spank me and he won't let Mac spank me, so I guess I'm safe." She glanced across the table at Zane. "You never did say how long you plan to stay."

"As long as I like. This is my home."

Addison relaxed back against Cade, then sent Zane a sideways glance. "I wasn't expecting you, so I put Ravyn in your room. You'll have to sleep on the couch in the family room."

"No, Ravyn can share with me," Zane said.

"Aren't you afraid sharing a room with me will compromise you?" Ravyn asked.

"I don't think anyone here is going to talk about where I sleep, or with whom."

"Maybe I don't want to share a room with you."

Marisol drew her attention when she leaned around Thor. "You're welcome to move your clothes into my room and use my shower. My room only has one twin bed in it, but maybe Addison has a cot or something."

"Logan moved his furniture to his house," Addison said. "So, I had one of the twin beds from the guest room moved into Logan's old room for Thor. I don't think we have any cots. Sorry."

Zane smiled. "Then it looks like you'll be sleeping on the couch, princess."

Ravyn smiled and pretended she didn't care. She was tempted to share a bed with him and grab whatever happiness she could, while she could. Only the knowledge that doing so would end with both of them being hurt kept her from begging him to let her share his room. "I'm fine with that, Zane. It's your room." She smiled across the table at Cassie. "I want to know why Luc and Logan had you locked up."

"They thought I was a drug-dealing murderer," Cassie said. "But it turned out I was being framed by the traitor in Thor's office, Dale Miller."

Jenna giggled. "Cassie is an artist. She drew two pictures of Luc and Logan with smiling dickheads instead of faces and she framed them. Now, every time they act stupid—"

"Which is daily," Zane said, then grunted when Logan elbowed him.

Jenna laughed again. "When they act stupid, she hangs them in their office until they smarten up."

Luc hugged Cassie. "We didn't really believe you were a drug-dealing murderer, sugar. That was Thor's fault for showing us that DVD."

"Right," Cassie said, then kissed him. "I forgive you, even though I shouldn't."

"Well, now that we have that settled, I need to let you know to save room for dessert," Addison said. "Jane made peach pies before she left for Maggie's."

* * * *

Ravyn made sure the sash on her silk robe was tied, then hurried down the stairs. Addison was just coming out of the family room as she stepped off the last step.

"I made up the couch," Addison said.

"Thank you, Addison," Ravyn said.

"If you need anything, just ask. Mac will be with you and you know not to open the doors or windows because of the security system. Right?"

Ravyn nodded, then hugged Addison. Mac appeared in the open door and smiled at her. He was wearing pajama bottoms that hung low on his hips and her mind went blank.

Addison laughed. "He's really hot, huh?"

"Oh, yes. Wow, who knew? I mean, I knew, but I didn't really, really know. Until now." Ravyn sighed. "Does that make sense?"

Addison laughed, nodded, and then waved as she walked away.

Ravyn stared at Mac as she approached him, then scooted by him. The huge sectional was made up and she saw a yellow rose lying on the pillow. She picked it up and held it to her nose. The scent of roses always reminded her of her mother and the many hours they'd spent in their garden. She saw Mac watching her, so she smiled, then untied her sash and let her robe fall from her shoulders, revealing a short, sage-green silk nightgown. Blushing because Mac was staring, she tossed the robe over the back of the couch, then slipped beneath the covers on the couch. She fluffed the pillow, then curled up on her side facing him. "Night, Mac."

Mac chuckled, then dimmed the overhead lights before he moved to the couch across from her. A second later, he laughed again. "Don't get too comfortable over there, Ravyn. By now, Addison has told Zane that I'm sleeping here, too, and he should be storming in about—"

"What the hell do you think you're doing, Ravyn?" Zane asked from the open door.

"—Now," Mac said, then laughed.

Zane stalked into the room and leaned over her with one hand on the back of the couch and the other pressing into the cushion by her hip. Ravyn rolled onto her back. "I'm sleeping on the couch. Remember?"

"The hell you are," Zane said as he scooped her into his arms. "You're not sleeping in a room with Mac."

"Mac is a gentleman."

Mac laughed. "Whoa, don't be saying things like that. I had a plan to get under the covers with you, pet."

"Fuck off, Mac." Zane carried Ravyn out of the room. "He sleeps with every woman he meets."

"I do not," Mac said, then laughed. "I sleep with every other one, and there's no sleeping involved."

Ravyn smiled at him over Zane's shoulder, then waved. "Zane, put me down."

"Be still or we'll fall." He climbed the stairs two at a time.

"Where are you taking me?"

"My room."

"That's not a good idea," she said, even as her heart leapt with anticipation.

Zane kicked the bedroom door shut, then moved to the chairs by the fireplace. He set her down in one, then took the chair across from her. He stared at her for a moment and she fidgeted as his eyes ran over her silk gown. "Are you wearing panties?"

"No. You said it wasn't allowed." Ravyn looked around the dimly lit room. "Are we going to share the bed?"

"No. Mac's getting a new roommate." Zane smiled, then sobered. "I'm not going to let you hurt anyone in my family and that includes Thor and Ben, and even that bastard Mac."

Ravyn curled her legs beneath her, then smoothed her gown over her knees. This was going to be another one of their conversations that left her heart shredded. "I don't intend to hurt anyone, Zane."

"Look at me."

Ravyn folded her arms over her chest before she looked at him. He was dressed in jeans and nothing else. Even his feet were bare. He hadn't shaved in several days and dark stubble covered his chin and cheeks. He appeared to be relaxed as he slouched in the chair with his legs spread apart, but his eyes were narrowed and focused on her.

"Did you know what your father and Dolman were doing? Tell me you didn't, then maybe I'll believe your intentions are good."

"Zane." She looked away, then, without hesitating, she slid to her knees and crawled over to him and knelt between his legs. She ran her hands up and down the well-washed material of his jeans. "I would rather die than do anything to hurt you or your family."

Zane caught her hands and held them flat against his legs. "You didn't answer my question."

Ravyn could feel the heat of his body radiating through the material and she wanted to rest her head on his leg and just let time slip away. Instead she pulled her hand out from under his and slid it up and over his erection. "You told me not to tell you anything."

"Ravyn." His voice held a warning.

She fiddled with the button on his jeans until she had it undone. When she grasped the pull tab on the zipper, he covered her hand. She looked up at him. "You said you wouldn't make love to me, but you didn't say anything about me pleasuring you." Zane reached out and ran his hand over her hair and she felt the pressure of the hand covering hers decrease. She finished pulling the tab down, then grasped his cock when it sprang free and squeezed it as she stroked it.

He groaned. "You're killing me."

The drops of pre-cum on the head tempted her and she kept her eyes on his as she licked them away, then took him into her mouth and flicked her tongue over him. Zane's eyes dilated and the muscles in his face tightened with arousal. A rush of joy filled her as she saw a nerve by his lips jump as she licked him. She slid her lips down the shaft, and he threaded his fingers through her hair.

"Ravyn." His voice broke on her name. "Damn."

She tugged on his jeans, and he raised up so she could pull them off him. The flesh covering his dick was silky and she traced a throbbing vein down the side of his shaft to his balls, then took one into her mouth. She sucked on it for a moment, then released it and licked around the base of his cock. Zane's fingers fell from her hair to his knees. His fingers opened and splayed as if he had no energy left to move them.

Ravyn wrapped her hands around his cock and held him prisoner as she slid her lips over the head again. Zane's breathing sped up and he groaned as she worked her lips down his shaft until the spongy head touched the back of her throat. She pulled back, then took him deeper and swallowed, then hummed with pleasure, over and over again. She played with his balls until she felt them draw up, then she stopped sucking on him and licked up and down the shaft. He groaned and she sucked the head into her mouth then teased him by flicking her tongue over the slit.

Finally, he gritted out her name, plunged his fingers into her hair, pushed to the back of her throat, and held still. A moment later, a long, tortured moan echoed around the room, followed by her name.

Hot semen hit the back of her throat. She swallowed then licked the head of his cock and felt another spurt of cum fill her mouth. Zane's hands slid from her hair as he slumped in the chair. She licked him clean and felt him shiver again just before he pulled her up onto his lap and claimed her with a kiss. His kiss had no soft lead-in and no fumbling. It was a complete invasion and takeover of her senses that left her lying limp in his arms. When he ran his hand over the silk covering her breasts, she froze, then jumped from his lap before he could stop her.

"Ravyn?" He reached for her. "Come here, pet."

With a small shake of her head, she backed away from him. "If anyone asks if you made love to me, you can honestly say no." She ran her hands up and down her arms as exhaustion consumed her. "I'm not sure what you can say if they ask if you fucked me." She laughed then bit her lip. "You can say 'not at the ranch,' I guess." When she bumped into the bed, she stepped to the side, then wrapped her hands around the intricately carved post and leaned against it. "I'm really tired."

Zane stood up. She saw the intention in his eyes and held out her hand to stop his approach. "Don't, Zane. I don't expect anything from you. I just wanted to give you"—she paused while she asked herself if it was time to bring this up, then added—"pleasure. That's all."

Zane pulled his jeans on, buttoned them, and walked toward her. "Why?"

"Charles took me to a club in Houston three years ago. I saw you there. He wanted to show me what a real woman could give him. I watched you and learned what a man could give me instead." She didn't tell him she'd probably begun falling in love with him that night, or that his image had haunted her dreams ever since.

"Planning on blackmailing me, princess? It won't work. My brothers know what I'm into and I don't give a shit what anyone else knows."

Ravyn jerked away from him. "Why can't you just once think kindly of me?"

Zane tipped her face up to his and stared into her eyes before he kissed her. "Damn it, Ravyn. You tempt me at every turn." He hugged her to him, then sighed. "I'm staying the night, then I'm returning to Dallas. I want you to stay here at the ranch. Will you do that for me?"

"Yes. If that's what you want." She couldn't resist wrapping her arms around his waist. "I'm sorry, Zane."

"What are you sorry for?"

"For this mess I've gotten you involved in," she said. "I wish I could change the past."

Zane rested his cheek on the top of her head. "What would you change?"

Ravyn thought about all the times she had let her father and Charles bully her into doing things she didn't want to do, including marrying Charles. But if she wished that away, then she and Charles wouldn't have lived in Colombia the first year of their marriage and she never would have met Maria, and there would be no Harper. "I would have been braver."

Zane lifted her into his arms, then laid her on the bed and pulled the covers over her. He gently tucked her in, then planted a little kiss on her lips. "You're brave enough for me. Get some rest and I'll see you at breakfast."

She watched him walk toward the door. He opened the door, then glanced back at her before he flipped off the overhead lights. A moment later, the door closed behind him and she thought of something else she would change. "I would have told you I love you."

Chapter Four

The next morning Ravyn hurried downstairs, expecting to see Zane. When she entered the dining room and saw his empty chair, she almost burst into tears until she noticed that only Cade and Addison were present. She sat down then smiled at Addison. "Zane's running late this morning."

Addison reached over, grasped her hand then gave it a little squeeze. "He left sometime during the night."

Ravyn smiled with trembling lips, then picked up her orange juice and sipped it. "So, what are we going to do today?

Addison passed her a basket of biscuits while giving her a sympathetic look. "We're going to choose some paint colors and tiles for Jenna and Jackson's new rooms." She glanced at Cade, then added, "Online, of course, and then we're baking cookies this afternoon."

"And pies," Cade added. "Lemon meringue."

Ravyn smiled. Cade was a notorious pie addict and thief. "I can bake, but I don't know how to ride. Do you think I could learn while I'm here?"

Addison leaned forward. "Yes, I'll teach you. I taught Jenna."

"Great," Ravyn said. "I've always wanted to learn."

"Learn what?" Jackson asked as he and Jenna entered and sat down.

"To ride," Ravyn said.

Jenna laughed. "Addison and I will teach you. Cassie and Marisol already ride. We'll be able to get out of the house and tour the ranch." She turned and looked at Jackson. "Right?"

"Close to the ranch with an armed escort."

"You sound like you're expecting trouble," Ravyn said.

"Always." Jackson leaned Jenna back, said something that made her laugh, and then kissed her before he sat her back up.

Ravyn watched them and envied them their happiness, then felt bad for being jealous. She knew they'd had a misunderstanding early in their relationship that had kept them apart for several years. It had only been in recent months that they'd finally gotten back together and now they were planning a winter wedding. While she'd been thinking about Jenna's wedding plans, Cassie had entered the dining room, followed by Luc and Logan. They'd barely sat down when Thor and Marisol entered and took the two chairs left on her side of the table.

Ravyn glanced across the table at Luc, Cassie, and Logan. She found it deeply disturbing that her ex-husband had been involved in Cassie's father's death, and she knew he was being controlled by Carlos Mendez. As she looked around the table, she began to realize that all of their stories seemed to be connected to Carlos Mendez in some way, including Marisol, as her father was Mendez's bitter enemy.

"Where's Mac and Ben?" Cade asked Thor.

Thor laughed. "We played poker with Nate last night at Club Mystique. He refused to play for money and insisted on playing for favors, so they're outside washing his truck."

Luc set his glass down with a sharp click. "How'd Nate get into Club Mystique?"

Addison rubbed her tummy, then smiled. "I asked Logan to give Isabella a membership so she could learn about D/s. Nate won't let her go alone, so he needed a membership, too."

Luc looked at Logan, one brow up. Logan gulped his orange juice, then set the glass down and shrugged. "I checked them out. They cleared all our background checks, so I didn't see any harm in it. Besides, you've said yourself Isabella needs a spanking. Maybe Nate will give her one and get her to behave. She chased me out of the kitchen last week with the mop. How was I to know the floor was wet?"

Lines fanned out around Luc's eyes and the edges of his lips curved up in a fleeting smile. He nodded, then went back to eating.

"If Nate plays poker then Isabella probably does too," Ravyn said.

"Do you play?" Addison asked.

"My grandfather taught me," Ravyn said. "He used to play all over the world."

Addison's reddish-gold brows drew down as she pursed her lips. "Samuel Templeton?"

Ravyn nodded. "Yes. He was my grandfather."

Addison laughed. "My dad was Cooper Matthews. He used to curse your grandfather all the time."

"You're kidding," Ravyn said, then got a thoughtful look on her face. "That means your mother was Fiona O'Rourke, the singer. Right?"

Addison nodded, then smiled.

"I met her once. She told me all about you but she called you Addy and said you had the voice of an angel."

Everyone at the table laughed and Cade covered Addison's mouth. "Don't you dare sing, baby. I'm trying to eat."

Addison nodded and Cade removed his hand. Addison laughed then told Ravyn, "I'm don't sing but I do play poker."

"Great! We'll play after breakfast." Ravyn said.

"No," Jenna said. "First, we pick out my paint and tiles."

"And bake cookies and pies," Cassie said. "Then, we play poker."

"We'll see if Isabella wants to play," Addison said. "That gives us six."

"Excellent," Cade said. "That will keep you in the house where Mac and Ben can keep an eye on you."

"Eight," Ravyn said. "My car needs to be washed, too."

"What makes you think you're going to win?" Addison asked. "The beige tank Cade bought me, and swears is a car, needs to be stolen and set on fire so I can have a Porsche."

Cassie giggled and Jenna said, "That is one ugly car."

Cade frowned. "It has a high safety rating and it's not that bad, and, baby, you're never getting a sports car of any kind."

Addison smiled, then winked at Ravyn. "My dad beat your grandfather in Monte Carlo. Twice."

Ravyn smiled. "My grandfather beat your dad on his own turf in Ireland. Twice."

Cade slid his hand over Addison's mouth again. "Here are the rules. No getting Ben and Mac to do things Thor and I won't like. Do you understand, baby?"

Addison mumbled something, then nodded her head and Cade dropped his hand.

Marisol set her coffee cup down. "I don't know how to play poker."

Ravyn and Addison said, "What?"

"The nuns didn't teach us how to play poker," Marisol said.

Thor growled. "Don't start with that nun business again, *skjebne*."

Marisol glared at him. "It's true. My sister, Valentina, and I went to school at a convent. Actually, we lived there and they didn't teach us how to play poker. They sort of frown on gambling, farmer."

Thor smiled. "One of these days I'm going to plow you, then sow some seeds."

"You'll have to have a complete physical first. I saw the picture in the Sunday paper of you and the socialite." Marisol laughed when the other royals gave her a thumbs-up gesture.

"It's not a problem," Ravyn said. "We'll teach you. We can do that and bake at the same time."

Once everyone had finished eating, Marisol started clearing the table. The other four women got up to help her. After kissing their men good-bye, they pushed the cart into the kitchen. Isabella turned around and smiled at them. "You didn't have to do that," she said as she stood up. Across from her, Nate sipped his coffee, then set the cup down.

Ravyn smiled at him. For an older man, he was really good looking, and the scars on the right side of his face only made him appear more intriguing. From his description, she'd expected him to be bald. Instead, his hair was cut really short, but she could tell he had dark hair with silver wings on the side. His smile was a little crooked and for some reason she felt drawn to him. She sat down next to him, then couldn't resist reaching out and touching his arm. "Hi. I'm Ravyn Templeton. We haven't met yet."

Nate covered her hand and gave it a little squeeze. "Nate Grant."

Ravyn's smile widened. His voice was deep and gritty and reminded her of her favorite treat, chocolate-covered coffee beans. "Nice to meet you, Nate." She glanced around. "Have you met everyone?"

"Everyone except this dark-haired beauty," he said, pointing toward Marisol.

Marisol smiled. "Marisol Rios. I'm a friend of the family."

Nate laughed. "You mean you're one of the royals?"

The women laughed and Cassie gave Isabella a thumbs-up, then said, "That group includes Isabella now. After we bake cookies and pies, we're teaching Marisol to play poker."

Nate nodded, then stood and hugged Isabella. He mumbled something to her, then swatted her on the bottom and left the room. The back door slammed shut behind him.

"I hope we didn't run him out of here," Ravyn said as she watched him walk across the backyard toward a large, black truck with a huge chrome bumper. Ben and Mac waved at him, then pointed to the truck.

"No, he has things to do," Isabella said. "He checked out Club Mystique last night. He's taking me there Friday night."

"I thought since you started the Southern Women Against Terrible Spankers society, you were against the lifestyle," Ravyn said.

Isabella laughed and shook her head. The aqua color in her hair caught the light and shimmered. "I started S.W.A.T.S. to mess with Luc and Logan."

Addison laughed, then clapped her hands. "We'll all go. That will be fun."

Jenna moved the laptop to the table. "The sooner we pick out a paint color and tile for my new rooms, the sooner we can start playing poker." She brought up an interior designer's website and logged in. "What do you think? Light blue or light green?"

"Neither," Ravyn said. "Somehow I don't see Jackson in either color. What did he say he wanted?"

"He said to keep the bed big, and high enough to whip my ass or, uh, you know?" She blushed. "He also said if he has to walk around something to get to me, he'd take a crop to my bottom."

Ravyn grinned. "So, essentially he wants a room with a big bed and nothing else?"

Jenna nodded, then clicked the mouse and pursed her lips before she turned the laptop to face them. "How about a plaid? Jackson likes plaid shirts."

"Jackson likes anything he can get off in a hurry." Addison nudged Jenna's shoulder. "Including you."

Jenna blushed then joined in the laughter. "Okay, what color should the plaid be?"

"Neutral creams with dark brown leather chairs and ottomans," Marisol said. "You can have the pillows made in an open plaid pattern."

Ravyn looked at Jenna's platinum hair and jade-green eyes. "No, you need this." She reached out and clicked on a picture, then quickly began pulling items into the room. The furnishings were dark chocolate brown, but everything else in the room was silver and jade blue with touches of a neutral cream. "There. It will remind Jackson of you, Jenna." She stepped back so the others could see it.

Jenna touched the screen, then looked up. "I love it. It's perfect."

Ravyn reached forward and added some tiles to the bottom of the screen for the bathroom. "I've used this designer in the past. She's really good. If you like the colors, just send this screen to her and she'll do the rest."

Cassie glanced at Ravyn, then pushed the laptop in front of her. "Do mine now, please?

Ravyn smiled, then examined Cassie for a moment and started clicking. A few minutes later, she turned the laptop around and Cassie smiled.

"Yup, that's you, Cassie," Jenna said.

Addison and Marisol nodded.

"Almond walls with cyan-blue and gold." Ravyn pointed to the pillows and rug in the room that had touches of black in them. "You need the black to ground the room."

"Perfect," Cassie said.

"Do mine now, please. I need two spare rooms in neutral colors. Add pillows and things like that in colors I can change out for each season," Addison said.

Ravyn worked for a few minutes while Isabella and Cassie began gathering the ingredients for several kinds of cookies. When she was done, she turned the laptop around and Addison nodded her approval.

"I'm glad that's done." Addison retrieved a pitcher of iced tea from the fridge while Jenna grabbed some glasses.

"I hate decorating." Addison began pouring six glasses of tea while Jenna added ice. "I'd rather shop for clothes and shoes."

"Me, too," Marisol said.

"Not me," Isabella said. "I'd rather shop for a new gun."

"Me, too," Cassie said. "Or knives."

"I don't know how to shoot a gun," Ravyn said, drawing all eyes her way.

"How can that be?" Marisol asked. "You live in Texas."

"We don't all own a gun or know how to shoot it," Ravyn said, then waited for Addison and Jenna to agree with her.

Addison looked at Jenna and shrugged. "I can't think of anyone I know who doesn't own a gun." She looked at Jenna. "Can you?"

Jenna shook her head. "Maggie?"

"No, Cade and I bought Maggie a new one for her birthday." Addison patted Ravyn's shoulder. "We'll teach you that, too."

"Teach her what?" Mac asked as he entered the room with Ben behind him.

Addison pointed to Ravyn. "She doesn't know how to ride or shoot a gun. We're going to teach her."

Mac hooked a chair with the toe of his boot and pulled it out before he dropped into it. "You can teach her to ride, but there's no way Cade, or any other man on this ranch, is going to let you anywhere near a gun, Addison."

Ben snorted as he heaved himself up on a stool at the central island. "You ladies don't need guns when we're here to protect you." He reached for a chocolate chip in the bowl Cassie was stirring and she slapped his fingers with the spatula.

Cassie shoved a small pile of chocolate chips toward him. "Eat those."

Jenna laughed, then asked, "Cassie, how many weapons would you say you have hidden in this house?"

"Guns, knives, or both?"

"Both."

"Nine guns, thirty-six magazines, and twelve knives." Cassie smiled, then looked at Ben. "Don't bother looking. You won't find them."

"I'll take that bet," Ben said. "How many downstairs?"

"Four guns, twelve magazines, and six knives."

Ben nodded, then got up and left the room. Jenna and Addison started mixing the oatmeal cookies while Marisol and Ravyn began mixing the ginger cookies.

The fragrance of baking drifted out into the house and brought the four Ramsey brothers to the kitchen. Luc grabbed the milk from the fridge while Logan grabbed four glasses. Cassie had just placed a platter of cookies in the middle of the table when Ben returned with a gun and two magazines in his hands.

"Where'd you find those?" Cassie asked.

"The downstairs powder room," Ben said. "Taped up behind the water tank on the toilet." He held up a key to the trigger lock. "I found this taped up beneath the sink along with this rod. What's it for?"

"It's another safety device." Cassie took a magazine and removed one of the bullets, then held it up. "If you don't know it's there and you try to fire the gun this will lock it up. Then, you have to remove it with the rod before you can fire the weapon."

Ben looked at the bullet-like gadget then passed it around the table.

Addison slid onto Cade's lap and brushed her hand over his neck. He caught her hand and held it down then grinned at her. "None of that, baby. Whatever you're going to ask the answer is probably no. You're pregnant."

"We want to go to Club Mystique Friday night with Nate and Isabella, and besides, I'm only a little bit pregnant." Addison smiled. "Please, Master?"

Cade chuckled. "You only call me that when you want your way."

"That's because I'm a smart sub." Addison moved her hand back to his neck and stroked it.

"Not a bad idea," Jackson said as he hooked his arm around Jenna's waist and pulled her down onto his lap.

Luc grabbed a cookie then reached out and settled Cassie on his lap before Logan could grab her. Logan set the alarm on his watch, then held up three fingers. He bit into a cookie while he and Luc held a silent conversation with a cocked brow here and an eye blink there. After several seconds, Logan said, "If you're going to the club we'll take Cassie, too."

Thor settled back in his chair and crossed his arms over his chest. "Marisol?"

"Sure. Why not?" Marisol smiled. "I might meet someone who'll take me off your hands."

"Don't even think about it. You're staying with me until we figure out who the other traitor in my office is and who's in command of him, or her."

"Suit yourself," Marisol said, then smiled at Ravyn. "I think we should wear our matching outfits to the club."

Ravyn laughed. "Yes. Good idea."

"What about you, Isabella?" Cassie asked. "We're wearing red. Do you have a red corset?"

"Sure. I'll see you there. In the meantime, I'm going to start lunch." She disappeared into the pantry.

"Nap time, baby." Cade picked Addison up and carried her from the room.

Jackson pulled Jenna toward the door. "Come help me in the stables, angel."

Jenna squealed as Jackson picked her up and placed her over his shoulder, then swatted her bottom.

Logan took Cassie from Luc. "You can play poker later. Luc and I told Cade we'd drive over the land where he wants to build the new office building for The Larkin Agency. We've narrowed it down to four places and we want you to help us decide."

"Sounds like fun," Cassie said, then waved at Ravyn and Marisol as she left the room with Luc and Logan.

Marisol smiled at Ravyn, then pointed to the back door. "Go grab a sunhat, then let's take a walk."

Isabella came out of the pantry. "There's a collection of hats hanging on the back porch. You're welcome to choose from them."

Marisol led the way toward the back porch, and she and Ravyn each chose a hat, then left through the back door. As soon as they were a few feet away from the house, Marisol took her arm and led her toward the rose garden.

"Let's look at the roses." Marisol stopped at the first rose bush, then bent over and smelled a coral bloom. "Cade has the entire place wired for video and audio. Be careful how loud you speak and be sure to look down so they can't read your lips." She smiled, then stood up and pointed to the roses.

Ravyn smelled them, then said, "Have you managed to get a message to your father yet?" She stood up and smiled then moved to a large, yellow rose bush and carefully pulled a bloom toward her and sniffed it. "This one is lovely."

"I sent the information to him last night. He's going to have one of his best men check into the situation."

Ravyn nodded. "I'll never be able to repay you and your father for your help."

Marisol took her arm and moved toward a red rose bush with a bench beside it. She leaned down and smelled the roses. "No need. My father loves to mess with Mendez. He's going to free all of the prisoners and destroy the house."

Ravyn sat down and smiled as she fisted her hands on her lap, then smoothed them out and made herself appear relaxed. She wanted to fidget or scream, but knew to control herself. "This is wonderful." She saw Marisol smile and knew she realized that she was actually commenting on her father's plans.

"Yes." Marisol grabbed a closed bloom. "Peaceful. Hopefully, no ringing phones will disturb us."

Ravyn understood that everything that could be done was being done. She nodded, then changed the subject. "Have you ever been to Club Mystique before?"

"I've toured it, but it wasn't open at the time." Marisol examined a red bud.

"My ex-husband took me to a club in Houston once. He went off with one of his women to play in the dungeon. I sat in a booth with a couple of his bodyguards standing over me. It was a little scary."

"Club Mystique is nice and not scary." Marisol plucked the rose and held it to her nose, then handed it to Ravyn. "The Ramseys have a large booth, and we'll all sit there together."

"It's big enough for all of us?"

Marisol laughed. "These men are true Texans. They don't do small."

Ravyn smiled, then looked toward the house when the back door slammed.

Addison waved at them as she walked toward them. Her flip-flops made a slapping sound on the sidewalk as she reached them. "Cade fell asleep and I snuck out. I swear, I sometimes wonder which one of us is pregnant." She smoothed her gown over her tummy and turned sideways. "What do you think? Do I look bigger today?"

"Huge," Marisol said.

Ravyn laughed. "Humongous."

Addison laughed, then said, "ah oh," when Cade yelled her name. "Caught again. I swear he has a buzzer or something that lets him know when I move more than ten feet away from him."

Ravyn looked toward the back door where Cade stood with his arms crossed over his chest. "Why do you let him boss you around, Addison?" She laughed, then added, "I mean, other than the big, bad Dom thing."

Addison looked in Cade's direction, then back at her, and Ravyn thought she'd never seen the tiny Irish beauty more serious.

"There's things you don't know about Cade. Things even his brothers don't know—about what happened to him when he was younger." Addison looked at Cade again, then moved to the rose bush and leaned over and smelled it. "Did you know when Jake and Katherine Ramsey adopted them that Cade didn't talk to the Ramseys for several years? He began talking to Jake when he was thirteen, but he didn't talk to Katherine until he was fourteen."

"Why not?" Ravyn held the bloom to her lips. "Couldn't he talk?"

"He could, but he only talked to his brothers and even then, only when they needed something. He said the teachers used to yell at him because he couldn't answer them. Jake told them Cade would talk when he had something to say and not one damn day before then." Addison laughed, then her smile disappeared and she crossed her arms over her chest and clasped her elbows with her hands as she looked in his direction.

"But what about the tradition they have of celebrating the anniversary of their adoption every year? Zane told me Cade started it when he was twelve," Ravyn said, then explained to Marisol that the five brothers celebrated the date of their adoption by the Ramseys every year with cake and iced tea, sometimes beer.

Addison smiled. "He started it because he knew his brothers were safe with Jake and Katherine. He told me there were many times he wanted to run away because he didn't feel worthy of Jake and Katherine's love for him."

"I know their mother was an alcoholic and she neglected them, but was she physically abusive? Did Cade have to protect his brothers from her?" Ravyn asked, then watched Addison's blue eyes darken with rage as her hands fisted.

"He protected them. Except one time when Luc was sick and stayed home from school. Joan got drunk and took a belt to Luc. She left cuts on him. Cade said he should have known to stay home that day, but there was a birthday party at school and he wanted to go. They had cake, you see?" Addison blinked her eyes to clear the tears from them, then glanced toward Cade as she stroked her hands over her belly. "He was really happy about the baby at first, but now he worries that something will go wrong and he'll lose me. I need to reassure him. Can you all help me do that? Please?"

Ravyn glanced in Cade's direction again, then stood and hugged Addison. "Only happy baby stories with happy endings. And, definitely no teasing. Okay?"

Marisol laughed. "You realize he has this whole place bugged and might have recorded part of what you've just said?"

Addison smiled, then nodded. "Of course," she said and her smile turned secretive. "Cade's an amazing man, but I'm going to have to change him. Just a little."

Marisol and Ravyn laughed as Marisol took Addison's arm. "It's probably time for lunch, and you and Limo need to eat. Then, after lunch, you can teach me to play poker."

The three of them walked back toward the house, but Ravyn's mind wasn't on lunch or poker. Instead, it was on the Ramsey brothers. Cade was one of the toughest men she'd ever met. At first, she'd wondered if he was really capable of loving Addison. Being with them, though, had convinced her that he loved his wife with a fierceness that couldn't be broken. It made her wonder, though, what kind of childhood baggage Zane was carrying around and how it would affect his chances for a happy future. With someone else, she reminded herself, because sooner or later, her phone would ring and she'd have to destroy any chance she had of ever being with him.

* * * *

Zane paged through the brief in front of him, then looked up when his boss, Harry Jennings, cleared his throat.

"We've set the date for Charles Dolman's trial. There's no evidence that his ex-wife had any intention of having him killed," Jennings said.

"What about Dolman's allegations that his father-in-law, Douglas Benson, was laundering money for Carlos Mendez?"

"There's no evidence that either Benson or his daughter were involved in that." Jennings flipped through his file, then asked, "What last name is Ravyn Dolman going by now?"

"Templeton," Zane said.

Jennings wrote something on the inside of the file, then nodded. "The FBI is investigating Dolman. I've met with the special agent in charge of the case, Jan Michaels. She hasn't been able to find Ravyn Templeton to speak to her. She did track down the Bensons' previous housekeeper, Ellen Clark. She had a lot to say about Dolman and none of it was good."

Zane sat forward, eager to hear anything that would clear Ravyn of any involvement. "Like what?"

"Ms. Clark said Dolman was a friend of Ravyn Templeton's mother, Margaret Templeton. He moved to Texas and began working for Benson after Margaret Templeton was kidnapped and murdered fourteen years ago."

"What?" Zane knew his surprise showed on his face. "I didn't know her mother was murdered."

Jennings nodded. "I looked up the case. Fourteen years ago, Margaret Benson was kidnapped while she and Ravyn were vacationing at their beach home near Corpus Christi. The investigators said the only reason they didn't get Ravyn was because she was at a friend's birthday party. Benson paid the ransom against the FBI's advice. His wife's body was found on the beach a few days later. Ms. Clark told the FBI that Douglas Benson became obsessed with keeping his daughter safe after that."

Zane sat back while he thought about this new information. "That answers why she didn't have a social life of any kind. Might also explain why she married Dolman."

Jennings shook his head. "Ms. Clark said Benson had been diagnosed with cancer and was afraid he wouldn't be around to protect her. He forced her to marry Dolman. After a very private ceremony held at their home, Dolman took Ravyn to Colombia for their honeymoon. They were supposed to be gone for a week but they ended up staying longer and only returned to America after Benson died a year later."

Zane could feel his anger with Ravyn growing. She'd lied to him when she'd said she thought Dolman had had her father killed. "So Benson died of cancer?"

Jennings shook his head. "He died in a hit-and-run accident when he was crossing the street after meeting a client at a restaurant. Ms. Clark told the FBI that Benson gave up control of his company to Dolman right before his death."

"Did she say why he did that?" Zane asked.

"No, but she said that Dolman and Ravyn lived in a home owned by Carlos Mendez during the year they spent in Colombia."

Zane was beginning to get a clearer picture of Ravyn's life with her father and Dolman and none of it looked good. "Where did Dolman live before he married Ravyn? Did he have a home of his own?"

"Ms. Clark said when he first moved to Texas, he had an apartment, but by the time Ravyn was fourteen he'd moved into the Benson home."

"Do we know anything about Dolman before he moved to Texas?"

"I'm sure the FBI is looking into that." Jennings glanced at his watch, then slid a card across the table to Zane. "That's Special Agent Michael's contact information." He stood up. "I promised my wife I'd be home for dinner on time, for once."

Zane gathered his files and followed him to the door. "Looks like you're already late."

"As usual." Jennings nodded. "Keep me in the loop. I'll see you tomorrow."

Zane stuck his files beneath his arm, then headed for his office. He had a lot to think about before he drove to the ranch Friday night to see Ravyn.

Chapter Five

Zane slammed through the saloon-style doors at Club Mystique. What the hell did Ravyn think she was doing, going to Club Mystique without him?

The receptionist, Carly, smiled at him, then lowered her eyes and let him pass without the usual sign-in process. In the main room, he turned to the left, then stopped. Hands on his hips, he stared at the new half-moon table that had replaced the booth he and his brothers usually shared. It seemed there were a lot of things going on that he hadn't been consulted about, and his anger increased.

Ravyn sat in the middle, facing him, with an empty chair to her right. Addison sat on Cade's lap with Jackson next to them. Jenna's back was to him as she straddled Jackson and nuzzled his neck. There were two empty chairs at their end of the table. Luc and Logan sat to Ravyn's left and apparently, Luc's turn to hold Cassie had just ended as he was in the process of passing her over to Logan. The two chairs next to them were occupied by Isabella and a man he assumed was Nate Grant. When he saw the matching outfits the women wore and the club collar around Ravyn's neck, he clenched his fists and gritted his teeth until they ached.

Ravyn saw him, smiled, and waved. He glared and wondered how many drinks she'd had tonight as she dropped her hand and the smile on her face disappeared. He stalked toward the table and planted his hands on the smooth top, then leaned over until he was almost nose-to-nose with her. "Get up. We're leaving."

Ravyn leaned back, then lifted her glass of wine and took a sip.

"Did you hear me?"

She licked a drop of wine from her lips as she set the glass down. "Yes, but I don't want to leave. I'm having a good time, Sir."

Zane glanced at Cade and Jackson. "How many drinks has she had?"

Before the men could answer, Ravyn said, "This one." She held up the almost-full glass of wine. "I'm happy to see you, Zane."

Zane ignored her and focused on Cade. "You shouldn't have brought her here."

Cade smiled, then spoke to Ravyn. "Do you have a contract with Zane?"

"No, Sir." Ravyn smiled, then touched the club medallion that hung from the collar around her neck. "It's just little ole me, all by my lonesome self."

Cade smiled again and Zane thought he looked way too satisfied with the situation, which meant Addison was involved. He glanced at her and frowned when she smiled at him.

"Then Ravyn's free to do as she pleases." Cade smiled again. "Would you like to join us, little brother?"

Zane sighed, then nodded. As far as he was concerned, Addison was turning out to be a really bad influence on Cade and was causing him to lose his edge. "What the hell happened to the booth?"

"Logan and I decided it was too confining." Luc smoothed his hand over the top. "This table is on hinges so we can flip it over if we need to, and it's bulletproof."

"Are you expecting trouble?" Zane looked around the club while wondering if they were being targeted, then gave himself a mental shake. God, his brothers, and their crazy women, were turning him into a paranoid bastard. He straightened up, then prepared himself for more of their insanity.

"Cassie likes to be prepared." Logan pulled Cassie toward him. "Don't you, sugar?"

"Better safe than sorry," Cassie said.

Zane smiled when Luc and Logan nodded in agreement like well-trained monkeys. In his head, he pictured them wearing tiny red caps and holding out little tin cups with the words "Help, Cassie's taken our balls" printed on them. He laughed and they looked puzzled. His attention moved to Cade when he slapped the table then pointed to Isabella and her companion.

"Zane, you've met Isabella, but you haven't met Nate Grant. Nate, this is our youngest brother, Zane."

Zane's manners kicked in and he reached over and shook the large man's hand before he turned back to Ravyn. Before he could say anything, Jackson stood up, then pulled Jenna to her feet.

"Dance with me, angel," Jackson said as the band began playing a slow country song.

Cade stood up, then slid Addison down until her feet touched the floor. "We'll join you."

Zane loosened his tie and jerked it off as he walked around the table. He shrugged out of his suit jacket and hung it on the back of the chair next to Ravyn. Once he was settled, he scooted his chair closer to hers. "You shouldn't be here and you know it."

Ravyn twisted to face him. "Why not? It's not like I'm breaking the law or anything."

"Sir." Zane leaned toward her, crowding her. He grabbed her glass of wine, took a sip, and moved the glass out of her reach. "If you want to play at being a sub, then follow the rules. I'm sure the *royals* have taught them to you by now."

Ravyn sucked in a deep breath. "How do you know about that?"

"I told you, Cade bugs everything. That includes the area around the pool."

"Then I'll be careful what I say anywhere on the ranch, Sir Jack." Ravyn smiled, then sobered. "Why are you here?"

Zane frowned at the new nickname she'd given him. "Watch it, or you might find yourself over my lap." He saw her shiver of arousal and had to force himself to remember why he'd wanted to see her tonight. "I want to talk to you about your ex-husband and the year you lived in Colombia after you married him." Zane saw the color drain from Ravyn's cheeks and a red flag went up. She was hiding something and didn't like that he was closing in on her secrets.

Ravyn lowered her eyes. "There's nothing to tell. I married Charles because my father insisted I marry him. He took me to Colombia for our honeymoon. He said it was a working honeymoon because he had some business to take care of there."

Zane went on the offense. "Did you know you were going to stay in a home owned by Carlos Mendez?"

"No. Charles said he'd leased it for our honeymoon."

"How many times did you meet Mendez?"

Ravyn leaned back in the chair and crossed her arms over her chest. "I only met him once, very briefly, when he came to dinner. He frightened me."

"Did you know you were going to be in Colombia for a year when you went there?"

"No. Why are you asking me all these questions?"

Zane ignored her question. "Did you know your father turned his business over to Dolman right before his death?"

"He had cancer and he wanted to make sure his business would be okay."

Zane felt his anger increase when Ravyn looked away from him, and he knew she was only telling him part of the truth. "What about you? Did he want you to be okay, too?"

Ravyn blinked her eyes to clear the tears away. "Stop it, Zane."

"You told me you thought Dolman had your father killed. Why do you believe that?"

Ravyn tried to stand up, but Zane grasped her wrist and kept her seated.

"Dolman already had you and the business. Why kill your father when he was already dying?"

A heavy mug hit the table, drawing everyone's attention to Nate. "That's enough. You're badgering the witness."

"Stay out of this, Nate." Zane turned back to Ravyn. "Answer the question. What did Dolman have to gain by killing your father?"

"Zane—"

"Do you know what I think, princess? I think Dolman and Mendez were holding you hostage in Colombia and your father had either threatened to go to the police or had gone to the police. Maybe he talked to the wrong people and that's why he was killed."

The sound of a chair tipping over and hitting the floor drew Zane's attention back to Nate.

"I said *that's enough*." Nate's voice was deep, the words grated out as he stood up. "In case you haven't noticed, your woman is in tears."

Zane stood up, his eyes level with Nate's. "She's not my woman. If she was, she would have known not to come here without me."

Nate moved behind Ravyn. "Are you sure she's not your woman?"

"Absolutely positive." Zane waited to see what Nate's next move would be. The guy was the same height as him, but big, like a moving mountain, all hard muscle and sharp lines. The scars on his face pulled the right side of his mouth up in a permanent smile, but it was the look in his narrowed blue eyes that revealed what he was really thinking. This wasn't the kind of guy any sane man wanted to tangle with, but Zane wasn't sure he was in his right mind, so he refused to back down.

"In that case, Ravyn, I'm offering you my protection." Nate put his hand on Ravyn's shoulder.

Zane knocked his hand away, then slid his hand around Ravyn's neck in a show of possession. "Fuck off, Nate."

"I'm asking you one last time—is this your woman?"

Ravyn shoved Zane's hand away and stood up between the two combatants. "Thank you, Nate, but I'm not his woman. He thinks I'm a criminal, and he's trying to protect his family." She glanced at Zane. "I'm ready to leave."

Marisol and Thor returned from the dance floor just as Ravyn finished speaking. Marisol moved to Ravyn's side and grabbed her hand. "If you're leaving then I'll come with you."

Ravyn shook her head. "No, but thanks for offering, Marisol." She turned to Zane. "I'll get my things and meet you in the entrance."

"You don't have to go with him if you don't want to," Cassie managed to say before Luc covered her mouth.

Ravyn sent Cassie a trembling smile, then hugged Marisol. "Zane and I have some talking to do, and we might as well get it over with tonight."

* * * *

Zane drove toward the ranch, his mind on the woman sitting beside him. He didn't know what he was going to do. He'd intended to see her tonight and force her to tell him the truth, but all he really wanted to do was take her to his bed. The red-and-black corset she wore outlined every curve of her lush body and forced her breasts up into a mouthwatering display. He wanted to pull them from the cloth concealing them and play with them. He wanted to pinch, then suck on them, then clamp them and watch her passion grow.

The questions he wanted to ask her disappeared from his mind. All he could think of was how beautiful she would look draped across the bed in the playroom, surrendering to him, with her legs spread and her cunt and ass offered to him.

As soon as he parked the car, he released his seatbelt, then ran his hands over his face and looked at her. She turned to face him and he couldn't bear the fact that he'd caused the look of fear on her face. Knowing what he knew now about her father and ex-husband, he had to wonder just who, if anyone, had ever protected and cherished Ravyn. What had she been like as a little girl? Dolman had moved into her home when she was a child. Had he threatened her even then? Had she had to hide from him in her own home? The way he and his brothers had hidden from their mother when she'd gone out and gotten drunk then returned home angry and out of control?

"Did Dolman scare you when you were a little girl?"

Ravyn bit her lip, then looked down.

"Answer me, pet."

"He—he was odd. When we would go to Boston to see my grandfather, Charles would always show up. I don't think my mother liked him."

"What else did he do?" Zane asked, then saw her clench her fists on her lap.

"He insisted on keeping my mother's portrait in my father's study. I wanted to move it to my sitting room, but he refused to let me."

Zane was surprised. "The portrait in the study is of your mother? I thought it was you."

Ravyn shook her head. "No. I look a lot like my mother. Charles used to call me by her name when he tried to vis—"

Zane saw the muscles in Ravyn's neck spasm as she swallowed, then looked away, and her hair slid forward and hid her face from him. "When he what?" he asked, then felt rage sweep through him as he put more of the puzzle pieces together that made up Ravyn's life. "He used to visit your room? Is that what you were going to say, Ravyn?" He reached out and released her seatbelt, then pulled her onto his lap. "Baby, how old were you?"

"Zane." Ravyn felt tears flood her eyes. "Don't."

Zane held her tighter. In that moment, he wanted to kill Dolman. "It's okay. You don't have to talk about it if you don't want to." He kissed her cheek and held her while he tried to rein in his temper.

Ravyn trembled, then rested her head on his shoulder. "I was thirteen. He came to my room. He scared me. Our housekeeper, Ms. Clark, came in with clean sheets for my bed and he let me go then left. She told me to lock my bedroom door from then on. I did, but he would still try to get me to open the door. Sometimes he would corner me in other rooms in the house and hug me or try to kiss me. I learned to hide out in the kitchen with Ms. Clark after he moved in with my father and me. He hated her because she protected me and the first thing he did after my father's death was fire her when we returned from Colombia."

Zane felt Ravyn tremble and he knew it was because she'd brought the conversation back around to Colombia. He could jump in now and question her again, but somehow he just couldn't do that. Cade wasn't the only one losing his edge. All he wanted to do tonight was hold her. "It's okay. We'll talk tomorrow." He kissed her and she slid her arms around him, almost in a stranglehold.

"I love you, Zane. No matter what happens, I want you to know that I love you."

Before he could ask her what she thought might happen, her lips slid across his. He caught them and deepened the kiss. She tasted like a combination of the wine she'd been drinking earlier and his woman. He'd lied to Nate when he'd said she wasn't his woman. She belonged to him and it scared the hell out of him. The justice system was something he believed in wholeheartedly, but if it came down to her or his job, he would have to give her the benefit of the doubt. He would talk to his brothers and Thor in the morning and then make sure Ravyn understood that he would protect her from her ex-husband's accusations. But tonight he was going to make sure she understood that she belonged to him and from now on, he was in charge.

He threw open the car door and carried her into the house and up the stairs. At the top he hesitated. Which way? Right to his room, or up the stairs to the playroom? He looked at her and saw she was waiting for him to decide. He smiled at her, then dropped the vanilla facade he wore most of the time, revealing his true character. Her eyes dilated, and he knew he'd made the right decision as he took the first step to the third floor.

The door swung open. "If we go in here, I'm going to expect you to not only submit to me but be my full-time slave. Are you willing to do that?"

"Yes, Master."

Zane smiled and held her closer. "I know your limits. Have any of them changed?"

Ravyn ran her hands over his neck. "No, Master."

"Your safe word is *guilty*. Do you understand?"

Ravyn smiled, then looked down. "Thank you. I understand."

Zane stepped across the threshold, then set her on her feet and flicked on the light. He kicked the door shut and they were alone and surrounded by an almost unlimited choice of objects for sexual gratification.

Ravyn toured the room, trailing her hand over the spanking bench then the St. Andrew's cross. She stopped by the medical exam table and smiled at him.

One dark brow flicked up as he shook his head, then opened the doors on a large armoire and chose an outfit for her. "Go behind the screen and put this on. Fix your hair appropriately, young lady, then I want you to join me. Do you understand?"

Ravyn held the outfit up, then smiled. "Yes, Master."

Zane chose a few more items from the cabinet, then took a seat behind the large desk and arranged them in front of him while he waited. He wanted her to see them and feel anxious arousal. He could hardly wait to see her. This was his favorite fantasy and he'd never played it out with another sub. He'd saved this one for someone special. For Ravyn.

When she stepped into view, the zipper on his dress slacks bit into his cock. The sheer white blouse revealed the color of her nipples and the extremely short plaid skirt barely covered her ass. Her slender legs were incased in white stockings that ended mid-thigh, and she wore Oxford loafers on her feet with four-inch heels. Her hair was in a long ponytail down her back with a black velvet ribbon at her nape. He left her standing until she shifted, then he frowned. "Stand in front of my desk, young lady."

Ravyn moved to the spot he pointed to, then looked down at his hands and the items arranged in a straight line between them. She glanced at him, then back down at the items.

"Do you know why you've been sent to my office, young lady?"

"No, Headmaster."

Zane frowned. "You will address me as Sir, and lying will only earn you more swats. Now, tell me why you're in my office today."

Ravyn looked at him, then said, "Because I got caught kissing Johnny behind the bleachers, Sir."

Zane frowned. "Because you got caught? Do you believe it's okay to kiss Johnny as long as you don't get caught doing it?"

"No, Sir, I meant I was kissing Johnny." Ravyn clasped her hands together in front of her.

Zane saw her knuckles turn white. Good, he thought, she's getting caught up in the game. "So, you were caught skipping a class and making out with Johnny? Is that correct?"

"Yes, Sir."

"I suspect if you've kissed Johnny then you've kissed other boys as well. Probably the entire football team?"

"No, Sir, only Johnny."

"I see." Zane tapped the desk, drawing her eyes back to the objects. "How many times have you fooled around with Johnny?"

"Four times, Sir."

"Has he touched your breasts?"

Ravyn nodded but kept her eyes down.

"Answer me." Zane made his voice stern. "Has Johnny touched your breasts?"

"Yes, Sir."

"I see. Has he played with your nipples? Has he sucked on them?"

"Yes, Sir."

"Has he touched your pussy?"

Ravyn blushed. "Yes, Sir."

"Has he fingered you?"

Ravyn blushed. "Only a little, Sir."

"Only a little?" he asked. "What do you mean by that?"

"I only let him put one finger inside me, Sir."

"I see. Has he played with your clit and given you an orgasm?"

"Yes, Sir."

"Did Johnny touch your ass?"

Ravyn shook her head and the ponytail brushed over her back, giving her goose bumps and her nipples hardened. "Oh, no, Sir, I would never, ever let him do that."

"I see." He rubbed his chin. "We have a very strict policy at this school about students and their behavior. Are you aware of it?"

"No, Sir, I'm new. I just transferred in last week."

"A week and you're already causing trouble. I'm afraid your punishment is going to be quite severe." He pointed to the items on his desk. "Name these as I point to them."

Ravyn watched him point to the first object. "A wooden ruler." He pointed to another object and she licked her lips, then swallowed. "I don't know what that is, Sir."

Zane smiled, then held the object up. "This is a butt plug." She followed his movements as he picked up the last object. "This is lube. Do you know what I'm going to do with them, young lady?"

Ravyn shook her head. "No, Sir."

Zane chuckled and held up the lube. "I'm going to spread this lube all over your tight little asshole. Then, I'm going to finger it and make sure to get you nice and slick before I slide this"—he held up the plug—"into you." He put the two objects down and pointed to the last object. "What is this?"

"A condom, Sir."

Zane nodded. "There's a stool by the wall. Fetch it and place it in front of my desk. Then I want you to face away from me, lift your skirt and bend over the stool. I want you to spread your legs and then reach back and pull your cheeks apart so I can see your pussy and ass. Do it now, young lady."

Ravyn slowly walked over to the stool and pulled it across the room. She stood between it and the desk, then inched her short skirt up to her waist.

"Tuck the hem into your waistband, young lady. I don't want any mishaps blocking my view." He settled back in the chair and stretched out his legs, then unzipped his pants. His cock was killing him and he felt as if it would have the impression of the zipper teeth on it for days. He saw Ravyn glance over her shoulder and assumed she'd heard the hiss of the zipper being lowered. "Did I give you permission to look at me?"

"No, Sir."

"That's five more swats with the ruler. Now, get to it and bend over. I'm waiting."

Ravyn lifted the skirt, tucked it into the waistband, then bent over the stool and walked her feet out until they were far apart.

Zane watched her slide her hands down her hips, then over her ass cheeks. Her fingertips disappeared between the rounded globes, then she spread them and he sucked in a deep breath. Damn, he thought, as he stroked his hand up and down his cock. *She has a great ass.* It was heart-shaped and rounded in all the right places. High and tight, and her hole was perfect, tight and puckered, and he knew he was going to have to fight for control if he ever got into it.

"Pull those sweet cheeks as far apart as you can," he said, his voice tight but demanding. He saw the distance increase and waited for a moment before asking, "So, you've never had a finger in your ass?"

"No, Sir." Ravyn's voice was muffled from her head hanging upside down over the stool and her weight on her belly.

"We'll have to do something about that. We'll begin stretching your hole today so I can get my cock into it. We can't have students running around breaking the rules without getting the appropriate discipline." He stood up, shrugged out of his clothes, then picked up the ruler and tapped it against his palm as he moved around the desk. "I believe you've earned twenty swats. Move your hands now."

Ravyn dropped her hands to the bottom rail of the stool and gripped it as he stepped up beside her. He ran his hand over her back then down over her bottom. "Be still now, young lady, and I expect you to keep count for me. If you miss one, we'll have to start over." He rubbed the ruler over her ass, first up and down, then in circles. "Here we go."

He swatted her, once on each cheek, then again on each cheek. A pink mark about an inch wide appeared on her ass and his cock jumped and grew harder as a drop of pre-cum appeared on the head.

Ravyn let go of the rail and began to reach behind her then put her hands back and said, "One, two, three, four Sir."

Zane swatted her four more times, and then rubbed his hands over her pink-striped bottom as she counted out the swats.

"Five, six, seven, eight, Sir."

He gave her four more.

"Nine, ten, eleven, twelve, Sir."

He moved in front of her and ran his hand up and down his cock. She looked up at him and licked her lips.

"Do you know the proper way to suck cock?"

"No, Sir, but I'm a fast learner."

Zane slid the ruler beneath her chin. "I just bet you are, you naughty girl. You'll have to earn the right to suck my cock and swallow my cum." He moved back into position, then swatted her ass four more times.

"Thirteen, fourteen, fifteen, sixteen, Sir." The tears glazing her eyes made her voice husky.

Zane laid the ruler on her back, then rubbed his hand over her ass and held his palms against it, sealing in the heat, and she wiggled. He slid his fingers between her legs and swirled his fingers in the moisture he found there. "You're enjoying this even though it's meant as a punishment." He picked up the ruler and swatted her four more times, then tossed it on his desk and squatted down and looked into her eyes. He tutted, then shook his head. "What am I going to do with you? I can't have you telling the other students you enjoyed your punishment, now, can I?"

"I'm not enjoying it, Sir, really, I'm not." Ravyn sniffled.

Zane smiled, then reached over and ran his fingers between her legs, then held them up where she could see them before he rubbed them over her lips. He kissed her and hummed his approval as he tasted how sweet she was, like honey. He slid his lips away from hers, then smiled, stood, picked up the ruler and swatted her five times. "No lying allowed, young lady. You better remember that or your bottom is going to be a lot redder before the night is through. Do you understand?"

Ravyn sniffled again, then ran her hand over her face. "Yes, Sir."

"Excellent." Zane picked up the butt plug, then disappeared into the bathroom for a moment. When he returned, he picked up the tube of lube, then squatted down behind Ravyn. He tapped her left hand. "Hold this, and don't drop it." He waited until she had a grip on the plug, then he let it go and flipped the cap of the tube open and squeezed out a generous amount. It ran down her ass crack and she wiggled, and he smiled. "Cold, huh?"

"Yes, Sir."

"Here, I'll warm it up for you." Zane ran his fingers up and down and around her hole, smearing the lube until she was covered. "Hold still now. We're going to start with one finger." He began pressing his index finger into her and she moaned and wiggled. He swatted her on the bottom and she squealed. "Be still or you'll earn more swats with the ruler." He ran his other hand over her butt cheeks. "Your ass is the prettiest shade of rosy pink." As he talked, he pressed in deeper until his finger was inside her up to the second knuckle. She wiggled and he chuckled. "More?"

"Yes, please, Sir."

"You are a very bad girl. I may have to have you visit my office every day until you learn the rules." Zane pushed in until his finger was in her all the way. He pulled his finger out, then pushed it back in. He didn't think she realized she was rocking back and forth and making little moaning sounds. He took the plug from her hand and pressed it against her tight little rosette. She froze for a second, then wiggled, and he heard her whisper a litany of "please, please, please, Sir."

Zane pushed the plug against her bottom hole, then twisted it and pulled back before pressing it in again. Little by little, he slid the plug farther into her. "Relax now and let me get this in you, then we're going to see if you really are a fast learner." Zane pushed the plug against her, firmly, and it slid in the last little part. She gasped, then stiffened her legs and screamed as she came. He stood up, stared at her in disbelief for a moment, and then swatted her hard, five times.

"I'm going to, to, oh." Ravyn shivered again and gave a little satisfied moan of pleasure.

Zane reached beneath her and jerked her back. The little devil had had her clit up against the stool seat and had just given herself two orgasms. He pinched her clit and she squealed. With his other hand, he grabbed the ruler and swatted her five more times. Her ass was glowing red. "Beautiful."

He arranged her on the stool with her clit several inches back from the edge, then placed his hand on the small of her back. "If you move I'll use my belt on your ass. Do you understand, young lady?"

"Yes, Sir."

"Good, now, look at my cock." When she lifted her head, he rubbed the large, red tip over her lips and she licked the drops of pre-cum from it, then licked her lips and looked at him. "Good, now I want you to lick the head. All over like an ice cream cone."

Ravyn adjusted her position on the stool then obeyed him. She licked him softly, then stiffened her tongue and gave him a harder swipe before she swirled her tongue around the head. Finally, she slid her lips over it and sucked as she pulled off him with a little pop. She looked up at him for his approval.

"Keep doing that until I tell you to stop." He threaded his fingers into her hair and pulled her head up. "Feel free to take as much into your mouth as you can."

Ravyn surprised him when she slid her lips over the head of his cock and took him all the way to the back of her throat. She hollowed her cheeks and sucked on him as she flicked her tongue over his shaft. Her mouth was heaven and he already knew her pussy was hot and tight. Fucking her ass when she was ready was going to test him to the limits. He rocked back and forth, and she followed his movements, keeping his cock in her mouth. Her tongue was everywhere, up and down the sides and flicking over the bottom of his cock. He pulled out of her and she tried to follow, then mewed with disappointment when he moved out of her reach.

She looked up at him and frowned. He glared at her. "If you don't want me to take my belt to your ass, you better get that frown off your face, young lady." He almost laughed when her facial expression quickly smoothed out. "Now, stick out your tongue."

Ravyn smiled, then stuck out her tongue a little bit, then a little more, and then a little more until the tip touched her nose. She slurped her tongue back into her mouth, then giggled.

Zane felt himself shake with arousal and he barely managed to say, "Open."

Ravyn opened and nearly wrapped her tongue around his cock before she pulled him into her mouth.

Zane dropped his head back and stared at the ceiling, but his focus was really on Ravyn's mouth and what she was doing to him. He closed his eyes and concentrated on the feel of her tongue running over his shaft, then remembered he was supposed to be in charge and pulled out of her mouth just as he felt his balls draw up.

He pulled her up from the stool, held her in front of him for a moment while he tried to decide what to do with her, then said, "Fuck it," and bent her back over the stool. The condom on his desk drew his attention and he grabbed it, tore it open, and rolled it on. In seconds, he was behind her and thrusting into her. "Do you want this?" he asked, as he drew in a deep breath, unsure what he would do if she said no.

"Yes, oh, yes. Please, Sir."

"What's your safe word?" He cursed himself for asking, sure she would use it.

"Guilty, but I'm not saying it. Just telling you what it is, Sir." Ravyn wiggled her ass, tempting him "Is this part of my punishment for being a bad girl, Sir?"

"Does the thought of it turn you on?"

"Oh, yes." Her voice was a breathy whisper of sound.

Zane pressed into her. "Then, yes, young lady. I'm going to fuck you so hard you're not going to be able to walk out of here." He paused for a moment, then added, "After you stand in the corner for five minutes and think about what a bad girl you've been."

Ravyn shivered and goose bumps appeared on her silky skin.

"What did you just think?" Zane asked.

"I, uh, I thought if you weren't using a condom then when I stood in the corner with my legs apart your cum would run down my thighs and you would see it."

Zane grasped her hips and raised her slightly, then pushed into her. She wiggled and he slipped in deeper. Her slick cunt slid over his shaft and he pressed forward until he was balls-deep in her. His fingers bit into her soft flesh as he began fucking her.

"Harder, please, Sir, harder."

Zane lifted her hips and pounded into her. His cock made a slapping sound as he pressed forward, then a slick, wet sound as he pulled back. Two sounds he loved. He groaned and pumped harder, faster. Ravyn was moaning so often it sounded like one long purr of pleasure. He fucked her until he felt her tighten, then he stopped and waited until she relaxed and began again. After the third time, she was begging him to let her come.

"Can I come…can I come…can I come, please, Sir, please?"

"Not yet," he groaned. "Almost." He stopped for a moment, then pulled out until only the rounded head was in her, then slammed forward. "Now. Come now." She moaned, then screamed his name as she came. He pressed in deep, froze, and then let himself come as she pulsed around him.

He leaned over her and rested his chest on her back as he nuzzled her neck. "Good girl."

Ravyn hummed with pleasure. "I don't think I can stand, Sir."

Zane chuckled when he heard the wheedling tone in her voice. "I'll prop you in the corner and if you fall, I'll give you twenty more swats with the ruler." He kissed the back of her neck. "We need to do something about that pussy. Students at this school have bare mounds."

"But, Sir, I'm well-groomed and I like my landing strip."

"Ms. Templeton, I don't believe you've learned your lesson yet." He lifted her up and carried her to the corner. "I believe tomorrow we'll have a spa day."

Chapter Six

Ravyn opened her eyes, then had to bite her lip to keep from laughing with joy. Zane's face was only inches from hers on the pillow they shared. During the night, he'd slid one of his legs between hers and wrapped his arm around her waist, and she could feel his hand pressing into her back, holding her against him, belly to belly. Asleep, he looked younger than his twenty-nine years. The worry line between his brows had smoothed out and his lashes formed small, black fans beneath his eyes. His nose was slightly crooked and she wanted to kiss it, then lay a line of kisses down his chest and legs all the way to his feet and back up.

His morning erection pressed into her and she thought about waking him by rubbing herself all over him. Then she remembered what he'd said about grooming the night before and she froze. It wasn't that she didn't trust him, but the thought of anyone near her little pink parts with a razor made her want to run. Which she intended to do, as soon as she could free herself from the hold he had on her.

At least that was her plan until she moved and his leg slipped, putting a tiny bit of pressure on her clit. She gasped and wiggled, and Zane's eyes popped open. This close up, she could see a darker line of bluish-green ringing his irises as his eyes darkened with passion. She smiled and the hand on her back slid down, then settled on her bottom and patted her once, then again.

"Going somewhere, princess?"

Ravyn nodded her head. "Bathroom."

Zane searched beneath the covers for her hand. When he found it, he wrapped her fingers around his cock and held it there. “You have five minutes, then we’re taking a shower together.”

Ravyn squeezed his cock, then scrambled from the bed, squeaked when she realized she was naked, and hurried into the bathroom. She silently counted the seconds in her head as she used the facilities, and had just finished brushing her teeth when the door opened and Zane walked in. He punched the buttons on the shower control. “Go ahead and hop in,” he said, then swatted her on her bare bottom as he passed her.

She couldn’t help the hum of pleasure when she moved beneath the spray. The temperature was perfect and the force of the water was exactly what she needed after a night with Zane. The man was insatiable, and energetic. He’d not only put her in positions she didn’t think were humanly possible, he’d held her in them while he’d fucked her until she’d literally passed out in his arms. She turned, enjoying the massaging effect on the back of her neck and shoulders when Zane’s arms slid around her and pulled her slightly off balance. She relaxed and leaned against him, knowing he could hold her weight.

He kissed her neck, then moved her a couple steps back before he handed her the bottle of shower gel he used. “Wash me, slave.”

“As you wish, Master.” Ravyn squirted a small pool of gel on her hand, then rubbed them together before she began stroking her hands over his body, beginning at his shoulders. Zane held her waist as she rubbed circles on his chest, then down his arms. She dropped to her knees and washed his legs, paying special attention to his feet. He had gorgeous feet, long and narrow and so masculine. She pressed her fingertips between his toes and wiggled them. “Lift your foot, please.”

Zane pulled her head back until their eyes met. “Sir, pet.”

“Sir.”

He nodded, then released her.

She washed his foot, then made sure the suds had been rinsed away before she moved onto the second one. Once his feet were clean, she crawled around him and heard his groan of approval. He loved a woman willing to serve him and she was a woman who loved to serve. This was working out for the both of them, she thought. Now, if she could only get this business with Charles and Mendez out of the way, they might be okay.

She washed the backs of his legs, then his ass. He had a great ass. Hard and muscled, with tempting dips and curves. As she massaged his cheeks, the muscles flexed and rippled. She rinsed the suds away, then kissed his buns. Without thinking, she nipped him and he gave her a warning growl. So, she nipped him again, harder, and felt him shudder, then place his hands on the shower wall to brace himself.

Ravyn leaned between his spread legs and looked up. His head hung down, eyes closed. She smiled, then licked the inside of his left thigh, then his right thigh, then flicked her tongue over his scrotum. He groaned and she licked up his crack, over his anus, and up to the top of his crack, then back down.

She slid her hand around his hip and found his hand wrapped around his cock. She wrapped her hand over his and copied his movements as he stroked his dick. When he reached the mushroom-shaped head, he squeezed it, then moved his hand and placed it over hers. She continued to stroke his dick while she nipped his butt again, then licked up his crack then down to his balls. She sucked one into her mouth and ran her tongue over it before releasing it and taking the other one into her mouth. Zane groaned and her arousal grew. Knowing she was pleasing him…serving him…was making her so horny and wet, and she didn't known how much longer she could continue teasing him. Her pussy was empty and she needed him to fill her. To fuck her. She flicked her tongue over him again, then released him and slid between his legs and looked up at him. He moved his fingers apart and she slipped her tongue into the gap between two of them and licked the silky flesh of his dick.

"Open your mouth."

Ravyn rose to her knees and took his dick into her mouth as she grasped his hips. She knew what he liked now. She flicked her tongue up and down the length of his shaft, then sucked on the head. Slowly, she took him deeper and deeper with each plunge until he pressed against the back of her throat. She tightened her lips around his shaft and glided up and down, and heard him groan as he slid his fingers into her hair. Each time she reached the head, she slicked her tongue over it several times before sliding down the shaft again. She played with his balls, gently rolling them, but just as she felt them draw up, he pulled her head back and forced her to release him.

* * * *

Zane looked into her eyes. They were dark with arousal. He pulled her up and took her mouth in a devouring kiss. She moaned into his mouth and rubbed her belly against his cock. He smiled against her lips.

"Do you remember what I said I was going to do today?"

"Yes, Sir."

He stroked his finger over her lips. They were red and swollen from sucking him, and from his kiss. She looked good, kissable, so he kissed her again, then grabbed the shampoo. "I love your hair. Don't ever cut it." He wet her hair, then squirted some shampoo in his hand and rubbed them together, then smoothed the creamy suds down her hair and into her scalp. Ravyn dropped her head back and sighed with pleasure. A moment later, he tipped her head beneath one of the sprayers and rinsed the suds away before he stroked conditioner through the strands. When it had been rinsed away, he used the citrusy shower gel and washed her. Once she was clean, he hugged her, then patted her bottom. "Dry off and dry your hair. You can wrap a towel around yourself, but nothing else."

He watched her as he washed himself, then rinsed off. She had the most beautiful body. Lush, with curves in all the right places and a slender waist with curvy hips. The kind of hips a man could hold onto when he was inside her. With his cock throbbing, and his balls begging for release, he grabbed a towel and dried off. He'd just tossed the towel toward the hamper as she shut off the blow dryer, then ran the brush through her long, sleek hair. Her hair was true black, without a hint of blue. It flowed down her back and over her shoulders in sharp contrast to the white towel she'd wrapped around herself. Her eyes met his in the mirror and he easily identified the need in them as he slid his arms around her waist then picked her up.

He expected her to ask him where they were going, but was pleased when she rested her head on his shoulder instead. The show of trust pleased him and he held her tighter as he left their room and carried her to the playroom. Once inside he laid her down on the exam table, then loosened the towel and let it drape down on either side of her. He smoothed his hands over her legs, then moved to the end of the table. In seconds, he had the knee rests and stirrups adjusted.

"Scoot down and place your legs here." He patted the knee rests and stirrups, then smiled when she wiggled down a few inches and slowly spread her legs and moved into position. A soft blush covered her cheeks as he restrained her legs with straps above her knees and around her ankles. He tested the tightness. "Too tight?"

"No, Sir. They're comfortable."

Zane ran his hands down the insides of her thighs and felt her leg muscles ripple beneath his palms. He ran his fingers over her pussy, then circled her clit with his fingertip. She was already glistening with moisture and he knew she was still aroused from their time in the shower. He slid his hands back up to her knees and she shivered, and goose bumps rose on her skin.

"I'll be right back." He felt her eyes on his back as he walked toward the bathroom. Once inside, he filled a small tub with warm water, then got a cloth, shaving cream, a brush, and a new razor, which he set in a cup of cold water. As he carried the items back to the exam table, he saw Ravyn's eyes widen as her luscious mouth formed into a little pout. He placed the items on a rolling table, then moved it and an adjustable stool to the end of the exam table. Before he sat down, he moved up and leaned over her. Her beautiful, soft gray eyes were dilated with arousal and a soft, rosy blush covered her cheeks. She licked her lips and he couldn't resist kissing her, then stroking his finger over her soft skin.

Ravyn smiled, then asked, "May I speak, Master?"

He gazed into her eyes for another moment. This woman pleased him more than any other. "Permission granted."

"I thought I was supposed to serve you."

"You are serving me. I own you. If I want to shave your pussy, I will. If I want to roll you in the mud and then fuck you, I will. I'm your Master and you belong to me. Understand?"

Ravyn smiled, then nodded. "Yes, Master, I do now."

"Good, then let's get started."

He didn't wait for her agreement. As soon as he was settled on the stool, he rolled closer to her spread legs, then wrung out the cloth and laid it over her mound. While he waited for the warm cloth to soften the hair and open the pores, he touched her legs, letting his touch reassure her. After a few moments, he removed the cloth, then rubbed a few drops of shaving oil into her skin to help prevent razor burn. Ravyn wiggled and he saw a few drops of cream slip down the seam between her labial lips. He fought to keep the grin from his face. His princess liked having him play with her pussy even when she pouted and pretended she didn't like it. He wiped his hands, then opened the shaving cream, wet the brush, and worked up a lather that he applied to her mound before he picked up the razor, and slowly drew it over her. Little by little, he shaved her until her skin was smooth and bare. He wrung out the cloth again and washed the residue away, then leaned down and licked her and heard her gasp of surprise.

"Sensitive, pet?" He opened a jar of aloe and rubbed the cooling gel into her bare skin.

"Yes, oh, yes." Her voice was breathy, the words barely loud enough for him to hear.

Zane ran his tongue down her slit, then slid it into her. She tasted tangy and good. He wiggled his tongue deeper and Ravyn cried out and wiggled again. As he licked her, he played with her nipples, pinching them and strumming his fingers over them. Ravyn strained her hips upward, and he placed his hand on her belly and held her down. "Be still."

He continued to run his tongue over her swollen lips and into her sleek pussy until her clit was red and poking out from its hood. He swiped his tongue over it, then sucked it into his mouth. He stiffened his tongue and ran it over her clit again and again. She shivered, then froze right before she screamed his name and came on his tongue. He licked her, unable to get enough of her taste and she came again, then collapsed into a sprawl.

He kissed her pussy, then looked up at her. Her breasts rose and fell with her rapid breaths. Her arms hung over the sides of the table. Everything about her screamed that she was a woman who'd been taken to the limits of her desire and satisfied. He stood and kicked the stool, and it rolled several feet away as he gently stroked his cock up and down her slit, coating himself in her cream. Slowly, gently, he slid into her, then pulled back and slid further into her until he was as deep as he could go.

Ravyn moaned and reached for him. He grasped her hands and held onto her as he began fucking her. He focused on her eyes, then looked down and watched his cock disappear into her. Damn, the sight made his heart pound in his chest as his breaths rasped in and out. He pulled on her hands until he lifted her. "Watch me fuck you."

Ravyn looked down, then gasped.

He slid out until only the head of his cock was inside her, then slowly slid back in, and she gasped again and glanced up at him, then down again.

"Haven't you ever watched a cock fucking you, princess?"

Ravyn shook her head and her silky hair slid over her chest and covered her breasts. Her rosy red nipples peeked out between the strands. "Just the one time when you fucked me in your kitchen, Sir." She wiggled, then curved her pelvis upward. "Please, please."

Zane released her hands and she held herself up on her elbows while he played with her clit, flicking his finger over and around it. "What do you want?"

"You. I want you to fuck me. Hard and deep and fast. Oh, please, Master."

Zane plunged into her, then pulled out and slammed back in again.

"Oh, yes, oh, oh."

"Watch." His fingers tightened around her thighs as he continued pumping into her and she strained upward, encouraging him to take her. He couldn't resist her invitation and began fucking her, hard and deep. Watching his cock disappear into her had his heart slamming in his chest. He drew in another deep breath, felt the beginning signs of a pending orgasm, and told himself to hold back, nearly failing when he felt her pussy ripple around his cock.

Ravyn reached down and touched Zane's cock as he pulled out of her, then slid back in. She lifted her fingers to her mouth and licked them.

"God, Ravyn." Zane slammed back into her, then grasped her clit. "Come, now."

Ravyn dropped like a stone onto the table as she came, screaming his name, and he exploded inside her. He felt as if the orgasm was being torn out of him. He planted his hands on either side of her waist and collapsed over her, and felt her shiver. Her hand slid into his hair and she held him against her. The pounding pulse in her throat caught his attention. He licked it and heard her moan.

"Kiss me," he said, then waited.

Ravyn lifted her head until their lips met. The kiss was soft, inviting intimacy. Zane slid his hands beneath her head and held her mouth to his. When he raised his head, he smiled at her, then stood up and released the restraints on her legs. She swung around until her legs hung off the side of the exam table. Zane lifted her into his arms, carried her into the shower and quickly washed her, then himself. After she dried her hair, he ordered her to clean up the playroom, then watched her. He nodded his approval and then wrapped a towel around her and carried her back to their room and into the closet. He searched through her clothes and chose a white wrap dress with little red roses on it for her to wear. He handed it to her, then patted his hard belly. "Get dressed, then time for breakfast."

Ravyn slipped it on, then went into the bathroom where Zane was shaving. She watched him in the mirror while she brushed her hair.

"Can I ask you something?" she asked as she put her hair up in a ponytail.

"Sure." Zane lifted his chin and scraped the razor over his neck.

"Did your mom—Joan, I mean—beat you?"

"Shit." Zane dropped the straight razor, then bent over and splashed cold water on his jawline before he grabbed a tissue and held it to his neck.

Alarmed, Ravyn reached for his hand and lifted the tissue away. A small scrape on the curve of his jawline seeped several tiny drops of blood. She glanced up at him, but he avoided making eye contact, a move that only increased her curiosity as she dabbed at the scrape. "It's not too bad." She pressed the tissue against it, then lifted it. "It's already stopped bleeding."

Zane took the tissue from her and threw it in the trash before he picked up the razor and continued shaving.

Ravyn waited for a moment. "Are you okay?"

Zane slid the razor over his chin. "Mmmhmm."

Ravyn scooted up on the counter and watched as he rinsed the razor. "Are you going to answer my question?" she asked while wondering if he would tell her the truth.

He gave her a sideways glance, then went back to shaving. He rinsed the blade again. "I don't remember much about her."

"Did she beat Cade?"

Zane sighed. "I think so. When she was drinking, Cade would send us upstairs with Jackson while he kept her downstairs."

"Did you ever see marks on him?"

Zane snorted and Ravyn took that as a yes. "Did she beat you?"

"No, but she hurt Luc once. The neighbors called the police. After that, John came home and we moved to Long Valley. Things were better then."

"You remember him? John, I mean?"

Zane dried the razor and put it away, then washed the rest of the shaving cream away. The towel he used to dry his face muffled his voice. "Not very well. Mostly I remember that after he came home, we didn't go hungry anymore and Cade didn't have as many bruises."

Ravyn was surprised by his answer. Why didn't his dad put an end to the abuse? "She still beat Cade even after he came home?"

"John worked nights. Joan drank nights. When she drank, she beat Cade." He tossed the towel into the hamper. "Why are you asking me all these questions?"

Ravyn shrugged. "You asked me about Charles last night and it made me wonder if you knew what it was like to be scared like that."

Zane spread Ravyn's legs and stepped between them. He grasped her ponytail and pulled her head back until their eyes met. "Did he ever do more than touch you or try to kiss you?"

"There were some close calls, but I was pretty good at hiding from him." Ravyn wanted to look away from him but made herself hold his gaze. She hadn't planned on being on the receiving end of the questioning. "Did your mom bring men home with her?"

"Sometimes." Zane narrowed his eyes.

"Do you think one of your mom's boyfriends went after Cade…in a bad way?"

Zane slid his thumbs beneath her chin and she shivered. He was controlling her movements with just the touch of his hands. His eyes had darkened, but he wasn't aroused. Her nerves twanged when he didn't answer and she did what she always did when she was nervous…she started blabbering. "That happens, you know? To boys and not just girls. More often than people realize. I read this article and it sa—"

Zane slid a finger over her lips and she stopped talking.

"I have an idea, princess—why don't you ask him?"

"Uh, no." She fidgeted, wondering if questioning him had been a bad idea and if she should stop. She still hadn't asked him the one question she really wanted to ask though.

"Are you done now?"

Ravyn licked her lips, saw him track the movement, and rushed into speech. "I heard that when the Ramseys adopted you and your brothers, Cade didn't talk to them for several years. He doesn't talk much now, either."

"He doesn't have anything to say." Zane gave her a hard little kiss, then nipped her bottom lip. "You women talk to each other too much."

"We talk to each other because you *men* won't tell us everything we want to know."

"There are things you don't need to know." Zane shifted his hands to her waist and pulled her off the counter. "Breakfast, then we're going riding."

"I don't know how to ride."

"Now, princess, we both know that's not true. You've ridden me several times."

"It's not the same thing, Zane."

"Sure it is. You just spread your legs and hop on."

Chapter Seven

Ravyn covered Zane's hand, then strummed her fingers over his fingers. He pressed his hand into her tummy and pulled her back against him. She tipped her head to the side and looked up at him, and he leaned down and brushed his lips over hers. He was dressed in jeans and an old, faded T-shirt with worn cowboy boots and a hat that looked as if it had been dropped and stepped on several times.

"What are you thinking about, princess?"

She smiled, then reached up and touched the bent brim of his hat. He'd pulled it down low, shading his eyes. "You look like an outlaw."

"Does that turn you on?"

"Oh, yes."

"Tell me a story and make it filthy."

Ravyn felt a blush of heat on her cheeks and Zane laughed. She glanced to her left. Cade rode his gelding, Sarge, a few feet away from them with Addison held safely in front of him. Thor and Marisol rode next to them, each on a horse of their own as Marisol had refused to double up with Thor. Jackson and Jenna were to their right with Luc and Logan beyond them. At the moment, Cassie was riding with Luc.

"Well, I was just thinking that you look like an outlaw with your hat pulled down like that. And, then I wondered what it would be like to ride across this land if you'd just raided my home and taken me."

"Start over. What year is it? What's your name?"

Ravyn leaned back against him, closed her eyes, and let her imagination soar. "It's 1867 and my name is Daisy Darling."

Zane laughed, interrupting her story, then squeezed her as he chuckled. "Go on, Daisy Darling."

Ravyn laughed, then continued, "The Civil War ended two years ago. My father died in the war, leaving my mother and me in the guardianship of her evil brother, Bedford. He and his friend, Halbert Smythe the third, want my father's land, and he's trying to force me to marry Halbert. My mother is very ill and knows she won't live long, so she came up with a way for me to escape. I've been writing to a gentleman in Texas who wants a wife. He sent me the money for the train."

"So, you're a mail-order bride, huh?"

"Yes, from New Orleans."

"Me, too," Addison said.

Ravyn gasped and sat up. She hadn't realized that the others had ridden closer and had been listening to her. Addison smiled at her and the sun turned her eyes into sparkling sapphires. "Okay, what's your name?" Ravyn asked.

"Lily Lovely," Addison said, then laughed. "But, I'm a dance hall girl trying to escape her disreputable past and settle down."

Cade laughed and kissed the top of Addison's reddish-gold hair. "Good for you, baby."

Jenna drew their attention when she said, "If Addison is playing then I want to play, too. My name is Honey Houston. I'm a friend of Lily's from the saloon."

Jackson laughed. "You naughty girl. You need a whipping."

Jenna laughed then hugged her arms around his neck. "I bet you're just the man to give me one. Aren't you, mister?" Jackson tipped Jenna over his arm and kissed her.

Marisol rode closer. "I want to play, too. My name is Magnolia Mercy. I was on my way to the convent when I was kidnapped by this outlaw." She pointed to Thor.

Thor grunted then laughed. "I'm of Viking decent, Magnolia. Prepare to be pillaged."

"You wish," Marisol said, then guided her horse a few feet away from him. "I got away from him once and got on the train at the last stop. I sat down next to Lily Lovely and we started talking."

Ravyn turned to Cassie, who just stared back at her for a moment, then rolled her eyes.

"Oh, all right. I'm Rose Round-heel. I'm a working girl." She winked, then laughed. "I was coming west because I heard the pay was better in Texas for girls like me. I have no intention whatsoever of changing my ways."

Luc kissed Cassie, then handed her over to Logan. He settled her in front of him, nuzzled her neck, and then kissed her. "You're my kind of lady, Rose."

"Okay, now that that's settled, everyone settle down," Zane said. "You invited yourselves along on this ride, so be quiet and let Daisy tell her story."

Ravyn grinned as she looked at the royals. During breakfast, the minute Zane had said they were going riding, Addison had insisted she and Cade join them. Within minutes, Addison had talked everyone into coming along for a swim in the river and a picnic. She knew Zane had had his own plans for them, but apparently, the other men did, too, as they each had a bedroll tied to their saddles. She could see the leather-wrapped handle of a riding crop sticking out of Jackson's and she wondered what Zane had planned for her. Out of curiosity she asked, "How many men do you have stationed around the picnic area at the river?"

"Enough to make sure you're safe," Zane said, then tapped her tummy. "Start talking, Daisy."

Ravyn laughed. "Okay. The five of us met on the train and as we talked, we realized we were all going to the same small town. Rendezvous, Texas. Before we could get there, though, the train was stopped and the conductor said we were being robbed by six outlaws. You all came aboard with your guns cocked and ready to fire." She had to stop and wait for the royals to stop giggling.

Zane leaned down and nuzzled her neck. "That's not all that's ready to fire, Daisy."

Ravyn tipped her head to the side to give him better access and he kissed, then licked that one little spot that always made her panties wet, if she was wearing panties. She squirmed and felt her jeans grow wet. Zane slid his hand up the inside of her jean-clad leg to her crotch and she rushed into speech.

"You claimed you were ranchers and you weren't there to rob anyone. All you wanted was brides, because you were so lonely and you'd heard there were brides on the train."

"What? Their horses weren't enough for them?" Jenna asked, in her best southern belle accent. "In my experience, cowboys love their horses."

"Horses, brides, same difference," Jackson said. "The more spirited they are, the better the ride."

"I do declare, Sir," Jenna said. "Why, you just make my little ol' southern heart yearn for a nice, long ride."

Ravyn laughed then continued her story. "You spotted us sitting in the back corner of the train car and surrounded us. In seconds, we were over your shoulders and off the train. Our screams and tears didn't bother you, nor did our begging to be set free. You"—she pointed behind her at Zane—"threatened to tie me up and gag me if I didn't quiet down. Something a true southern gentlemen would never threaten to do."

"Daisy, you haven't met the right kind of southern gentlemen," Zane said, his breath warm on her neck. Goose bumps rose on her arms and she shivered, even though the day was warm and sunny. Zane pulled his horse up and the other men moved into a circular formation, facing him. "I think we need to give our southern belles a fighting chance." He grabbed Ravyn's leg, then lifted it over the saddle horn and lowered her to the ground. She looked around and saw that Marisol, Jenna, and Cassie were still mounted. Addison was standing next to Sarge, and Cade was leaning down and talking to her.

She nodded her head, apparently agreeing to something he said, then walked over and mounted in front of Marisol. Cassie rode closer to Ravyn, then pulled her foot out of the stirrup and offered Ravyn her hand. Ravyn took it, then lifted herself onto the horse behind Cassie. Jackson doubled up behind Cade.

Zane leered at her, then chuckled. "Okay, ladies, you have now escaped us. Here are the rules. You ride directly to the river and you stay on this side of it. You can follow the river for three hundred yards in either direction to hide. We will be hunting you. You can only be caught by your man, but when you're caught, you will be punished, then fucked. Do you understand?"

Ravyn fanned herself and fluttered her lashes at Zane. "Why, Sir, how dare you threaten to put your hands and other interesting parts on me."

Zane laughed, then nodded toward the river. "Get going, Daisy. You have fifteen minutes before we come after you."

Ravyn laughed, then held onto Cassie as they rode toward the trees in the distance. Once in the shade, Cassie guided the horse to an open area that had been landscaped with grass and flowers. A thick bed of sand lined the riverbank and there were picnic tables located on each side of the clearing. A large, covered fire pit sat in the center surrounded by eight benches with thick cushions on them.

"Wow, this is nice," Ravyn said as she dismounted, followed by Cassie, who walked the horse over to a rope strung between two trees and tied the reins to it.

Jenna tied her horse next to Cassie's, then walked back to Ravyn. "This is where I caught Jackson skinny-dipping when I was twenty-two." She looked around, then pointed to a tree limb. "He'd hung his clothes on that branch. He caught me spying on him and we had a really hot encounter. Afterward, he got dressed and told me if I was still here when he turned around he was going to use his belt on my ass." She laughed. "I ran away, but looking back, I wish I'd stayed."

Ravyn felt her heart speed up and wished she'd been there to see that. "So, he built this as a memorial?"

Jenna nodded. "Yes. All of the brothers are really romantic in their own way."

Addison and Marisol joined them and Addison laughed. "Did you see the big white monument on the hill?"

Ravyn nodded. "The Ramsey cemetery is up there, right?"

Addison laughed. "Yes, but the big white monument is in memory of my stallion, Diablo. I always thought Cade had it built because I loved Diablo so much, but now I know he built it because he loves me so much. You see, one time when I was about fourteen or so, he and I were out checking fences and some men tried to kidnap me. Cade made me ride away on Diablo while he stayed back and shot at them to keep them from following me. He said that Diablo saved my life that day and that's why he built the monument. Because he wouldn't want to live without me."

Cassie joined them. "I can hardly wait to see what Luc and Logan build for me. I know they're planning something because twice now, they've clammed up when I've walked into their office."

Jenna smiled. "It will be something wonderful, Cassie."

Cassie laughed. "I know." She sighed, then said, "We better get going or they're going to find us standing around yammering."

Addison hopped up on the picnic table and lay back with her legs hanging over the edge. She swung her feet in their shiny red boots back and forth, then smiled at the sky. Ravyn couldn't keep the smile from her face. Pregnancy had turned Addison into a lazy little Irish elf and Cade into a worrier.

"Are you staying here, Addison?" Jenna asked.

"Yes. I promised Cade I would. I'll see the rest of you after you're caught and punished."

"What makes you think we'll all get caught?" Cassie asked.

"Because I know you and you're no dummies. Who could resist the lure of punishment, then a good fucking?" Addison asked.

"You're right," Ravyn said. "The sooner we hide, the sooner they can find us." Before she could take off, Cassie grabbed her arm.

"Give me your boots, Ravyn," Cassie said, then winked.

Ravyn laughed, then slipped off her boots and handed them over.

Cassie stood up. "Stay here while I lay a false trail for Ravyn. Then I'll do one for each of you, and then we'll take off." She left, then returned several minutes later and changed boots with Marisol and disappeared again. The third time she returned, she put on Jenna's boots. When she returned, she gave Jenna's boots back to her, then put on Ravyn's.

"Okay, Ravyn and I are going east. Jenna, you and Marisol should go west. Travel together for part of the way, then separate and hide." She glanced at Ravyn. "I'm going to follow you and clean up our trail."

Ravyn stood up, then went east for a hundred feet before Cassie stopped her.

"Okay, we separate here. Do you want to go toward the river or away from it?"

"Away from it," Ravyn said.

Cassie high-fived her. "Good luck."

Ravyn glanced in the direction she intended to take, but when she turned back to wish Cassie good luck, she was gone. "Damn, how does she do that?" She shook her head, then carefully walked back toward the field. A few minutes later, she saw a good climbing tree, walked past it, and carefully hid her steps as she circled around as if she was lost, then crouched down by a bush, making sure to leave her knee marks in the ground before standing. She took several steps back toward the field, then carefully walked back to the tree she'd chosen. She glanced around, didn't see anyone, and reached up and grabbed the first branch, then heaved herself up. Off in the distance, a scream followed by laughter came from the river and she smiled as she climbed. Jackson had just found Jenna.

Once she was high enough off the ground, she found a large branch and sat down on it, then wrapped her arms and legs around the tree trunk. The branches below her hid her from view but she had a small glimpse of the path she'd taken from the clearing. She knew Zane would find her, and probably sooner rather than later, but at least he would have to search for her. She didn't expect him to use the path she and Cassie had taken and was surprised when she saw him, Luc, and Logan step into view. They searched the ground, then spoke for a moment before Zane moved in her direction while Luc and Logan moved in the direction Cassie had taken.

She held her breath as he drew closer. He paused by the base of the tree she was in, then moved past it. Minutes went by as she waited for him to return. When he didn't she smiled a self-satisfied smile and smothered a giggle, then gasped when she looked down and met his leaf-green eyes.

"Come down here and get your punishment, princess. You're getting extra for the trick with the boots."

"How'd you find me?"

"You didn't check your six. Once I moved past you I had a clear view of your back."

Ravyn looked behind her, and saw that he was right. "Oh, da—I mean dang." She began climbing down. Once she was at the lowest branch, she hung down from it, and Zane grasped her around the waist and lowered her to her feet. He smiled at her, then unbuttoned her jeans and slid the zipper down. A second later, he hooked the waistband with his thumbs and pushed the jeans down to her boots but left them wrapped around her ankles.

"Arms up."

Ravyn stuck her arms in the air and Zane grasped the hem of her T-shirt and stripped it from her. She was braless and he smiled at her before he held the shirt against the tree. "Breasts against the shirt."

Ravyn shuffled closer until she was in position and Zane placed her arms around the tree. Her fingers didn't touch, so she gripped the grooved bark. He adjusted her stance until her butt was sticking out, then he stroked his hands over her back and across her ass cheeks and the backs of her thighs. Several fingers slid through her ass crack, then over her pussy, and she knew without looking that they were wet when he held them up. A second later, she shivered when she heard him sucking her cream from his fingers. She wanted him to hurry, so she wiggled and he swatted her.

"No moving. We've discussed topping from the bottom, right?"

"Yes, Sir."

"Then you're getting five more for breaking that rule. That makes ten swats, but first, we're going to see how you like this."

Ravyn felt something soft trail over her back and then across her butt. Goose bumps rose on her flesh and she pressed harder against the tree.

Zane chuckled. "I thought you'd like this flogger."

Ravyn gasped as the first stroke of the soft leather strands swept over her back. She tightened her arms and rested her forehead against the tree. Gradually, stroke by stroke, Zane worked the flogger in a side-to-side pattern down her back then over her buttocks before moving back up and starting down again. She wanted to wiggle. Instead, she moaned.

Zane stopped and pressed his chest against her back. He nuzzled her neck. "Good, pet?"

"Oh, yes, Master. So good."

He kissed her nape, then stepped back and began again.

Ravyn felt her mind shift as she relaxed and floated in a soft, shadowy place. Gradually, her arms drifted to her sides and her weight rested against the tree as soft moans left her lips.

Zane pressed his chest against her back again, then nipped her shoulder. He grasped her wrists, then wrapped her arms around the tree again. "Hold on."

She wallowed in the pleasure of having his weight pressed against her, holding her helpless and controlling her. She tried to grip the tree but only managed to keep her arms up as he stepped back.

"I want you to keep count and thank me." He swatted her once on each ass cheek, then waited.

Ravyn forced herself to pay attention. "One, two, thank you, Master."

Zane swatted her once on each cheek, then again.

"Three, four, five, six, thank you, Master."

He repeated the same sequence. Ravyn counted them, thanked him, and he pulled her back until she was bent at the waist.

"Brace your hands on the tree and spread your legs."

Ravyn heard the hiss of a zipper being lowered, then felt Zane's hands stoke over her back and grasp her waist. He lifted her to her toes, then pressed the head of his cock against her pussy. She was so wet that there was no resistance as he slipped into her, pulled back once, and then plunged in all the way. She moaned, then wiggled, and he swatted her right ass cheek as a warning. She liked it, so she wiggled again and he pulled out of her, stepped back, and swatted her five times, hard, right on the crack of her ass. She screeched, and he grabbed her and thrust back into her.

"No topping from the bottom. If I have to tell you again I'm using my belt on your ass. Do you understand?"

"Yes, Sir." Ravyn forced herself to be still and let him fuck her. Apparently, her behavior pleased him because he began fucking her so hard she had trouble keeping her balance.

"That's it, baby. You know what I want. Press back and give yourself to me."

Ravyn braced her hands and pushed back toward him. She loved this. Loved serving him and giving herself to him. Zane began fucking her harder, deeper. The sounds his cock made as it slid in and out of her should have embarrassed her but they spiked her arousal instead. She tightened her vaginal muscles and tried to hold him inside her.

Zane groaned. “That’s it. Squeeze down on my cock while I fuck you.”

Ravyn began a squeeze-release rhythm and Zane stopped for a moment, then groaned. He slid his hand over her ass, gathered some of her cream on his finger, and spread it over her anus. She wanted to reach back and spread her cheeks to give him access to her, but there was no need. His finger gathered more cream, then pushed into her. Little screams of pleasure and need left her and she shoved back against him. The finger slid in all the way.

“Oh, oh, please, Master, please.”

“Not yet. Not yet.”

Zane pushed into her, then held himself still as he finger-fucked her ass. Ravyn shivered and goose bumps appeared on her back. He added another finger and she panted with pleasure.

“Please, please.”

Zane pulled his cock out of her, then plunged back in. “Now, come now.”

His demand exploded through her followed by an orgasm unlike anything she’d ever experienced before. The pleasure swept through her then rebounded, over and over. She screamed his name then lost her grip on the tree. Zane caught her and held onto her as he came and his hot seed flooded into her. He pumped a few more times and Ravyn felt her moisture and his seed running down her legs. The sensation threw her into another orgasm and she heard Zane groan when her vagina rippled and pulsed around his cock again.

He leaned over her, his breath hot on the back of her neck. He nibbled on her nape, then slid his hands around her and played with her nipples. She moaned and he chuckled, then pulled out of her.

“Sir?” Ravyn wiggled, wanting him to fuck her again.

He chuckled then swatted her ass. “Get dressed, princess. No more fucking for you right now.”

"Have I displeased you, Master?" Ravyn chewed her lip while she pulled up her jeans and fastened them. Was she too demanding? Was he changing his mind about keeping her? It took her only a moment to pick up her shirt, shake it out, and slip it on while she waited for his answer.

When she turned around, Zane shoved his shoulder into her belly and lifted her over his shoulder, then swatted her butt. "You please me very much, pet, but you're my prisoner now, so behave or I'll take a crop to your ass."

* * * *

After returning from the hunt, they changed into their suits and swam. Luc and Logan were the last to show up with Cassie tied up and thrown over Luc's shoulder. They quickly changed into suits and jumped in the water then started a game of war until Addison complained of being hungry.

The day was too warm to have a fire, so they left the cover on the fire pit and placed the food and drinks on it. Everyone helped themselves, then found a seat.

Ravyn snuggled up against Zane with a glass of iced tea in her hand. He was angled in the corner of one of the padded benches with her almost on his lap. He balanced a plate of food on her tummy and fed her a bite, then himself a bite, between sips of tea.

Ravyn looked around and smiled. It was turning out to be one of the best weekends of her life. Earlier, when she'd begun to worry about what would happen when the call from Mendez came she'd shut the thought down immediately. She was going to allow herself to have as much joy as she could before the situation became what Zane called FUBAR. Fucked up beyond all recognition. It was a good acronym and one she intended to remember.

"You okay?" Zane asked.

"Yes." She looked into his eyes and smiled. "I'm having a good time. I haven't done anything like this since my mother and I would go to our beach home by Corpus Christi. Every day we would swim, then eat our lunch on the beach."

Zane tightened his arm around her. "It must have been hard on you to lose her."

"Yes. It was horrible. I still have nightmares about the reporters surrounding my father and me while they yelled questions and tried to take my picture. After that, my father became really protective. I think he was scared something would happen to me."

"Did they ever figure out who had kidnapped her?"

Ravyn shook her head. "I've always felt guilty that they got her that day."

Zane smoothed his hand over her hair. "You were just a kid, princess. You wouldn't have been able to save her."

"You don't understand, Zane. They weren't after my mother. They were after me."

Zane sat up and the plate slid off Ravyn's lap to the ground. "What? Why do you think that, Ravyn?"

"Well, because my mother shouldn't have been at the park that day. My friend, Emma, was supposed to be holding her birthday party there and I wanted to go, but I was grounded. Charles told me he would take my mom to lunch and I could sneak out and go."

"Dolman was there?"

"Yes, he'd always show up when we went to the beach house. Anyway, Emma's party was supposed to be in the park, but they'd closed it because they'd found a huge African bee nest. I had to walk by her house to get to the park and her mom saw me and stopped me. Our housekeeper told my mom where I'd gone and she went to the park to find me. That's when she was kidnapped." Ravyn realized everyone had grown quiet. She looked around and saw that they were focused on her.

Cade drew her attention to him. "Where was Dolman when your mother was kidnapped?"

"The housekeeper said he and my mother had argued and he'd taken off before she went to the park to find me."

"Did you tell this to your father and the police, Ravyn?" Zane asked.

"I told my father. I guess he told the police. I know the police talked to our housekeeper. She probably told them, too."

"What's that housekeeper's name, and where is she now?" Thor asked.

"Her name was Lettie. I don't know her last name or where she lives. She was older then, so she may not even be alive now. It happened almost fourteen years ago."

Across from her, Addison squirmed, then settled when Cade gave her a suspicious look. Ravyn watch as Addison smiled at Cade, then seemed to find her bare toes fascinating.

Luc settled Cassie on Logan's lap, then leaned toward Ravyn. "You said that Dolman had a mistress and you'd found several long blonde hairs on his jacket."

"Yes. That's right," Ravyn said.

"Do you remember when you found the first hair?"

"Over two years ago. Why?"

"Dolman was arrested for trying to have you killed last November. The two of you were living apart at the time. Where was he living?"

"He kept an apartment downtown. A penthouse." Ravyn looked from Luc to Logan. "Why are you asking me all these questions?"

Luc narrowed his eyes. "Just a couple more questions. Did his mistress live with him?"

"I don't know."

"Did you ever hear him say the name Linda?" Luc asked.

Ravyn shook her head. "No." Ravyn saw Luc glance toward Logan, then a second later Logan nodded, then wrapped his arms around Cassie and whispered something to her.

Addison pushed Cade's hands away, then stood up.

"If you're going to talk about your horrible ex-sub, the woman the two of you shared with Cade before we were together, then I'm going swimming again," Addison said.

"I'll go with you," Cassie offered.

Cade pulled Addison back onto his lap. "We're just trying to keep all of you safe while we figure out what's going on."

Ravyn saw the frown on Addison's face and thought, ah, oh, the crap is about to hit the fan.

"By withholding information when you promised not to keep secrets from me," Addison said.

"Baby—"

"Don't you *baby* me, Cade Ramsey! You promised. What else are you keeping from me?" Addison turned to Cassie. "Did you know about this?"

"Not until just now, when Logan explained it all to me." Cassie elbowed Luc, then jumped to her feet. "You know, I think there's a lot of things going on that we women aren't being told about. Maybe I forgave the two of you"—she pointed to Logan, then Luc—"too quickly."

Logan stood up and grasped Cassie's waist. He pulled her onto her toes until they were almost nose to nose. "Come on, sugar, don't make me gro—" Logan stopped talking, but not soon enough.

Luc growled, then stood up next to Logan and confronted him. "If you've been groveling, I'm going to kick your ass. You're supposed to be a Dom."

Thor laughed and Cade and Jackson snorted, then chuckled.

Jenna stood up and moved next to Cassie. "I'm going swimming, too. If Cade, Luc, and Logan know what's going on, then so does Jackson."

Logan wrapped his arms around Cassie. "You said you forgave us. You can't take it back now." Before Cassie could move away, Logan sat down with his arms wound around her waist. Luc sighed, then sat down again and lifted Cassie's feet onto his lap.

"We're going to talk about this later tonight. At home," Luc said, and Cassie snorted, then slid off Logan's lap and sat between them. When Luc reached for her, she leaned away from him.

"Hands off the goods," Cassie said, and Luc growled, then sent Logan an evil look.

Ravyn lowered her eyes. Apparently, she wasn't the only person with secrets.

Jackson patted the area next to him, and Jenna moved back to the bench and sat down, but kept some distance between them.

Zane sighed. "I think we all need to lay our cards on the table. Together, we may know a lot more than we realize. For instance, it makes me suspicious that Dolman was in Corpus Christi the day your mother was kidnapped, Ravyn."

"You think he had something to do with her death?" Ravyn asked, realizing she'd never even considered that possibility because she'd always believed Dolman was in love with her mother.

"We know either he or your father had begun laundering money for Mendez," Zane said. "Were you being held hostage in Colombia by Dolman and Mendez?"

Ravyn thought about what she could tell them without incriminating herself. Not much, she realized, but maybe just enough. "Yes, but I didn't realize it for a long time. Once we got to Colombia, things got really bad. Charles was gone all the time and I wasn't allowed to leave the property. I asked him when we were going home and he got really mad and hit me. I didn't ask again after that."

"That son of a bitch," Zane growled. "I'm going to kill him."

Cade chuckled. "It's easy to throw that law book out the window when it's your woman being hit, isn't it, baby brother?"

"Fuck off, Cade. It's not the same thing." Zane frowned, then rubbed his hand up and down Ravyn's arm. "Do you think your father was involved with Mendez?"

Ravyn shook her head. "My father was controlling, but he wasn't evil. I know he wouldn't have worked with Mendez."

Zane's arms tightened around her. "Do you know how your mother died?"

"She was stabbed, but that's all I know. I was only twelve at the time and my father never talked about her after she died."

"When you were in Thor's SUV, you said you'd heard Dolman mention Barbie's name and that she'd cheated him out of some money," Zane said. "Did you ever hear him mention her name at any other time?"

"No, just that one time."

"How long ago was that?" Zane asked.

Ravyn thought about it, then said, "Right before he tried to have me killed. So, about nine months ago."

Thor had been texting someone for the last few minutes. A chime sounded from his phone and he read the text, then his lips curved in the smile of a predator. "I had Dania look at the police investigation of your mother's death, Ravyn. Her cause of death was reported as a knife wound to the back of the neck."

Ravyn let out a soft cry, then buried her face in Zane's shoulder. He threaded his fingers into her hair, shielding her as he whispered to her.

"The same way my father died," Cassie said, giving Ravyn a moment to compose herself. "That's Dale Miller's method."

"Yes," Thor said.

Ravyn felt a wave of rage sweep through her. Had Mendez ordered her mother's death, she wondered as she sat up. "Do you think it was him? That he killed my mother?"

Ravyn saw Addison squirm again and Cade pulled her onto his lap. "It's time to tell her, baby."

Addison nodded, then pushed herself away from Cade and stood up. "I want to talk to the royals first."

Thor growled. "Damn it, Ramsey, she's going to negotiate for information now. Do something."

Addison stomped her foot. "Tell me you and Cade aren't keeping some information back."

Thor shook his head. Cade sighed, then said, "I can't do that."

"Then, it's only fair we get an exchange of information."

"Addison, I'm going to whip your ass," Cade said, his voice threatening.

Addison covered her belly, then spoke to it. "Did you hear that, Limo? Mean old Daddy wants to whip Mommy." She crossed her arms and stuck her chin in the air. "Deal, or no info."

Ravyn watched as Cade looked around, got nods of agreement from his brothers, and Thor then said, "You tell us everything you know and one of us will answer any question you ask."

"No," Addison said. "We each get to ask a question. Cassie gets to ask two, because she has Luc and Logan. After each question is answered, I tell one thing I know."

"You don't know that much," Cade said.

Addison smiled, then shrugged and waited. A moment later, Cade growled, then said, "All right. An equal exchange, but first you tell me what you know about Lettie."

"I already told you part of what Maggie told me when she called earlier. I would have told you this, too, but there wasn't time."

"Okay, baby. Tell me now."

Addison smiled. "Her last name is Davis. She lives in Corpus Christi. I have her address and phone number at home."

Cade nodded, then waved her away. "Get going and don't keep us waiting too long."

Addison waved the royals to follow her. They huddled together by the riverbank. Every now and then, one of them would look at the men, then return to the huddle. After several more minutes, they returned to their seats.

Addison pulled her feet up onto the edge of the bench then hugged her knees. "You first, Jenna."

Jenna hugged Jackson. "Do you love me more than you love your horses?" she asked and the royals giggled.

Jackson cocked a brow then smiled. "Yes, angel. I love you more than my horses, but they're running a close second."

Jenna laughed then kissed him.

"Okay, baby, your turn," Cade said.

Addison cleared her throat. "Ravyn, you said the blonde hairs you found on your ex-husband's jacket were blonde. Did they have red tips?"

Ravyn nodded. "Yes, I'd forgotten about that but they had bright red tips."

Addison smiled and looked around. "Linda's hair. She was or is Dolman's mistress."

"Shit," Luc said, and Logan nodded in agreement. "We think Linda was sent by Mendez to spy on us. That's why she made a point to get involved with me and Logan. When she left, we stopped finding the drugs in the private rooms at the club."

Logan nodded. "I'm not sure she was leaving them for someone to pick up, though. I think Linda has a little habit of her own."

"You never thought to mention that until now?" Luc asked.

Logan grinned. "Just something I've been thinking about for a while."

Ravyn kept her eyes on Addison. It was uncanny how much the little redhead knew.

"Cassie, your turn," Addison said.

"I want to know how you got that mark on your hip, Luc," Cassie said.

"Oh, hell no," Luc said. "Ask something else."

"No. You all agreed to answer a question. That's my question," Cassie said.

Luc glared at her, then looked beyond her at Logan. After a few facial gestures, he said, "I stayed home from school one day. Joan got drunk and beat me with my belt. The buckle cut me." He glared at her again. "Satisfied?"

Cassie slid onto his lap even though he tried to hold her away. "I love you, Luc."

Ravyn waited to see what Luc's reaction would be. When he dropped his head and rubbed his forehead against Cassie's shoulder, she relaxed. While they'd been in the huddle, Cassie had said that Luc sometimes had nightmares about his childhood and then would pace the house at night. Cassie wanted him to get help, and she wanted to go with him.

After a short pause, Ravyn saw Addison slide off Cade's lap then move to stand in front of her. When she dropped to her knees, then slid her arms around her waist and hugged her, she knew she was right to be scared. Ravyn shook her head as tears glazed her eyes. She wasn't sure how much more she could take without falling apart. "Addison?"

"Ravyn, Cade and I decided that you deserve to be told the truth now"—she looked around—"while you're with people who love you."

Ravyn felt Addison take her hand and squeeze it but she was incapable of returning the gesture.

"Maggie told me something else today. Your mama didn't die of a knife wound. She died of a cocaine overdose."

Ravyn jerked her hand away. "My mother didn't use drugs, Addison. She was nice. I would have remembered if she used drugs."

"Of course she didn't, Ravyn. She was given an overdose, and that's what killed her."

"How the hell do you know that, Addison?" Thor asked.

"Maggie has a friend who works in the medical examiner's office in Corpus Christi. She called them today and they read the file to her. I told Cade, and we decided to tell Ravyn today."

Ravyn felt Addison take her hand again.

"I know you're sad, Ravyn, but what happened to your mama isn't your fault. You have to believe that."

Ravyn stood and pulled Addison to her feet, then hugged her. "Thank you for telling me, Addison." She held onto her for a moment, then let her go. She still had tears on her cheeks when she smiled at Addison. "Go ahead. You know you're dying to take a shot at the big guy."

Addison winked at her, then turned to Thor. "I don't know why you guys have so much trouble finding things out. It's easy."

"Ramsey, when that kid's born I'm using a paddle on Addison. I claim five swats," Thor said, and a litany of male voices also called dibs.

Addison moved back to Cade and sat down on his lap.

A moment later Addison said, "Your turn, Marisol."

Marisol crossed her arms over her chest. "I want to know what that word means—shebna?"

Thor laughed, then spelled it for her. "S-k-j-e-b-n-e. It means 'destiny.'"

Marisol smiled, then snuggled up to him. "I might like that."

"I've got news for you," Thor said. "I don't believe in destiny."

Marisol pouted and pulled away from him, and Ravyn hid her smile.

Addison cleared her throat, and Cade leaned forward and picked up his glass of iced tea, then handed it to her. She took a sip, then said, "The lab report on the cocaine that was given to Ravyn's mother proved that the drug came from Mendez."

"You're hired," Thor said. "I'll pay you five hundred thousand a year to work for us."

Cade took his glass back. "She's pregnant and she's going to stay pregnant. Maybe that will keep her busy and out of other people's business."

Addison rubbed her tummy, smiled, then nodded at Cassie. "Your turn again, Cassie."

"I want to know who Clint McCabe really is."

Thor grunted. "Aha, there it is! The real reason for this information exchange. I can't believe there's something you don't know, Addison."

Addison shrugged. "I haven't been able to find out anything about him except that his first name is really McClintock."

Ravyn saw Thor glance at Cade.

"Clint is the third partner in the new agency we're forming. Larking, Ramsey and McCabe Security. He has a special interest in our new project," Cade said. "And, no, I'm not telling you anything about that project, baby, so don't even ask."

Ravyn thought Addison was going to be stubborn and refuse to give her bit of information. Instead, she smiled, then said, "The man who walked by Cassie at Club Mystique and dropped his whip on her shoulder was really a woman dressed as a man. Linda."

"No fucking way," Luc said.

Addison rushed into speech. "I watched the video again this morning. All you have to do is watch the walk. It's Linda's walk. I'd recognize it anywhere. She drops her left hip."

Logan pulled out his cell phone and started texting.

"Your turn, Ravyn," Addison said.

Ravyn squared her shoulders, then looked at Cade. "Do you know how many children are molested by their mother's boyfriends in this country every day?"

"Don't, Ravyn," Jackson said, his voice worried.

Cade froze, then got up and walked away. Addison folded her hands on her lap then looked up. "Thor, Marisol hid a flash drive that her father sent to you in my jewelry box. It's at the house. It has information on it that you need to see tonight."

In the gathering dusk, Cade rode Sarge toward the fire pit. He pulled him up, then held out his hand. "Come here, Addison."

Addison got up, then let Cade take her hand and lift her in front of him. Without another word, they rode away.

Zane grabbed Ravyn's chin and turned her head to face him. "Why the hell did you do that?"

"Addison asked me to," Ravyn said.

Cassie jumped into the conversation. "None of you will ever heal if you don't start talking about your past. You've got to start dealing with what happened to you when you were children."

"We're going to talk about this later tonight, Cassandra," Luc said, and Logan nodded.

Jackson held up his hands when they looked at him. "Jenna and I have already talked about all this. As far as I'm concerned, how you choose to handle it is your business."

Thor drew their attention to him. "That just tied up a lot of loose ends, and proved the connection between Dolman, Miller, and Mendez."

"It still doesn't tell us why Dolman held Ravyn in Colombia, though," Jackson said.

Zane set Ravyn on the bench next to him. "Right before Benson was killed in a hit-and-run accident, he handed over control of his corporation to Dolman. I think Dolman used Ravyn to force him to do that, and then had him killed when he went to the police. Obviously he talked to the wrong people and that got him killed."

"He might have spoken to Don Wilson," Luc said. "He works for the DEA, and his daughter, Julia, tried to frame Cassie for running drugs. Or, maybe he talked to Dan Thompson. He works for the Drug Task Force and we think he's dirty."

"Maybe both." Thor stood up, twisted from side to side. His back cracked and he smiled. "Miller isn't talking yet, but he will. They always do. Eventually."

Ravyn watched him and trembled. The look on his face terrified her and she was glad she wasn't being questioned by him, because she knew she wouldn't be able to lie to him.

Zane patted her hip, then gathered her into his arms and stood up. "Time to go home."

* * * *

Ravyn turned off the bathroom light, then glanced around the bedroom. Zane sat, naked, on the side of the bed, waiting for her. She swept her eyes over him, then yawned and laughed. "All that fresh air has worn me out."

Zane sat up. "Show me your ass."

Ravyn twisted around, then ran her hands over her butt and cupped the bottom curves while she looked over her shoulder at him. "May I speak, Master?"

Zane narrowed his eyes. "Are you going to ask me more questions?"

Ravyn nodded, then said, "Yes, Master, but just two."

Zane leaned back on his elbows and his cock rose up into clear view. "Go ahead."

Ravyn turned around, licked her lips as she stared at his cock, and asked, "Do you think Cade and Addison are arguing in the playroom?"

"Probably, but Addison knew the question would piss him off, so that's her problem. Next question."

"When I saw you at that club three years ago, it looked like you had a slave. Didn't you keep her?"

"No."

"Why not?"

The look in Zane's eyes sent a hot wave of arousal and longing through her.

He watched her while he thought about her question. He'd played with a lot of subs, but he'd never wanted to own one until the day she'd walked into his office. She'd walked in and he'd wanted to rip her clothes off, bend her over his desk, turn her ass red and then fuck her until they both passed out. She hadn't helped any when she'd begun flirting with him and watching his every reaction with those soft grey eyes. He'd fought his own need as long as he could and then the day he'd decided to accept her blatant offers, Dolman had accused her of working for Mendez. Finally, desperate to have her, he'd told himself that an affair with her would be enough. He'd known even then he was lying to himself, but he'd gone ahead anyway. Now, he couldn't trust her, but he was determined to keep her because he wanted every breath she took, every smile, every tear, to belong to him.

"Zane?"

"I was waiting for the right woman. The one I had to earn. You."

His statement dropped her to her knees. She lowered her eyes and clenched her hands as a sob left her lips. A moment later she crawled over to him. Once she reached him, she wrapped her arms around his legs and leaned against him. She bit her lip to keep from sobbing while all she could think was, dear god, what do I do now?

Zane lifted her onto his lap and held her as tears ran down her cheeks. "It will be okay. Trust me."

A trembling smiled curved Ravyn's lips. "You all say that."

"That's because it's true. It's what our dad, John, used to say to us after he came home for good and we moved to Long Valley." Zane stroked her hair and let her cry. Several minutes later, when she had calmed a little, he reached over to the nightstand, picked up a small blue box and showed it to her. "Present yourself to me, Ravyn."

She recognized the box and knew it came from an expensive shop that designed jewelry for Dominants to give to their subs. "Zane, I want to accept that. More than you'll ever know, but I can't. Not until this is over and you're safe."

"Who do you think is going to harm me?"

"Charles or Mendez, or anyone they send after you." She hugged his neck as she touched the blue box with the elegant logo on the top. She saw the determination in his eyes and knew that, short of a confession from her, he was going to do this now. She nuzzled his neck to give herself time to make a decision. Maybe by morning Marisol would have good news for her about Harper. If not, then she would risk everything and tell him the truth. He wanted to be her Master and in complete control of her and her problems, so she would let him take care of this for her.

Zane kissed her, then released her. "Knees, now, pet."

Ravyn slid to the floor between his feet. She spread her knees, then placed her hands on her thighs, palms up. A second later, she felt something cold and smooth slide around her neck, then click into place. She reached up and felt a thick chain with a heart-shaped tag hanging from it. There were letters on it and she gasped as she realized they were written in gems of some kind.

Zane slid his fingers into her hair, then tipped her head back until their eyes met. "I had this made the day after I met you. You belong to me now. Do you understand?"

Ravyn's lips trembled with emotion. She licked them, then forced herself to smile. "Yes, Master. Forever."

Zane lifted her to his lap, then tipped her back on the bed. He grasped the medallion on the collar and lifted her lips to his. "Kiss me."

"Please, may I speak?"

"Later, pet. Kiss me."

Ravyn slid her arms around his neck and teased her lips over his. He caught her bottom lip between his teeth, then growled a warning to her. She smiled, then kissed him.

Chapter Eight

The next morning Ravyn sat on Zane's lap while he fed her breakfast. She smiled as she glanced around the table. The entire family, plus Thor and Marisol, were present. Jenna winked at her from her place on Jackson's lap and she giggled just as Cade's phone chimed. He pulled it out, read it, and then slid it back into his pocket. Beside him, Addison sat on her own chair. An unusual occurrence. Apparently, she was still mad at Cade or he was mad at her, or they were mad at each other. Either way, it looked like they had a standoff going on and there was no telling which one of them would give in first. Her eyes flashed back to Cade when he said, "The FBI is here to see you, Ravyn."

Ravyn trembled, then clung to Zane. This was it. Everything was over now. She reached up and touched the heart-shaped medallion that hung from the collar around her neck.

The men at the table moved quickly as they rearranged the room and moved the royals into their own seats. Zane slid her onto the chair that Luc placed next to him.

"Tell me why they're here," Zane demanded.

"Zane." Ravyn licked her lips. Tears glistened in her eyes. She blinked and one slid down her cheek and she brushed it away. "I'm sorry. So sorry." She'd been in such a hurry to talk to Marisol this morning, she hadn't taken the time to remove her phone from its hiding place and check it. She knew that if she looked at it now, there would be a message from Mendez on it. She looked across the table at Marisol and saw her looking back at her with an anxious look on her face.

The sound of the doorbell ringing echoed in the foyer. A moment later, Isabella appeared in the dining room archway with two men in black suits behind her. Ben and Mac silently moved up behind them. Ravyn glanced at Zane, but he refused to look her way. A nerve jumped in his jaw and the hand he'd placed on the table was fisted. She glanced at Cade and heard him tell Zane to hold it together.

She knew she had one chance to save Zane and she was going to take it. Before these two agents arrested her, she would have them convinced that she was a femme fatale and she'd used Zane and his family. She sat up straight and adopted an arrogant, disinterested expression.

Isabella drew everyone's attention to her when she snorted, then pointed over her shoulder at the two strangers. "These two rude bastards say they're from the FBI and they want to talk to Ravyn. I tried to take them to the living room, but they insisted on following me." The older man tried to push in front of her, but she blocked him with a well-practiced move.

"Lady, you're interfering with a federal agent. Now move, or I'll place you under arrest," he said as he pushed her aside and looked at them. "I'm Special Agent Johnson." He motioned toward his partner. "This is Special Agent Lake. We're her to speak to Ravyn Dolman."

"I'm Ravyn but my last name is Templeton now." Ravyn set her napkin down.

"Whatever," Johnson said. "My partner and I have some questions to ask you."

Cade stood up. "Gentlemen, you were allowed through the gates because you flashed your badges. The two men behind you will escort you to the living room."

Johnson and Lake twisted around and found Ben and Mac crowding up behind them. When they turned back to face Cade, the arrogant look on their faces was gone.

"Isabella will get you some coffee and we'll join you in a few minutes," Cade said.

"We want to speak to Ms. Templeton"—Johnson stressed the name—"alone." He glanced at Zane. "Don't you work in the District Attorney's office?"

Zane nodded. "That's right. I'm the prosecuting attorney in charge of Charles Dolman's case."

Ravyn noted the leer on Johnson's face before he glanced back to Zane. "Cozy setup you have here, counselor."

Luc stood up and placed his hand on Ravyn's shoulder. Across the table, she saw Marisol's eyes widen as she mouthed, "Oh, shit."

"Johnson, in this house, women are treated with respect," Luc said.

Johnson sneered. "You're interfering with an FBI agent."

Ravyn lowered her eyes. She touched the collar and medallion around her neck. Zane's initials were etched into the surface of the platinum heart, but her finger stayed on the half-carat pink diamond set in the middle. It had been cut in the shape of a heart as well.

"What happened to Special Agent Michaels?" Zane asked. "I was told she was in charge of this investigation."

"She had a sudden death in her family. The case was handed over to me and my partner," Johnson said.

"I'll have to give her my condolences." Zane flipped through his wallet, then pulled out a card. "Yup, I have her number." He held the card up and Johnson fidgeted.

Luc squeezed Ravyn's shoulder just as the doorbell rang again.

Isabella huffed, then swiveled around and stomped out of sight. A minute later, she reappeared in the archway. "This old guy's here."

A short, stooped man appeared behind Isabella. His gray hair was mussed and his suit disheveled. The attaché case beneath his arm was old and cracked and had several papers sticking out of it. "Sorry to be late," he said as he stuffed the papers back into the case. "I got lost." He laughed. "I've only driven out here a thousand times over the years. You'd think I'd know the way by now."

Ravyn saw Special Agent Johnson send the newcomer a smirk as Special Agent Lake snorted. "Who the hell are you?" Lake asked.

The newcomer held out his hand and rushed into speech as several loose papers drifted to the floor. "Augustus Rosie," he said. "I'm Ms. Templeton's attorney. Well, I really only work for the Addy Foundation for Children." He looked at Addison. "I was fishing when you called me. Caught a couple big ones in Old Man Muldoon's lake." He held out his hands and his briefcase dropped to the floor. Papers scattered everywhere. He didn't even notice. "A big, four-pound black crappie. Gave me a heck of a fight. That old fool Webber only caught a half-pounder. Just proves attorneys can always beat a judge with the right bait." He smiled, then looked down. Isabella had gathered his papers and was on her knees in front of him, holding them out to him. He put his hand on her head, then looked up. "Is this one taken?"

"The whole town is full of perverts," Lake said.

"And this guy's full of crappie," Johnson said, and Lake laughed.

Logan stood up. "While you're in our home, you'll show the proper respect for our guests or you can get the hell off our property."

The tension in the room increased and Ravyn held her breath. Johnson put his hands up in a cajoling gesture.

"No offense intended. Just trying to be friendly," Johnson said.

Ravyn saw Cade's nod, but realized he didn't smile. Not a good sign. She glanced at Addison and wondered how she'd known to call her attorney and have him here today.

Addison caught her looking at her and winked. "Gentlemen, you may use my living room to speak to Ravyn in the presence of Mr. Rosie."

Luc pulled Ravyn's chair back, then helped her to her feet. She walked out of the dining room, accepting that this was her last moment of freedom and happiness. It would be okay, though, if Harper and Zane survived.

At the archway, Mr. Rosie took her arm. "I need five minutes alone with my client," he told the agents, then escorted her to the living room. Mac followed them. The doors clicked shut and she could see his outline through the frosted glass of the French doors. Mr. Rosie seated her on the couch, then sat down next to her. "Don't answer their questions until I've given my approval. Do you understand, my dear?"

"Mr. Rosie, please believe me. I have to answer their questions. I have to confess, but thank you for trying to help me." Ravyn's hands were trembling and she clenched them on her lap and tried to compose herself. She knew Cade had the house bugged, so Zane would hear everything she said, and he would hate her.

Mr. Rosie patted her hand. "Call me Rosie, my dear, and please don't worry. Addison has explained everything to me. She's told me about Harper."

Ravyn cried out. "No, no, they'll kill him." She jumped to her feet. She didn't know what she intended to do but felt she needed to try to get to Harper. No matter what it cost her.

Mr. Rosie rose next to her. Even though his stooped shoulders were a few inches below hers, the hand he wrapped around her wrist was strong. "My dear, please don't worry. The plans to rescue Harper are already made and will be carried out within the next twenty-four hours. Right now, we need to get this *confession* over with and then have you placed somewhere safe. It's going to be okay, my dear. Trust me."

Ravyn tried to smile, but couldn't. She covered her trembling lips as tears began to slide down her cheeks. "He's safe right now? Are you sure?"

Mr. Rosie patted her shoulder, then pulled a monogramed hankie from his pocket and handed it to her. "As of this morning, you are testifying on behalf of the State of Texas. You've gotten a very good deal with the Attorney General and you're being placed in the protective custody of Clint McCabe. He should be here anytime now."

Ravyn dried her eyes. "I've never met Mr. McCabe."

"He's exactly what we need. Very scary. Just don't ever call him Clint. All those jokes about Dirty Harry, you know? Everyone just calls him McCabe or Boss." Rosie grinned and his sunburned face flushed redder. "I'd almost forgotten how much I love a good fight." Rosie chuckled, then pulled her down onto the couch beside him and kept hold of her right hand. "I want you to only answer with 'yes' or 'no.' If I squeeze your hand, do not answer the question. Say you don't know. Do you understand?"

"Yes, S—Rosie," Ravyn said.

Rosie's cell phone chimed. He read a text, then mumbled, "Excellent timing," and turned away from her. He raised his voice and said, "Mac, they can join us now."

Mac opened the door, then stepped aside. Special Agents Johnson and Lake entered the room, their movements somehow sinister and well-practiced. They claimed the chairs across from her and Rosie. Johnson rubbed his hands together and Ravyn shuddered. There was something about him that scared her. Maybe it was the emotionless look in his eyes that made her think he was not only capable of killing but had killed in the past. She glanced toward the doors and felt a wave of relief rush through her when she saw that Mac had left them open. She knew she couldn't run away from what was coming, but it made her feel better to know the door was open.

Johnson focused on her. "Let's get started. Mrs. Dolman, we—"

"Templeton," Ravyn reminded him. She may be screwed, but she'd be damned if she'd let him pin that name on her again.

Johnson ignored her. "Do you know a woman named Barbie Johnson?"

Before Ravyn could answer, she felt Rosie squeeze her hand just as the doorbell rang. She heard Cade's voice in the hallway, then the deep rumble of another voice. A moment later, Cade appeared in the doorway with a man next to him. She took one look at him and knew she was about to meet Addison's mystery man, Clint McCabe. He was the same towering height as Cade but appeared to be several years older. When he removed his sunglasses, Ravyn looked into his eyes. They were dark gray, almost black, then they changed to a light, frozen blue. She blinked, then shivered and lowered her eyes. *What the hell?*

"This guy's here to see you, Ravyn," Cade said, then walked away.

Ravyn glanced at Johnson and Lake and realized from their posture that they were on high alert like rats smelling an alpha predator tracking them.

McCabe approached the two FBI agents and stood over them. "Who are you?"

Johnson and Lake tried to stand, but McCabe crowded them and they were forced to drop back into their chairs. Faces red with anger or embarrassment, or maybe both, they flipped their badge cases open, then introduced themselves.

McCabe flashed a badge and said, "You can call me Sir."

The tension in the room thickened as he slid his badge back into the inside pocket of his suit jacket and Ravyn caught a glimpse of his shoulder holster. "I'm here to question Ravyn Templeton. You're welcome to stay as long as you don't interfere. Understand?"

The room fell silent for several minutes while McCabe waited for Johnson and Lake to answer him. Ravyn glanced at Rosie and wished she knew what Addison was up to, and how many of the Ramseys and their friends were involved.

"Gentlemen, I asked if you understand that I'm in charge of this interview."

Finally, Johnson nodded and Lake said, "Yes, Sir."

McCabe turned to face Augustus Rosie, and Ravyn saw an amused grin flash across his lips before he asked, "Who are you?"

Mr. Rosie stood and held out his hand. "Augustus Rosie. I'm Ms. Templeton's attorney."

McCabe ignored the extended hand, then sat down in the chair to Ravyn's right. He read her the Miranda rights, got her agreement, and then said, "Ms. Templeton, several nights ago the Dallas police received an anonymous call that your home was being vandalized. The police responded and searched the house for intruders. The intruders were gone, but the house had been ransacked. The officers found a locked room on the third floor and thought they heard someone calling for help. They broke down the door. Do you know what they found in that room?"

Ravyn felt Rosie squeeze her hand. "I don't know."

"You've never been in the room?"

"No."

"Do you know of a woman by the name of Barbie Johnson?"

Ravyn nodded then said, "Yes."

"Barbie Johnson was arrested last night during a drug raid. She stated that she picked up the drugs she sold from your home. Were you aware of that?"

Ravyn bit her lip, then said, "No."

"Were you aware that the money from the drug sales was being laundered through your late father's corporation?"

"Yes."

"Do you know a person named Harper Cortez?"

"Yes."

"We were told he was your love interest. Is this correct?"

Ravyn hesitated, then said, "I love him."

"Do you know his location?"

"Not exactly."

"Does he work for Mendez?"

Rosie squeezed her hand and she said, "I don't know."

McCabe stood up and removed a pair of handcuffs from his pocket. "Ravyn Templeton, you're under arrest for drug trafficking and laundering money."

Mr. Rosie rose to his feet. "I would like to make a deal for Ms. Templeton."

McCabe pulled Ravyn to her feet, then turned her around and put the handcuffs on her. "It's too late to make a deal now."

He began to escort her from the room, but Johnson tried to stop him.

"The FBI has jurisdiction here. She's going with us," Johnson said as he reached beneath his jacket.

"I wouldn't do that if I was you," McCabe said as he released her arm and took a step toward Johnson.

Ravyn couldn't see McCabe's face, but she saw Johnson drop his hand, then take a step back. From the agent's reaction, she knew McCabe was an extremely dangerous man and she thanked god he was on her side.

McCabe took her arm again and escorted her into the hallway. Behind them, she heard Johnson and Lake being distracted by a series of quick questions from Rosie. Once out the front door, McCabe helped her down the porch steps. She heard the door open behind them and then Zane called her name. She turned around, then stepped back when she saw the expression on his face. The look of hatred in Zane's eyes told her that he'd heard everything she'd said and he was furious. She didn't blame him. This was all her fault and whatever he did to her, she knew she deserved it.

He reached her and McCabe stepped between them. "Back off, Zane."

"Fuck off, McCabe. She's my sub. My slave." Zane's voice was cold and hard.

McCabe nodded, then said, "Thirty seconds."

Ravyn lowered her gaze to hide the devastation in her eyes. Zane grabbed her chin and jerked her head up.

"You lied to me."

"I know. I'm sorry. I was going to tell you the truth today."

"You should have told me the truth weeks ago," he said, his voice deadly. "You said you loved me and all the time you were really in love with another man."

Ravyn wanted to drop to her knees and tell him she loved him. She wanted to beg him to forgive her. Instead, she decided to free him. She corralled her feelings, then forced herself to meet his eyes. She knew she looked as if she didn't care that she'd lied to him, and hoped he didn't see that she was at the breaking point. "You can't blame a girl for trying to save herself."

"You should thank god you've been arrested." Zane reached for the collar around her neck. He unlocked it, jerked it off, then threw it as hard as he could. Ravyn saw a flash of light as the sun caught the pink diamonds on the medallion. She lost sight of it when it fell to the ground in the distance. When she looked back at Zane, he'd already moved away. Over his shoulder, he said, "Get her out of my sight before I hurt her, McCabe."

"Too late," Ravyn whispered, then jumped when the front door slammed behind Zane. She fisted her hands and straightened her shoulders. "I'm ready to go now."

McCabe took her arm and escorted her toward one of the three black SUVs parked on the circular drive. The first and third vehicles had two heavily armed men in dark sunglasses standing next to them. The middle vehicle only had one man standing by it. McCabe put her in the backseat, then buckled her in and slammed the door. She looked at the house through the darkened windows of the car. A movement in an upstairs window caught her attention. The royals were crowded next to each other, blowing her kisses and waving at her. Addison stood in the middle holding up a sign that said, "Trust me" in big, black letters. A moment later, she lost sight of them as she was driven away.

* * * *

As soon as they cleared the gates and were on their way to the highway, McCabe twisted around and smiled at her. "Don't look so sad, sweetheart. It will be okay."

Ravyn shook her head as tears dripped from her cheeks and ran down her chest. She rubbed her cheek on her shoulder to dry her tears. "Zane hates me." She faltered on the last word and it drifted into silence. A sob left her lips and the tears she'd been holding back wouldn't be held back any longer. She collapsed against the door and sobbed.

The driver said, "Boss, do something or I'm bailing."

"Stand fast, Deuce. We knew there would be tears," McCabe said, "and you lost the toss."

"Those fuckers rigged it."

"'Tears are the silent language of grief.'"

"Don't start that, boss. Thor cleaned me out while you were inside."

"You can owe me."

"Hell, I don't know. Shakespeare. Make her stop. Really, I can't stand the sound of a woman crying."

"I don't know who said it, but you owe me twenty for making me listen to you whine."

Ravyn sniffled and a hand holding a tissue appeared in front of her. She leaned forward and rubbed her face against it. McCabe pinched it around her nose and said, "Blow."

Ravyn shook her head.

McCabe sighed. "Turn around, then."

Ravyn trembled, then sobbed. "I thought you were going to protect me. Are you going to kill me now?"

"Why does everybody ask me that?" McCabe asked Deuce. "Do I look like a killer?"

"Well, yeah, boss, you do. It's the eyes, and well, let's face, it—we've killed a lot of people."

"I've never killed anybody who didn't deserve to die."

"I don't deserve to die," Ravyn said, then sniffled. "I just know too much."

McCabe held up the handcuff key. "Turn around and I'll take the cuffs off, and then we're going to talk."

Ravyn twisted around and felt McCabe remove the cuffs. She let her arms drop to her sides, then she rolled her shoulders a couple of times before rubbing her wrists. "Am I going to jail?"

"Yes, for a couple days," McCabe said. "While you're in jail, I'm going to Colombia. Juan Rios has already gotten a man on the inside where Harper is being held. He's going to help us free him as well as the other people being held by Mendez."

"How do you know about Harper?" Ravyn thought about it and decided Marisol must have told Addison about Harper. "Did Addison call you?"

McCabe smiled. "Addison is the biggest meddler I know. What do you think?"

Ravyn wrinkled her brow. "I think she told Cade and he called you."

"Smart girl. Now, tell me everything you know about your ex-husband and his business associates."

Ravyn leaned back, folded her hands on her lap, and gave him a summary of what she knew about Charles's business dealings. They'd reached the outskirts of Dallas by the time she finished talking. McCabe handed her a bottle of water and she took a sip then hesitated for a moment before she asked, "Did Zane know what was really happening?"

McCabe didn't answer her. Instead, Deuce said, "Don't tell her, boss. She'll start crying again."

"Deuce, you just told her." McCabe sighed. "Addison got Rosie and Judge Webber to swing a deal for you with the Attorney General, while Thor and Cade came up with a plan for me to take you into custody. I'm sure they'll explain it to him now."

"I hope not," Ravyn said through her tears. "I think I can convince everyone that I seduced him in order to save myself. Can you call and ask them not to tell him the truth?"

"Damn, the only thing worse than a crying woman is a crying woman who's trying to save the man she loves," Deuce said as he pulled over to the side. "That's it. I'm out of here." A second later, he reached for the door handle and McCabe stuck a capped water bottle against the back of his head.

"Don't open that door," McCabe said, his voice quiet and scary.

"Boss, tell me that isn't your gun," Deuce said.

"You'll only know that for sure if you open the door and force me to take action."

"You won't shoot me," Deuce said. "It would really piss Maw off."

"I'm the oldest and her favorite. She'll understand. Now, start the engine and let's go."

Ravyn bit her lip, then couldn't keep from asking, "You're brothers?"

McCabe twisted around to face her. "Two of six. The other four are here. Trey and True are at our twelve. Cin and Ace are at our six."

"Who are you? I mean, who do you work for?" Ravyn leaned closer when she realized McCabe's eyes were now a light green. He caught her staring and smiled. She smiled back, then said, "Your eyes change colors."

"It's a mood thing." McCabe shrugged. "All you need to know is we're on your side. If Johnson and Lake had gotten their hands on you today, you wouldn't have lived long enough to be booked. They're dirty and we're helping the DEA prove they're responsible for the deaths of at least two federal agents."

"So you're with the DEA?"

"You can say that—if you want to," McCabe said, then turned around as Deuce pulled up to a checkpoint, flashed his badge, then drove into an underground area. He parked by an elevator and waited.

Ravyn realized they were waiting for the men from the other two SUVs to take defensive positions around the vehicle. Several seconds later, McCabe got out and opened her door. He unfastened her seatbelt, then leaned in and dangled the handcuffs in front of her. She twisted around and put her arms behind her back and he snapped them into place, then helped her out of the car.

"Don't say anything to anybody, no matter what they ask you. Just tell them you need your attorney to be present." McCabe slid a business card into her hand. "That's Rosie's card. Refer anyone who asks questions to him."

"Okay, thank you, Sir," Ravyn said.

"Sweetheart, don't call me 'sir' in that breathy little voice of yours. You've got the kind of lush body Deuce and I can't resist, but touching you would get us killed." He chuckled. "Those damn Ramseys are too lucky." He led her toward the elevator as the doors slid open. "Game time. Try to look scared."

Deuce entered the elevator first. McCabe urged her to follow him then stood to her right.

"Now's the time for tears, baby," Deuce said, his breath warm on the back of her neck. She shivered and he chuckled.

Two of the other four men entered the elevator and took up positions in front of her. One of them had a short, groomed beard and the other had a mustache. They nodded in her direction, then turned their backs to her. They were as big as McCabe and Deuce and took up all the space in front of her. They didn't speak and McCabe didn't introduce them.

"Aren't they all coming?" She craned her neck, looking for the other two men.

"Cin and Ace are staying with the vehicles," Deuce said. "Trey is on your left and True is on your right."

Ravyn looked at Deuce over her shoulder, then gasped. He'd taken off his sunglasses and she realized he was an exact replica of Clint McCabe. "You—you're twins."

The two men in front of her chuckled. She turned around and looked at them. They twisted around, pulled their sunglasses down, and smiled when she gasped.

"There's four of you." She shook her head, then swung her gaze around to all of them. "Four."

"Six," McCabe said. "We're sextuplets. I'm the original. They're the copies. Don't tell anyone. It's a secret."

Ravyn could only nod.

"Maw says we're not copies," Deuce said. "You gotta quit saying that. You're damaging my self-esteem, boss."

His words were echoed by Trey and True.

"Stop whining or I'm going to punch you," McCabe said.

She almost smiled until she tried to reach out and pat Deuce. The cuffs on her wrists reminded her where she was and without any effort on her part, tears glazed her eyes and a she began trembling.

Chapter Nine

Zane slammed the door behind him, then stalked toward the stairs. Luc and Jackson were coming down them as he put his foot on the bottom step. They carried their field gear and sniper rifles.

"Where the hell are you going?" he asked as he climbed a few steps.

"We're going with McCabe to Colombia," Luc said.

"You're my fucking brothers and you're going after that son of a bitch Harper?" Zane asked.

"You're welcome to join us," Luc said.

Before Zane could say anything, Cade stepped out of the den. "Zane, I want to talk to you for a moment."

"If it's about Ravyn then forget it," Zane said.

"It's about Ravyn and Harper," Cade said.

"You, too, huh?" Zane asked. He turned back to Luc and Jackson. "You know, I think I will go with you. Maybe it's time I met this guy."

Cade walked over to the stairs and stared up at him. "Stop being a hardheaded idiot and come into the den and talk to me."

Zane snorted. "That's the kettle calling the pot black, isn't it, big brother?"

Cade nodded, then without another word he went back into his den. The door shut behind him with a soft snick.

"What's his fucking problem?" Zane asked.

"Addison," Jackson and Luc said, then high-fived each other.

Zane nodded his head, then pushed between them and took the stairs two at a time. "Wait for me," he told them over his shoulder.

Once in his room, he changed his clothes, then grabbed the bag he kept packed and ready to go. He left his room and took the steps down in leaps and bounds. Jackson and Luc leaned against the walls in the hallway. Jenna was kissing Jackson and Cassie was squeezed up to Luc, begging him to let her go with them. He heard her say something about Harper and it pissed him off. What the hell was it with his family and their concerns for this guy?

Cassie turned to him. "Zane, tell Luc and Logan to let me go. Harper might need a woman to be there."

"Fu—" Zane stopped himself before he could finish the curse in front of Cassie. "You, too." When she started to say something more, he held up his hand. "Not another word about this guy. You understand? All of you?"

Fan lines of amusement appeared beside Luc's eyes. "Three things cannot be long hidden, the sun, the moon, and the truth."

"Fuck off, Luc," Zane said and saw Luc frown.

"Buddha," Addison said from behind him.

Zane turned around and was shocked at her appearance. It was easy to see that she'd been crying. Without hesitation, he reached out and hugged her. "You okay, baby sister?"

Addison nodded, then shook her head. "No, but it's my own fault."

Zane hugged her again, then lifted her up and carried her down the stairs. At the bottom, he set her on her feet. "He'll get over it."

A tiny sob left Addison's lips. "Not anytime soon, he won't."

Zane hugged her again, then released her. "We're all here for you, Addy."

Addison's lips curved up in a tiny smile. "You haven't called me that in years." She glanced at the den door. "Time to face the music."

"If he gives you a hard time, let us know and we'll set him straight," Zane said.

"You've got problems of your own to deal with first," Luc said.

"I plan to do just that," Zane said, his voice deadly.

"You planning on beating this guy up?" Logan asked, then grinned as he pulled Cassie away from Luc.

Zane slung his pack over his shoulder. "He'll get what he deserves. But don't worry, I'll leave enough of him for you to bring home to Ravyn."

Jackson shrugged. "You're digging your own grave, but that's your choice. Let's go." He gave Jenna a quick kiss, then patted her on the bottom. "Be good, angel."

Zane patted Jenna's shoulder as he moved by her. Next to him, Luc paused then frowned at Logan. "No groveling while I'm gone, Logan. Understand?"

Logan shrugged and Cassie smiled. "Sometimes I make Logan pretend to be you when he grovels. I find it very satisfying."

"I'm going to use my belt on your ass when I get home, Cassandra," Luc said and Cassie laughed, then ran up the stairs with Logan on her heels.

Zane laughed. "You guys are a bunch of fuck-ups when it comes to your women."

Jackson laughed. "It's been a long time since I've looked forward to a hunt as much as this one." He shook his head, then waved his hand, indicating Zane should take the lead.

* * * *

Seven hours later, they landed on a small airfield owned by Juan Rios. Zane stood up and grabbed his field gear. Next to him, McCabe's brothers Deuce and True slung their packs over their shoulders.

"Did you ever think we'd be working with Rios?" Deuce asked.

"We're not working with him," McCabe said. "He's facilitating our mission."

"Same thing," Zane said.

"You a Marine or a lawyer?" McCabe asked.

"Both," Zane said.

"Nope, once a Marine, always a Marine," Deuce said. "Lawyering comes second."

"Both of you, shut up," McCabe said. "We got a job to do. We're going to do it, then get back home."

Zane followed McCabe off the plane. Several Jeeps were parked on the tarmac waiting for them. A tall, slender man approached them, his hand out. McCabe took it and Zane heard the man introduce himself as Javier Vega. He and McCabe had a short conversation in Spanish and then they headed for the first Jeep. They gathered around it and Javier spread a map out on the hood.

He pointed to their location, then to a location several hours away before he unfolded what looked like the ground plans of a large estate.

"This is the house. It's surrounded by a ten-foot wall with razor wire at the top. There's one gate"—he pointed to an area—"here on the east side. It's guarded by two men at all times."

"What about the walls?" McCabe asked. "Are they guarded?"

"Yes, but my brother Mateo is the guard here"—he pointed to the map—"and he is going to take care of the guard here. We should be able to get over the wall and into the compound without their knowledge. The prisoners are locked up in this shed in the back corner of the garden." He folded the maps, then gestured toward the Jeeps and they tossed their gear into them and took off.

Three hours later, they parked in a small clearing in the jungle.

"We walk from here," Javier said. "It's about a thirty-minute hike, but I'm familiar with the trail and my brother Mateo is waiting for us." He held out a small radio. "He will warn us if anything changes."

After several minutes of preparation, they moved out, rifles ready and faces camouflaged. Javier led the way with McCabe behind him. Jackson brought up the rear. Zane had Luc in front of him with Deuce and True behind him.

They passed through the jungle without making a sound. Several times, McCabe would hold up his fist and they would stop and listen, then move on. Ahead of them, they saw lights shining through the trees and Zane knew they were nearing the house. It wouldn't be long now and he could confront Harper. He was tempted to tell him what Ravyn had been up to while he'd been locked up, but just thinking her name made his heart ache.

Knowing she was in jail and probably scared sickened him, and he realized he should have stayed in Dallas and tried to help her. He was so lost in his thoughts that he didn't notice they'd stopped until he bumped into Luc.

"Get your head out of your ass," Luc said, his voice quiet.

"I should have stayed in Dallas," Zane said. "Ravyn needs me."

"Fine time to decide that now," Luc said. "You can be her hero when you take Harper to her."

Zane nodded. "As long as she's happy, then I'll be happy."

Luc made a gagging sound. "God, you're worse than Logan." He turned away and headed down the trail.

Zane smiled and followed him. He decided he'd never recover if he lost Ravyn so he wasn't letting her go. Not to Harper or any other man.

When they were close enough to hear music coming from the house, they regrouped. McCabe gave the orders for True and Jackson to cover their six while he, Deuce, Zane, and Luc went over the wall with Javier.

A few minutes later, they huddled in the shadows by the wall. Javier spoke into the radio and a second later, a rope came sailing over the wall. They heard a sharp click when something made contact with the razor wire.

"My brother put a length of chain on the rope," Javier said, then smiled and tapped his temple. "He is very clever."

McCabe smiled.

Javier grabbed the rope and scaled it, followed by McCabe, then Zane, then True and Luc. Once on the ground on the other side, they followed Javier along the wall to the back corner, where a small shed stood in the darkness.

The door had a heavy padlock on it and they could hear the muffled sound of several women crying coming from inside. Mateo produced a pair of bolt cutters and tried to cut through the heavy lock. After a moment Deuce stepped up, took the cutters from him, and picked the lock. Javier took it from him and a second later, Mateo opened the door and the crying stopped. The stench coming from the shed was horrible. A combination of fear, sweat, blood, and dirty humans. McCabe looked at Zane and waved him forward.

Zane turned his head away, took a breath then stepped into the doorway with Luc beside him. He flipped his night goggles down and examined the six people in the room. Three women and three men. He looked from man to man and wasn't able to identify Ravyn's guy. "We're here to rescue you. I'm looking for Harper."

A movement in the back corner of the building drew his attention. A second later, a little boy moved forward.

"I am Harper," he said.

The child was about seven years old. Skinny and dirty, with ragged black hair and Ravyn's eyes. Zane felt his heart stop, then stutter to life. He moved toward Harper and picked him up. "I've got you now," he said, and Harper slid a skinny arm around his shoulders.

"My Ravyn said you would come for me. She promised."

Zane hugged Harper closer and swore beneath his breath. He didn't know if he was angry because Ravyn had been suffering in silence for so long, or if it was because she hadn't trusted him with the truth. Either way, he was taking his belt to her ass until she told him if she was involved with Dolman and Mendez. If she was he would protect her, but this was the last time she'd ever keep secrets from him. He turned around and walked out of the building. Luc moved in front of him, guarding him and his precious cargo.

McCabe, Javier, and Mateo rounded up the other prisoners. They led them to the side of the building and Mateo and Javier picked up a heavy ladder, then propped it against the wall. Mateo went into the shed and grabbed the torn and dirty blankets. He shut the door, then handed the bundle to McCabe, who climbed the ladder and threw the blankets over the razor wire. He eased himself over it and dropped to the ground, then looked up and saw Mateo looking down at him.

A second later, he caught Harper as Zane lowered him. Jackson ran out of the covering of the jungle, grabbed the child, and disappeared back into the shadows. McCabe caught the next prisoner and the next until they were all on the ground on the outside of the wall. Zane dropped down beside him, followed by Luc, True, and then Mateo and Javier.

They joined Jackson and Deuce in the cover of the jungle and Zane took Harper from Jackson. "Let's get out of here. I don't want the bullets flying anywhere near Harper."

"So, you're not going to beat him up now?" Jackson asked.

Before Zane could answer him, Harper said, "My papa would never do that."

Zane smiled. "You have that right, son." He shoulder bumped Jackson as he walked by him. "Who would've ever thought I'd be the first in the family to become a dad, huh, Uncle Jackson?"

"Not Cade, that's for sure," Jackson said.

McCabe walked by them. "Let's move out."

It took them longer to return to the Jeeps. Halfway back to them, two of the women gave out and couldn't walk any further. Deuce and True picked them up, then moved to the center of the line with Zane. Jackson and Luc dropped back and watched their six while McCabe took point with Javier and Mateo behind him.

* * * *

Four hours later, Zane rinsed the suds off Harper with a handheld sprayer. "Turn," he said and Harper giggled, then turned around. He looked like a skinny drowned rat. All bones and matted, black hair.

Zane put down the sprayer and Harper protested. "When we get home you can play in the tub with bubbles as long as you like, but right now Uncle Luc needs to take a look at these cuts." Zane turned Harper, took note of the cuts and scrapes on him, then felt a wave of rage run through him when he saw the white scars left from a belt on Harper's lower back.

He wrapped a towel around him, then lifted him out of the tub and dried him. A moment later, he dropped one of his T-shirts over Harper's head and Harper looked down, then looked up at him and giggled. "Yeah, it's too big, but it will do until we get you to the ranch." Zane picked up Harper's filthy clothes and tossed them in the trash.

Harper ran over to the trashcan and grabbed them, then held them against him. "No, mine."

Zane hesitated. Should he let Harper keep them? He put his hand on Harper's shoulder. "Hey, if you want to keep them, you can, but when we get home we're going to buy you new clothes. Jeans and shirts and a cowboy hat."'

Harper hugged the clothes tighter, then looked down at Zane's boots. "Can I have cowboy boots?

"Yes, son. Any pair you want."

Harper hesitated then held out the bundle. "Okay."

Zane took the clothes, tossed them back into the trash, then lifted Harper and set him on the bathroom counter. He tried to run a comb through the ends of his hair but it got caught in the tangles. Harper let out a squeal of pain and put his hand on his head.

Zane stepped back just as Jackson walked into the bathroom.

"Problems?"

"His hair's a mess. I can't get a comb through it," Zane said.

Jackson nodded. "I could cut it."

"Like Papa's?" Harper asked.

Jackson chuckled. "I guess you've been adopted, Zane." He nodded to Harper. "Yes, sort of like your papa's."

Harper smiled and Jackson pulled out his knife. Harper scrambled off the counter, grabbed Zane, and hid behind him. "Don't let him hurt me, Papa."

Zane struggled to keep his rage from showing, but inside, he directed it at the people who'd done this to Harper. He picked him up and held him against his chest. "He's not going to hurt you, son. He's just going to cut your hair with the knife."

Harper raised his head, looked at Jackson, then at the knife. "Really? Promise?"

Jackson nodded. "Really. If I cut you then your papa can slug me."

"Okay," Harper said. "Can I slug you, too?"

"Absolutely," Jackson said, then chuckled and looked at Zane. "You're going to have your hands full with this one."

Zane smiled. "Fold up a towel so he can sit on it." Once Jackson had done that, he set Harper back on the counter, then wrapped a towel around his shoulders. Jackson stepped up and began chopping off the long tangles. When he needed to cut the back, he swiveled Harper around to face the mirror and Harper reached out and touched his reflection.

"Is that me, Papa?"

Jackson's hand shook and he stopped cutting Harper's hair for a moment. In French, he told Zane he was going back to the compound and killing every guard there. Luc appeared in the doorway and said he would go with him. Zane nodded and said he'd take point. Harper watched the exchange with a puzzled look on his face.

"It will be okay, Harper. Trust me," Zane said. "Finish cutting the back, Jackson."

A few minutes later, Jackson cut off the last lock, then ran the comb through Harper's hair. "There, all done."

"I'm going to treat your cuts and scrapes, buddy," Luc said, then held out his hands. Harper hesitated for a moment, then went into his arms and Luc carried him out of the room.

"I'll see you downstairs," Jackson said, then left.

Zane cleaned up the bathroom, then joined Luc and Harper in the bedroom. He smiled when he saw Harper standing still as Luc stuck a bandage on his arm. The T-shirt he'd put on him after his bath hung to the floor and slid off his bony shoulders. Just remembering Harper's reaction when he'd thrown his ragged clothes away was enough to make Zane shake with rage again. How could anyone treat their own child so horribly? Charles Dolman had a lot to answer for, and he was going to enjoy making him pay. He watched as Luc smeared an antibiotic cream on a cut on Harper's leg, then stuck another bandage on him before examining an old scar.

"I'm bad," Harper said. "I don't work hard enough and I drop things. That's why I get hit all the time."

Luc froze, then said, "I've got scars, too, Harper. But it's not because I'm bad, and neither are you." Luc stood, then undid his jeans and showed Harper the belt buckle scar on his hip. "My real mother did this when she was mad at me."

"Was she bad?" Harper asked.

"Sometimes, Harper," Luc said. "But you're not bad, buddy."

Harper touched the mark, then looked up at Luc with sad eyes. "Ravyn says mean people suck."

Zane watched Luc buckle his jeans, then squat down and put his hand on Harper's shoulder and hug him. "Ravyn's right, Harper." Luc saw Zane watching them. He hugged Harper again, then released him. "He'll do fine, Zane. He just needs good food and lots of it."

Zane noticed the cartoon bandages on several of Harper's wounds and smiled. "I see you came prepared."

Luc chuckled. "We tried to tell you, but you wouldn't listen."

"Next time, if there is a next time, try a little harder."

Luc laughed and walked away. "I smell food."

Zane heard Harper's tummy growl. He smiled and picked him up. "Time to eat."

"Can I have lots?"

"I want you to eat a little bit now, but not too much or it will make you sick. Okay, son?"

"Are you really my papa now?"

"Yes. If that's okay with you?"

"Yes, okay. Will Ravyn be my mama now?"

"She is your mama."

Harper giggled. "No, she isn't, silly. She's my sister."

* * * *

Zane saw Cade waiting for them as the jet landed. He knew immediately from the look on his face that he had bad news. His gut clenched with nerves as he walked down the steps with a sleeping Harper in his arms. McCabe was one step behind him.

"McCabe," Cade said.

"Cade. It went well. We got the kid and the other prisoners, then helped Rios destroy the compound. He wants out. I told him we'd see what we can do for him."

Cade nodded. "That would make Marisol happy."

"I'll be in touch," McCabe said.

"Addison is expecting you at the house."

McCabe laughed. "Oh, no, I know her reputation and I'm not getting anywhere near your wife and her matchmaking plans."

"Good luck, but it's probably already too late," Cade said with a grin. "Stay in touch."

"Will do," McCabe said, then walked back to the jet. A moment later, it taxied away.

Zane watched until it took off, then he turned to Cade. "What's happened?"

"We'll talk at the house. Addison, Jenna, and Cassie are waiting for Harper. Marisol is with them in case he needs a translator."

"He speaks Spanish and English," Zane said, the pride of a new father in his voice. "He's a smart kid for his age."

"For his circumstances," Cade said, then frowned. "Was he raped?"

"Hellfire, Cade, why would you ask something like that?" Zane asked, his voice too loud. Harper lifted his head and blinked sleepy eyes. Zane patted his back. "It's okay, son, I've got you."

"Papa," Harper breathed the one word as his eyes closed again and his head relaxed back onto Zane's shoulder.

Zane slid his hand over Harper's head. "God, I hadn't even thought of that. Damn it. He didn't seem to mind me giving him a bath." He frowned. "Would that be a sign?"

Cade shrugged. "We'll have Dr. Stephens talk to him."

"Who's that?" Zane asked, his voice suspicious.

Cade waved them toward the SUV parked by the airport building. "Turns out there are two Dr. Stephens. David Stephens is taking over Dr. Marshall's practice when he retires and his wife, Melinda Stephens, is opening a child psychology clinic. She specializes in abused and neglected children."

Zane saw a silent message pass between Cade and Jackson.

"So, in other words, Addison's been up to her old tricks?" Jackson asked as he opened the back of the vehicle and they stashed their gear before getting into the car. He and Luc took the backseat while Zane got in the front passenger seat with Harper on his lap.

"Seems so," Cade said. "They had dinner with us last night. We were expecting you to show up then."

"We had an errand to run," Zane said, and Luc and Jackson grunted.

"A killing kind of errand?" Cade asked.

"A revenge kind of errand," Zane said, then added, "I want Harper checked over. Is Doc Marshall at the house?"

Cade nodded. "He's waiting for you to arrive."

"We need to equip some vehicles with kids' seats," Zane said, then asked, "Tell me what's gone wrong? Is it Ravyn?"

Cade glanced at him. "She was removed from her cell around six last night. Mendez has her."

Fear slammed into Zane and he clutched Harper tighter to him. Harper protested and he forced himself to loosen his grip. He wanted to bellow with rage. Instead, he forced himself to remain calm. It was the only way he had a chance of saving Ravyn. "What do we know?"

"Thor, Ben, Mac, and Nate are on it." Cade glanced at him.

"Nate? I thought he was a cook," Zane said.

"Marine," Cade said. "He reminds me of someone, but I can't think who."

"I don't care who he is, as long as he's good. I'll take all the help we can get," Zane said.

Cade nodded. "We'll find her. We managed to track the vehicle they were in until they left Dallas going east. We have a good idea of the area they're in, but we don't think Mendez is still with them. We picked the vehicle up again going back into Dallas about an hour later. We're searching a forty-mile section."

Zane refused to face the possibility that they wouldn't find her in time. A wave of shame washed through him when he remembered what he'd done the last time he'd seen her. "Did someone pick up Ravyn's collar?"

"Addison did," Cade said, "right after she told me I was a stubborn ass and she was leaving me and going home to Ireland."

"You've got to get control of her before she becomes a bad influence on Cassie," Luc said from the backseat.

Cade growled. "Addison is not a bad influence on anyone. She's done nothing but try to help every one of us, including you. Do you think you'd have ever met Cassie without Addison's help?"

The tension in the car grew when Cade stopped the SUV at the end of the ranch driveway. He turned in the seat, looked at each one of them, and said, "When I was nine, Joan got drunk and brought a man home. He raped me. She knew and didn't care because he supplied her with drugs. When Dad found out, he decided to take us and leave. It's my fault he told her he was leaving her. It's my fault he died."

"Cade," Jackson said.

Cade interrupted him. "After the third attempt on Addison's life when she was seventeen, I got drunk and went to see her. I told her about the rape. I told her I loved her but could never be with her because I wasn't good enough for her. She's known all this time, and she's loved me and plotted to save me. Don't criticize her in my presence ever again."

"Cade," Zane said, "we didn—"

"I don't want to talk about it," Cade said. "Dr. Stephens said confronting it is part of the healing process. It's been confronted." He started the engine and drove on to the house. Addison and Jenna were waiting on the front porch. Before Cade could open the door, Luc leaned forward and grabbed his shoulder.

"Thank you for protecting us, Cade."

Cade nodded, then got out of the car and walked toward Addison. Zane was a couple steps behind him when Cade grabbed Addison and hugged her. She whispered something to him and he nodded his head, then carried her into the house.

Zane saw Jenna hug Jackson as he walked up to her. Cassie and Logan were waiting for Luc in the foyer. He watched them hug each other and missed Ravyn even more.

Doc walked out of the living room. "In here, Zane. I've got everything set up for Harper."

Zane followed Doc into the living room.

"Step on the scale," Doc said.

Zane stepped on it and Doc wrote down the number. Jenna held out her arms and he looked at Harper, then shook his head. "I don't want him waking up with someone he doesn't know."

Logan stepped forward. "Give him to me. If he wakes up, he'll just think I'm Luc."

Zane handed Harper over and Doc wrote down the new weight, then frowned. "Lay him down here and let's see how tall he is."

Logan laid Harper on the couch, then stepped back. Cassie helped Doc measure him.

"He's tall for his age, but underweight. He needs to gain at least ten pounds. Twelve would be better."

Jenna took Harper's pulse, then his temperature. "He has a low grade fever," she said.

"He has a lot of cuts and scrapes," Zane said. "Luc cleaned them and treated them with antibiotic ointment, but he was living in a filthy shed with six other people and no toilet facilities."

Doc nodded, then listened to Harper's heart. "Jenna, see if you can get some blood from this little guy without waking him."

"Let me hold him in case he wakes up." Zane sat down and lifted Harper into his arms.

"He's really sound asleep." Jenna brushed his hair back, then stuck him and watched the tube fill.

"Probably the first time he's felt safe enough to sleep in a long time, if ever," Doc said.

As soon as Jenna handed Doc the vials of blood, he put them in his case. "When he wakes, see if you can get a urine sample for me. I'm going to run these to the lab at the hospital. If I find anything that needs urgent treatment, I'll let you know. Otherwise, I'll be out to see him tomorrow. In the meantime, lots of fluids and small meals every two to three hours. Jenna, you know the list of foods for him."

"I do, and I've already been to the store to get the food he needs, including a children's vitamin."

"Good girl." Doc shut his bag.

"Doc, do you think Harper needs to talk to a child psychologist?" Zane asked.

"That's up to you, Zane, but I'd say it couldn't hurt." Doc put on his jacket, then left.

"There's food in the kitchen, Zane," Logan said. "I'll stay with Harper while you eat. Thor may be calling any moment and you'll need to go after Ravyn."

Zane nodded, then placed Harper in Logan's arms. "If he wakes up, call me."

"Will do," Logan said.

Chapter Ten

The sound of a man yelling somewhere down the corridor woke Ravyn and she sat up on the side of the cot. Yesterday she'd been fingerprinted, had her picture taken, and then she'd been searched. That had been the most embarrassing and humiliating experience of her life. She understood why they'd had to do it, but it still left her nerves shattered and she'd been in tears by the time it ended.

Afterward, she'd been given an orange, knee-length, shapeless sack to wear, then she'd been locked in this small, windowless room. The walls were a flat beige color with pewter-gray trim on the metal frame of the metal door. It held a cot with a thin, but clean, mattress, and a sink and a toilet tucked away in the corner. There was a slot in the door that was used to deliver food trays to a prisoner, to her, she thought. She was the prisoner now. The room smelled strongly of cleansers with a tiny hint of the food someone slid through the slot on a regular basis.

McCabe had said she'd have to stay a couple days. If it turned out to be longer than that, she thought she'd go insane. There wasn't anything in the small cell to stimulate her mind. No pictures and no sounds other than the sharp clanging sound of a metal door slamming somewhere in the distance. The only other contact she'd had was one of the guards banging on her door, demanding she push the tray through to him. She'd done that, then returned to the cot where she'd passed the time by tracing the grooves between the concrete blocks and counting the imperfections she found. She was up to sixty-nine when she'd fallen asleep.

The dream that number had inspired had left her panting and aroused. It was a position she and Zane had never gotten around to trying in reality. The knowledge that they never would now made her bottom lip tremble as tears flooded her eyes.

She pulled her feet up onto the edge of the bed and hugged her knees to her chest then rocked back and forth, comforting herself. One of her hands touched her neck, searching again for the collar he'd given her. She wondered if he knew the truth now, and if he did, would he forgive her?

The sound of her door being opened drew her attention. A hard-faced guard stood in the opening and summoned her with his hand. Ravyn hesitated for a moment, then stood up and slipped her feet into the soft shoes they'd given her.

"What's happening?" she asked.

He frowned. "FBI is here to question you."

"Johnson and Lake?" she asked, scared, as she took a step back.

He took a threatening step toward her and pulled out a nightstick. "You can come with me or I can put chains on you and take you. It's up to you."

Ravyn didn't know what she could tell him. She wanted to say that the two special agents were dirty, but if the guard was involved with them then that would alert them. She couldn't take the chance on them doing anything to harm Harper.

The guard held up a pair of cuffs and she approached him then held out her wrists. He snapped them on her then took hold of her arm and led her down the corridor to the elevator. Once inside, he kept her in front of him and her gut instinct kicked in and told her something was wrong. She watched the numbers flash by until the elevator stopped at the basement level. When the doors opened, she saw a black limousine waiting for them with its back door open. The guard shoved her ahead of him, then threw her into the vehicle. She banged her head on the opposite door and fell to the floor.

Ravyn groaned and raised her cuffed hands to rub her forehead. When she looked up, she looked into the smirking face of Mendez. Before she could sit up, a large foot landed on her back and held her down.

Mendez leaned toward her. "Señora, you are going to tell me everything that you have told the authorities."

Ravyn trembled with fear as her stomach rolled. She swallowed the bile that filled her mouth and fought to keep from puking. "I didn't tell them anything. I confessed. That's all."

Mendez tutted, then laughed and pulled out his phone. "With one call, I can have your young friend taken care of," he said. "Now, tell me everything you have told the authorities."

"Nothing, only what you told me to tell them." She struggled to get up and saw Mendez nod at someone behind her. The foot on her back slid away and she rolled over and sat up. Johnson and Lake sat on the seat across from Mendez. "Ask them," she said, nodding toward the two agents. "They were present when that other man questioned me."

"What about on the drive to Dallas?"

Ravyn shook her head. "I was alone in the backseat of the car. Crying."

"Ah, Señora, I'm afraid the thought of you in tears only excites me," Mendez said, then indicated the guard with his hand. "This is Dolor. Do you know what his name means?"

Ravyn shook her head, even as she knew it couldn't be anything good.

"It means sorrow," Mendez said, "because he brings sorrow to my enemies."

Before Ravyn could absorb the word, a hand connected with her left cheek. She fell sideways and her face hit Mendez' knee. The inside of her cheek split and blood filled her mouth as she cried out. Before she could catch her breath, Mendez buried his fist in her hair and jerked her head back.

"Now, Señora, I ask you one last time. What did you tell the authorities?"

"Nothing, nothing," Ravyn mumbled as tears of pain and fear rolled down her cheeks. She licked her lip and realized it was cut as well. "I swear."

Mendez shook his head. "You have disappointed me. I ask you to do one thing for me and you betray me." He turned to Dolor. "Get the truth from her, but do not kill her. She will bring a high price in the auction, and, Dolor, no sampling the goods. Understand."

Johnson sat forward. "Let's just get this over with. They've got the kid and from what I saw at the ranch, they don't give a shit about her."

Lake nodded. "We did everything you told us to do. We need our money so we can get out of the country."

"Gentlemen, the game is not yet over. The Ramseys are men of honor," he said the last word with contempt, "and they will come after her. Then, I will have my revenge." He rubbed his chest. "I owe Cade Ramsey a bullet to the chest, but I'm afraid mine will be fatal." He laughed.

Ravyn shivered with terror. Mendez had always scared her, but now he seemed even more evil, as if something putrid had taken over his soul. Dolor smiled and Ravyn looked down. She was going to die or at least wish she was dead, but that was okay because now she knew Harper was safe with Zane. She looked back up just in time to see a fist flying toward her face.

* * * *

The room she woke in was quiet and smelled old and damp. Ravyn rolled her eyes while she wondered why kidnap victims always ended up in places like this. She smiled around the gag in her mouth and the cut on her lip stung. Apparently, all bad guys followed a similar pattern. Kidnap a person, beat them up, take them to an old smelly house and—she tugged on her hands, then tried to laugh. True to form, she was tied to a bed and had been left to wake up alone and scared. She snorted. Surely, her death should be more interesting than this after all she'd sacrificed.

She rolled over, then groaned when her cheek rubbed on the bed and she realized her left eye was swollen shut. She looked across the room and screamed around the gag when she saw what was left of Johnson and Lake. They were dead, but they hadn't gone easy, and she knew this was the work of Dolor and that he'd be coming for her soon.

She raised her head and looked around the room. She had no idea where she was or what time it was, and only a little moonlight was coming through a small window high up on the wall. The window was wider than it was high, and she figured if she could reach it, she could wiggle through it. The door was the only other option and Dolor was probably on the other side of it so that route was out. She moved, then froze when the bed squeaked. When she didn't hear the sound of footsteps approaching the room she relaxed and looked at her wrists.

The handcuffs were gone and she was tied with rope. A mistake on their part. Slowly, without moving and causing more squeaks, she began to twist her wrists. A few minutes later, her skin was rubbed raw and bleeding. She bit down on the gag and forced herself to continue. Eventually the blood acted as a lubricant and her wrist slipped free. She grimaced with pain then removed the gag, and quickly untied the other one. She eased up and the bed gave another tiny squeak. She moved as slowly as she could and managed to reach her right foot and undo the rope. She eased her foot to the floor, then stood up with the other ankle still tied to the bed.

Only then did she notice she was naked. "Bastards," she whispered, then untied her left foot as she did a mental survey of her body and decided she hadn't been raped. Apparently Dolor followed Mendez's orders a lot better than she did. She looked around for her orange dress and didn't see it, or her shoes. She could wrap herself in the blanket, but it would be bulky and impede her if she had to run. Ravyn looked at Lake. He was small and about her height.

She tiptoed over to his body, then carefully removed his shoes. His socks were stiff with dried blood but she took them anyway. She undid his pants, then slipped them off him and stepped into them. They had wet spots of blood on them and she gagged. After several deep breaths, she looked around for his shirt and found his and Johnson's shirts piled in the corner. Lake's was white but Johnson's was a checkered green-and-black pattern. She chose it and put it on, then tucked it into the pants she was wearing. They were too loose, so she used Lake's belt to hold them up. A second later, she had the socks on and carried the shoes over to the window.

Ravyn reached up and realized she was about a foot short of touching it. The only furniture in the room was the bed and she didn't dare try to drag it over to the window. For a moment she felt defeated then straightened her shoulders and thought, hell no, she wasn't giving into despair. There had to be something she could do.

She looked at Johnson and Lake. God, could she? Determined to escape she grabbed Johnson and pulled his body over to the wall. The smear of blood she left on the floor gagged her and she swallowed, then grabbed Lake. She pulled him over next to Johnson, then stacked him on top of Johnson. The smell of blood in the room was strong and she gagged again, then forced herself to step onto Lake's back.

She reached up and unlatched the window, then pushed on it. A whispered curse left her lips when she realized it was stuck. She pushed again and Lake shifted beneath her feet. She caught her balance, then took a deep breath and pushed again, and the window broke loose and slid up a few inches. She pushed again and it opened all the way. Satisfied, she got down, grabbed the shoes, and dropped them outside the window, then held her breath and hoped they didn't make a sound. When she didn't hear anything, she grabbed the ledge, then began to pull herself up with a soft grunt. Little by little, she lifted herself until her belly was resting on the bottom ledge. She wiggled and looked around. There was nothing to hold onto and only the ground below her.

Nothing for it, she thought, and grasped the ledge and tried to bend her leg and force it through the window and couldn't. She hung from the window, then let go and dropped toward the ground. Her hands hit first and she managed to tuck herself into a ball and roll onto the ground. After she caught her breath, she searched for the shoes and found one nearby but had to pat around the ground for the second one. Once she found it she slipped them on and stood up.

She looked around and saw that she was at some kind of old farmhouse. She could see fields around her and, off in the distance, a line of trees. She listened for a moment and thought she could hear the sound of cars in the distance. She asked herself what Cassie would do, realized she didn't know and decided when she got back to the ranch, she was going to have Cassie begin training her.

If Dolor discovered she'd escaped he'd think she headed for the trees and the sound of cars on a highway so she decided she would go that way but then change direction and go either left or right. She'd decide when she got that far, if she didn't get caught in the meantime. She stuck to the shadows as she moved past the house and heard snoring coming from one of the rooms as she slipped away into the darkness. When she ran into a barbed wire fence and the barbs stabbed into her belly and hands, she bit her lip to keep from crying out. The wire was sagging, so she held one strand up and slipped through it, then hurried across the field.

* * * *

"We have movement on the east side of the house," Jackson said into the mic as he scoped the house in the distance.

"It's Ravyn," Luc said from his position. "She's going to walk right into you, Zane."

"I see her," Zane said. "As soon as I have her secured, we'll move in. I want that bastard Mendez alive, if he's here." A series of clicks was his only answer.

* * * *

Ravyn scrambled across the open field. Ahead of her, she saw what she thought was a ditch and she ran toward it. Just as her foot hit the edge, a dark shadow rose up and grabbed her around the waist as one hand covered her mouth, muffling her scream. She kicked and dug her nails into the arm around her waist, then heard a cursed grunt. A moment later she was on the ground with a heavy body on top of her.

"It's me, Ravyn. We're here to rescue you." Zane kept his hand over her mouth. "Do you understand?"

Ravyn nipped his hand and Zane removed it. "This isn't a rescue. It's an escape. You scared the crap out of me when you grabbed me. Couldn't you have just said something like, 'Psst, over here' or something?"

"For someone who's been kidnapped, you seem pretty relaxed."

"So what are you going to accuse me of doing now?" Before he could answer her, she asked, "How'd you find me anyway?"

"Nate found you." He hushed her, then said, "I've got her."

Ravyn looked and didn't see anyone else with them. "Who are you talking to?"

"Jackson, Luc, Thor, Ben, Mac, and Nate. How many men are in the house?"

"Dead or alive?"

"There are dead people in the house?"

"Johnson and Lake."

"Are you sure they're dead?"

"Well, when I dragged them over to the wall and stacked Lake on top of Johnson so I could stand on them and reach the window, they didn't protest. So I'd say yeah, they're dead."

Zane froze and looked down at her. "I am going to beat your ass if you don't stop with the smartass remarks."

Ravyn rolled her one good eye and snorted.

"Who hit you?"

"A guy named Dolor. I think he killed the agents. I think he's in the house asleep. I heard snoring coming from the back window of the house when I escaped."

"Anybody else in the house?"

"I don't know. There was only Mendez and Dolor and the two agents in the limousine when Dolor hit me and knocked me out. When I woke up, Johnson and Lake were dead and I was tied to the bed."

Zane hugged her. "It will be okay. Trust me."

"Like hell. You didn't trust me. You wouldn't even listen."

"You confessed to loving another man."

"Harper's seven years old, Zane." Ravyn realized she hadn't even asked about her little brother. She tried to push Zane away but didn't even manage to budge him. "Get off me."

"No."

"Did you rescue Harper?"

"Yes."

"Good. As soon as I get out of here, I'll go get him and we'll get out of your way."

"You can't. I've told him I'm his papa. He belongs to me now."

"You can't just claim him."

"Too late. He belongs to me and so do you."

Before she could stop him, she felt the collar slide around her neck and lock into place.

Ravyn reached up and tugged on it. "You Ramsey men think you can do as you please, but I'm here to tell you I refuse to be claimed like…like lost baggage."

"I didn't lose yo—"

"Uh, could you two lovebirds bitch at each other later?" Thor asked as he slid into the ditch next to them with Nate beside him. "Right now we need to play 'let's catch a bad guy.'"

"There's nothing more to talk about." Ravyn pushed at Zane again.

"You've got that right, pet." Zane slid off her. "I want you to stay here with Nate and keep your head down until I come back for you. No running off. Do you understand?"

Ravyn snorted. "Really, Zane. I'm wearing the bloody clothes of a dead man. Where do you think I'd go? Shopping? Out to dinner?"

"You're getting five for every smartass remark you make, so keep it up."

"You wish. I have a safe word."

"Then use it."

Next to them, Thor growled then looked toward Nate. "Get between these two before I decide to take Zane out."

"You're welcome to try," Zane said.

Nate reached over and grabbed Ravyn and pulled her toward him. He stuck an earpiece in her ear, then put a mic on her and added a pair of night goggles. She let out a little screech when he brushed her sore eye. "Sorry," Nate said, then turned on the goggles. "How's that?"

Ravyn looked around, amazed at what she could see. "Wow, I want to keep these."

Thor grunted again. "Zane, come with me. We're going to go get the bad guy now, if you have the time to spare."

Zane rose into a crouch. "Fuck off, Thor." He disappeared over the edge of the ditch.

Thor chuckled. "I love fucking with these Ramseys in love." He chuckled again. "'The fool who persists in his folly will become wise.'"

"William Blake," said Addison on the radio, then added, "Ah-oh."

"Addison, how the hell did you get your hands on a radio?" Cade asked on the radio.

"Uh, uh, I can explain," Addison said.

"Turn it off and get down here to my den right now," Cade said.

Thor snorted, then followed Zane.

Ravyn watched them move toward the house. From her position, she couldn't see them once they reached the side of the building. She tried to move farther to her right, but Nate blocked her.

"Keep your head down," Nate said.

"Can they hear us?" Ravyn asked.

"Yes."

"Stop the chatter," Thor said.

Ravyn grimaced, then waited for something to happen. For several minutes, there was silence, then she heard a soft squeak of old boards and Zane said, "Okay, I'm on the front porch."

Thor said, "I'm outside the bedroom window. This guy's still snoring."

Ben said, "Mac and I are right behind you, Zane."

Ravyn could hear the snores of the guy in the house. She listened, then froze. "Wait. There's something wrong."

"Everyone freeze," Nate said.

"What is it, Ravyn?" Zane asked.

"Thor, hold your mic up to the window," Ravyn said.

A moment later, she heard the snores more clearly. She listened for a moment, then gasped. "I think it's a recording. It's the same snores over and over."

"Are you sure?" Zane asked.

"Yes. Get out of there, Zane," Ravyn said. She listened and heard Zane and Thor question if the house was rigged to blow up.

"One of you look through the window I used to climb out of the house," Ravyn said, her voice urgent.

A few minutes later, Thor cursed, then said, "Get the hell out of there. The door is rigged. Ravyn, didn't you even try the door?"

"No, I figured it was locked or they were on the other side of it. Either way, I wasn't leaving that way." Ravyn saw Thor move away from the house. A minute later Zane, Ben, and Mac joined him.

"We can't just leave it like this," Zane said.

"They've probably rigged the entire house," Thor said. "The window Ravyn used is too damn small for any of us to get through."

"I could go back in and you could tell me what to do," Ravyn said.

"Hell, no," Zane said. "I figure they've got someone close by, waiting to see if the house blows."

"Let's find the son of a bitch, then," Thor said.

"Nate, take care of Ravyn," Zane said.

"No," Nate said. "You come get your woman and take her home. I'm in the mood to go hunting."

"Get your ass in gear, Ramsey," Thor said. "We'll get this guy and meet you back at the house. Luc and Jackson, you've got our backs."

Ravyn heard a series of clicks and figured that was their way of answering.

Zane appeared in front of her. "Let's go. Stay low and if I tell you to stop, you stop. Understand?"

"Stay low and stop if you say to," Ravyn said. "I think I can manage that."

"That's five more."

Ravyn rolled her good eye, then followed him. Every now and then, she'd hear a series of clicks on the earpiece and she knew the others were communicating with some kind of code. In front of her, Zane stopped and held up his fist. She stopped, then glanced around and wondered why he'd stopped. Ahead of them, she saw a pile of tree limbs and brush. Zane stared at it. When he stepped back toward her and pushed her to the ground, she let him. He came down beside her with his body between her and the debris.

He put his mouth against her ear. "Stay here and keep your head down."

She nodded and a second later when a cloud blocked the moonlight he disappeared into the darkness. If she hadn't had the night goggles on, she never would have seen him as he belly-crawled toward the bushes. As she waited, each second seemed like an hour. She stared in the direction Zane had gone, then jumped when a gunshot rang out, followed by two more. Ravyn saw Zane stumble out from behind the debris, followed by Dolor. Zane attacked and Dolor thrust a large knife in his direction. Zane blocked it then kicked Dolor and connected with his lower legs. Dolor stumbled back, then caught his balance and attacked again.

Ravyn saw Zane stumble and realized he was hurt. The thought that he might die sent her into a panic and she looked around for a weapon and saw a large rock. She grabbed it, then, without thinking, she ran toward them. She saw Dolor stab Zane's arm but Zane didn't even pause, as if the wound hadn't registered with him.

Ravyn waited until Dolor went after Zane again, then she ran up behind him and hit him as hard as she could on the head. He turned toward her with the knife raised and she saw Zane's arm go around his neck and pull him back. Dolor struggled, but couldn't loosen Zane's chokehold on him. They struggled for several minutes but when Ravyn saw Zane falter she screamed, ran toward them and kicked Dolor between the legs as hard as she could. He squealed and Zane managed to cut off his air supply until he passed out. Zane dropped him to the ground, then planted his knee in his back and zip tied his hands and feet together. Zane looked up at her, then without warning he fell over onto his back.

Ravyn ran to him and dropped to her knees next to him. "Zane, Zane," she said then remembered she had a mic on. "Zane's been shot or stabbed. I need help now."

"We're on our way," Nate said, his voice calm. "Find the wound and put pressure on it."

"Okay, but come quick." She ran her hands over his body. There was blood on his arm where the knife had cut him. It was bleeding but it appeared to be a shallow cut. She felt over his chest and body armor but didn't find any blood. When she touched his left leg, his pants were wet and she could feel blood running from an open wound. She pulled off the belt she was wearing, then wrapped it around Zane's leg above the wound and twisted it until the bleeding stopped. "He's been shot in the leg about a foot above his knee. There's a lot of blood."

"Right or left leg?" Nate asked.

"Left," Ravyn said. "I've used my belt as a tourniquet."

"Good girl," Nate said. "I'll be with you in just a minute."

"Come on, Zane, don't you dare die. You still owe me an apology and some groveling," Ravyn said. She wanted to hold him but didn't dare let go of the belt.

"I'm approaching you," Nate said.

"Please hurry." Ravyn looked around when she heard a moan. "This bastard Dolor is waking up. Zane tied him up before he passed out."

Nate dropped down next to her and she jumped.

"Sorry, didn't mean to startle you," Nate said as he pulled something from his pocket and placed it around Zane's leg, then tightened it. "You can remove the belt now, Ravyn."

"Are you sure?" Ravyn asked.

"I've put a combat tourniquet on him," Nate said. "It will control the bleeding and you don't have to hold it. Did you check his head and torso?"

"Oh, no, I didn't check his head." She reached for Zane and Nate grabbed her hand and squeezed it.

"Stay calm, Ravyn, and let me check him. Okay?"

She nodded. "He has a cut on his arm, but it's shallow."

After a few seconds, Nate leaned back. "He has a knot on the back of his head. He must have hit it when he fell."

Thor's voice came over the earpiece. "I'm in the SUV and I'm on my way."

"Luc and I have you covered," Jackson said, followed by two clicks.

"McCabe is sending Bari to disarm the bombs," Mac said, his voice disgruntled. "Ben and I will stay and make sure there are no more of these assholes watching the house."

Thor chuckled. "How well does Addison know Bari?"

"She can meddle all she wants, but it won't do her any good where I'm concerned," Mac said.

"Watch your six, Mac, or Addison will have you walking down the aisle," Thor said, then laughed.

Ravyn heard the sound of a vehicle approaching. A door slammed, then Thor was next to them. He and Nate picked Zane up and carried him to the SUV. They laid him on the backseat and she climbed in beside him as they got into the front seat.

"How's he doing?" Thor asked.

"He took a bullet to the leg and he's going to need surgery to remove it, but he'll live," Nate said.

"I've called the hospital and they're waiting for him to arrive," Cade said on the radio. "We'll meet you there."

"Roger," Nate said.

The SUV bounced up and down every time they hit a rut. Ravyn crouched on the floor and held onto Zane to keep him from bouncing around. After several minutes, they turned onto a road and Thor sped toward the lights in the distance. Several miles later, he jerked off his night vision goggles and turned on the headlights.

Ravyn stroked Zane's cheek, but he didn't stir. "Shouldn't he wake up?"

"No," Nate said. "It's better if he stays out and stays still."

Ravyn nodded, even though she knew he couldn't see her. She leaned toward Zane. "You're going to be okay. Trust me." She kissed his cheek. "I love you, Zane." She stroked his hair back from his forehead, then realized they were both still wearing the mics, ear buds, and night-vision goggles. She felt her cheeks heat when she heard Thor chuckle followed by several clicks on the radio. She removed their equipment then held it out toward Nate. "Here, Nate."

She felt Nate take them from her hand just as they pulled beneath the emergency entrance of a hospital. Several people in white coats stood near a gurney. As soon as the vehicle stopped, Nate jumped out and opened the back door. He picked Zane up and laid him on the gurney.

Ravyn scooted across the seat and ran after them. As soon as she cleared the doors, the royals surrounded her.

"I need to be with Zane," Ravyn said as she tried to push by them.

Marisol grabbed her by her shoulders. "He's in good hands, Ravyn, but you're hurt as well. Let us help you."

Ravyn sent an anxious look in the direction Zane had disappeared. "Where have they taken him?"

"Surgery," Addison said.

"Oh, god, it's bad," Ravyn said as tears flooded her eyes. Her swollen eye stung and she tried to blink it and couldn't. A sob left her lips as the reality of the situation hit her. "Is he going to die?"

"No," Addison said. "Absolutely not. He just needs surgery right now and you need to be cleaned up and treated as well."

Ravyn nodded, then looked down at her clothes in the bright lights of the hallway and gagged. The pants she had on were covered in blood. She gagged again, then ripped at the clothes. "Get me out of these. Now. Now." She tried to calm herself but her breathing was going wacky and there were spots flashing before her eyes as she felt herself falling.

Cade caught her and lifted her into his arms. "Coming through," he said, his voice loud as a nurse rushed out of a curtained area, saw him, then quickly pointed at an empty exam area. He laid Ravyn down, then stepped back as the nurse called for a doctor.

Dr. Stephens rushed in, nodded at Cade, and began examining Ravyn. "What happened to her?"

"Kidnapped, beaten up, lost consciousness, woke up to two dead men, dressed in their clothes, and escaped," Cade said.

Dr. Stephens smiled. "Just another day at the ranch?"

Cade nodded.

"Okay, nurse, you know the routine. Blood pressure, temp, pulse, blood, and call CT. Let's make sure her head's okay. That's quite a shiner she has there." Dr. Stephens listened to Ravyn's heart, then examined her eyes. "Get someone down here to look at this eye."

"Yes, Doctor," the nurse said. "Do you want her cleaned up?"

"Not until we get the CT scan back," Dr. Stephens said.

"Bag the clothes for evidence," Cade said.

Dr. Stephens nodded to the nurse. "Go ahead and gather evidence on her skin and beneath her nails."

The nurse scooted by them. "I'll get an aide to help me."

Dr. Stephens turned to Cade. "Do you think she was raped?"

"I was listening to the rescue on the radio. She didn't say anything about being raped."

"I'll ask her when she wakes up," Dr. Stephens said.

The nurse returned, and Cade and Dr. Stephens stepped out of the exam area. Dr. Stephens pulled the curtain closed. "If you want to go check on your brother, I'll keep you posted on her status."

Marisol walked up to them. "I'll stay with Ravyn, Cade."

Cade cupped her shoulder. "Thanks, Marisol." He released her and took off.

Chapter Eleven

Ravyn felt someone squeeze her hand. She squeezed back, then opened her good eye. Marisol smiled down at her.

"Hi," Marisol said.

"Zane?" Ravyn asked.

Marisol gently adjusted the ice pack on her eye, then smiled. "That feel okay?"

"Yes. Zane?"

"He's fine. Came through the surgery with flying colors. He's in recovery."

"Can I see him?"

"Doc will let you know. You need to rest and heal, too."

The door opened. Addison, Jenna, and Cassie entered the room.

"Scoot over, Ravyn," Addison said, "I'm exhausted."

Ravyn scooted over and Addison lay down next to her and sighed. "Ah, this is so much better."

Jenna laughed. "I swear, Addison, that baby is turning you into a turnip."

The royals laughed and Ravyn managed a small grin. Addison hugged her. "It's scary being kidnapped, isn't it?"

"Terrifying," Ravyn said. "I thought I was going to die." A sob escaped, followed by another. Within minutes, they were all crying.

The door opened, Jackson stepped in, took one look at them, and backed out.

Jenna giggled, then Cassie and Addison giggled. Marisol laughed and squeezed Ravyn's hand again.

"At least now we know how to get rid of them," Marisol said. "Just turn on the tears and they head for the hills."

Ravyn's stomach growled and Addison sat up. "Lunch."

Jenna frowned. "If I even think about food, I gain weight and you eat all day, Addison, and you don't gain an ounce."

"You look better now that you've put on some weight," Addison said. "You were too skinny before. Now you've got all your lovely curves back."

"Jackson won't stop feeding me. It sucks," Jenna said.

"You know what really sucks?" Cassie asked.

"Craving pizza and being in the hospital," Ravyn said.

Cassie laughed. "I was going to say Addison getting us in trouble for listening to your rescue on the radio and then she never gets spanked, but pizza sounds good, too." She pulled out her phone and made a call. When she hung up, she said, "The pizza will be here in thirty minutes. I told them they'd have to sneak them in and they said they were used to doing that."

"When do you think they'll move Zane?" Ravyn asked.

"Doc said in the morning," Cassie said as she pulled a chair closer to the bed, then sat down and propped her feet on the edge of the mattress. "Aww, that's better. Luc caught Logan pretending to be him last night while he groveled. The backs of my thighs are still sore from the spanking he gave me."

Marisol and Jenna grabbed chairs of their own, then took up the spaces on either side of Cassie. Jenna laughed. "Every time Jackson gets his sniper rifle out, when he comes home we have a sex marathon. I swear handling that rifle makes him hornier than hell."

"Did you order pop?" Addison asked.

Jenna snorted. "All you think about now is food. You don't get pop. Remember the conversation we had about caffeine and sodium?"

"Doc said I could have a pop once a week and today's my pop day," Addison said.

"You had pop yesterday," Cassie said.

"Rat," Addison said.

Ravyn slid onto her side so she could see her friends. Addison winked at her and Ravyn laughed. She was alive and Zane was alive and she was surrounded by friends. "Where's Harper?"

"Luc and Logan have him," Cassie said, then sighed. "He's almost one of them now. It's spooky."

"Oh dear, already?" Ravyn asked.

Cassie nodded. "After Doc checked Harper, Zane went to eat, then got the call that they'd found you. When Harper woke up, Logan was with him. He took one look at him and asked him who he was. He thinks it's really cool that he has two uncles that look alike."

"He didn't want to see me?" Ravyn asked, even though she told herself not to be so pathetic.

"We had to bribe him to keep him away while you slept," Addison said. "He's had enough rides on their shoulders to last him a lifetime."

"Not to mention all the snacks they've been feeding him," Jenna said.

"Is he sick? Hurt?" Ravyn asked.

Addison hugged her. "He's a little thin, but Doc said other than that, he's healthy."

"Tall for his age," Jenna said, "and smart."

The door swung open and a teenager pushed a cart into the room with a pile of linens on it. "Somebody order pizza?" he asked.

Cassie held up her hand and the boy lifted the drape on the side of the cart and pulled out six pizza boxes."

"Set them here." Cassie patted the rolling cart at the end of the bed, then handed the teenager a wad of cash. "Did you bring it?"

The teenager laughed, then reached down and pulled out two bottles of sparkling grape juice and held them up.

Addison laughed then sat up. "I'll go get some cups and ice from the nurses' station."

The teenager pulled out a small tub with a bag of ice in it and a stack of cups. "No need. I brought them. You wouldn't believe how many pizzas we deliver here every week." He set them next to the food, then left.

Addison grabbed the first box and opened it while Cassie filled the glasses with ice and juice. They each had a glass in their hands when the door swung open again and Cade, Jackson, and Logan walked in. Ravyn smiled when she saw Harper on Logan's shoulders. When he saw her he let out a squeal of joy and nearly jumped down.

"Whoa, easy there, Harper. Your sister is hurt and you have to be careful. Okay?"

Harper nodded, then said, "Okay, Uncle Logan."

Logan let him down and he ran over to the side of the bed and grabbed Ravyn's hand. She leaned down, pulled him up onto her lap and hugged him. "Oh, baby, I've missed you so much."

"I'm not a baby," Harper said, then giggled. "I'm a cowboy. See my boots?" He stuck his feet out and clicked his boots together.

"Great boots, Harper," Ravyn said, admiring the black-and-brown boots on her little brother's feet. She stood him up and checked him over like an anxious mother. He was dressed in blue jeans and a T-shirt with a superhero on it. When she ran her hands over his tummy, he wiggled, then giggled, and she hugged him tight as tears filled her eyes.

"Do you hurt, Ravyn?" Harper asked as he carefully touched her bruised and swollen cheek.

"Just a little. I'm better now that you're here." She hugged him again, then looked over his shoulder toward Cade, Logan, and Jackson. "Thank you. Thank you."

They nodded, then Jackson grabbed Jenna and sat down with her on his lap. Logan settled Cassie on his lap while Cade pulled Addison from the bed and took the chair Marisol offered him. Marisol perched on the end of the bed and began handing out the pizza.

Ravyn offered Harper a bite and he sniffed it, then bit the tip of the slice off and chewed it. He smiled and opened his mouth again. She laughed and held him on her lap, unable to believe that he was finally free and safe. He finished off almost a whole slice of pizza and part of her juice, then snuggled down on her lap and fell asleep.

She ran her fingers through his hair and smiled at him, then looked up and met Cade's eyes. She took a sip from her glass, then licked her lips. "After I married Charles, he took me to Colombia. He kept me there so he could force my father to hand over his corporation. My father came to see me and he met Mendez's sister Maria. It was her house we were living in. They fell in love and she got pregnant and had Harper. Mendez had her killed because he said she was no longer valuable to him." Ravyn blinked her eyes to clear the tears from them. "I raised Harper. After Charles had my father killed, he brought me back to the States, but he made me leave Harper behind. He would let me see him several times a year." She glanced around at them. "My father didn't hand over control of the corporation to Charles. He was forced to give Charles guardianship of Harper, because Harper owns everything. The house, the company, all the money, everything."

Cade threw his head back and laughed. Addison shushed him, but too late. Harper sat up and rubbed the sleep from his eyes.

"Dolman just did himself in," Cade said. "He's had control of the corporation for seven years. That clears you of any wrongdoing, and there's no way he'll ever convince a judge that Harper has been in partnership with Mendez."

Ravyn smiled. "When I saw Harper ten months ago, I told him I was going to send a friend to rescue him. I'd heard rumors about you and Thor, Cade. I intended to ask you to help me, but then Zane and I got involved, and Charles accused me of working with Mendez. Then Mendez started threatening me. He sent a message that he would let me know when he wanted me to confess so Charles could be released. He said if I didn't then he would ki—" She glanced at Harper and saw him watching her intently.

She brushed her hand over his hair again and smiled. It looked like someone had hacked away at it with a knife. Harper reached up and touched the medallion hanging from the collar around her neck.

"Did Papa give you this?"

Ravyn was startled, then realized Harper was talking about Zane. "Sort of, Harper, but just for a little while. When he's better, I'll return it to him."

"It's pretty." Harper let it go, then climbed down. "I have to go."

Logan laughed. "Through that door, buddy. Do you remember what I taught you?"

"Yup," he said. "Seat up, seat down. Don't forget to wash my hands."

"Yup," Luc said, then chuckled as Harper clomped into the bathroom. "That kid loves the noise those boots make."

The room door opened and Doc walked in, followed by Dr. Stephens. Doc smiled and flipped through the boxes of pizza, then chose a slice. "Thank you, I don't mind if I do," he said, then laughed. "Better grab some, David, or these guys will eat it all."

Doc leaned against the end of the bed while he ate. "Zane is doing very well, Ravyn. The bullet nicked a vein. I got the bullet out without too much trouble. The knot on his head is the reason he was unconscious. He's awake now and complaining about a headache. Since he's a Ramsey, I'd say he'll be up and running around in a few days."

Ravyn felt a rush of relief. She'd been so worried about Zane. Now that she knew he was going to be okay, every injury she had made itself known. Her eye ached and her head and face were throbbing. Eating, and smiling, had reopened the cut on her lip and it stung. Without warning, she felt herself sinking into the pillow as she lifted her hand and grabbed the collar around her neck.

She saw Dr. Stephens standing over her with a concerned look on his face. She tried to reassure him but only managed a small smile and one mumbled word. "Tired." She sighed, then let herself drift away.

* * * *

The next morning when Ravyn walked out of the bathroom after showering, she found McCabe sitting by her bed, working on a laptop. Deuce sat next to him, sipping a cup of coffee while he worked the crossword puzzle in the paper. Thor sat on the end of her bed, eating her breakfast.

"Was that for me?" she asked Thor.

"It was getting cold." Thor smiled at her. "The nurse said she'd have another one brought to you."

Ravyn tied the belt of her robe, silently thanked Addison for bringing her some clothes, then sat down on the side of her bed and reached for the covers.

"Here, let me get them," McCabe said. "You want to sit up?"

"Yes." Ravyn grabbed the sheet and pulled it up as the bed rose behind her. McCabe adjusted her pillow and she thanked him.

Dr. Stephens entered the room, glanced around, and said, "Give me a few minutes, guys."

McCabe stood up. "We ran a check on the doc. He's okay, Ravyn. Deuce, let's step out."

Deuce folded the paper then set it on the chair. "You want breakfast now, Ravyn?"

"Yes, please, Deuce."

Thor strolled toward the door. "I'll see if we can get four breakfast trays."

"You already ate," Deuce said.

"I'm a growing boy," Thor said as he passed through the door.

"We'll be right outside the door," McCabe said, then grinned at her and followed Thor with Deuce on his heels.

Dr. Stephens waited until the door closed, then stepped closer to her. "How are you doing this morning?"

"Better. My eye still hurts, though."

Dr. Stephens shined a light in her eye. "The swelling is going down, but you've got a nice shiner there."

"How's Zane?"

"Giving the nurses fits. He's demanding to see you."

"He can move around?"

"Not yet, and I told him when he's discharged he'll have to use a cane for three to four days." Dr. Stephens smiled. "That was a battle I wouldn't want to fight again."

"He can be a total as—uh, mule."

Dr. Stephens smiled. "I told him he could see you only if you agreed to see him. Do you want to see him?"

"Sure. I need to thank him for saving my little brother's life before I leave."

Dr. Stephens wrote on her chart, then slipped it back into the holder. "If you have pain, use an over-the-counter pain reliever."

"Okay."

Ravyn's thoughts moved to wondering what Zane was up to as Dr. Stephens continued talking about her condition. She only heard him say she should be okay before she wondered how she was going to convince Zane to remove the collar. Her attention was drawn back to the doctor when he cleared his throat.

"I'll write the orders out before I discharge you later this morning," he said.

After he left, McCabe entered with a wheelchair. "We're going to see Zane. Hop in."

Ravyn decided she might as well get this over with now, so she slid off the bed, stuck her feet in her slippers, and sat down. She smoothed her hands over her hair and wished she had a pair of sunglasses. She knew she looked as good as she could, all things considered, but there was no ignoring her swollen lips, bruised cheek, and black eye.

Deuce held the door open as Thor stood guard. As soon as they were in the corridor, they surrounded her. Two men in dark sunglasses with dark stubble on their faces held the elevator doors open. Once inside, McCabe pushed the button for the fourth floor, then stood to her right.

The two new guys had the same color hair as McCabe and Deuce, and they were the same size. "Are you Cin and Ace?" Ravyn asked.

The one on her left turned around and his lips curved upward. He pointed to his companion. "That's Ace and I'm pure sin, Princesita."

"Cut it out," McCabe said. "She's wearing Zane's collar."

Ravyn felt the tension in the elevator increase. "What's going on? Why are you guys so tense?"

"We'll let Zane explain that to you," Thor said as the doors slid open.

A minute later, she was sitting by Zane's bed. The room was crowded by the time they all got inside. "Where's True and Trey?" Ravyn asked.

"Around," McCabe said.

Ravyn nodded, then looked back at Zane and caught him staring at her. "You wanted to see me?"

"Have you been told about the threats Mendez has been making?" Zane asked her.

Ravyn felt the blood drain from her cheeks. She shook her head, then wished she hadn't as a wave of dizziness washed over her. She tightened her hands on the arms of the chair. "No, what's he threatening to do?"

"We've got him on the run. While he was here going after you, Juan Rios and his men attacked his main compound. They destroyed, it along with most of his warehouses, but he still has access to his bank accounts. We've managed to shut down access to your father's corporation, and they're on the run."

"They?" Ravyn swallowed, fearing the worst news was yet to come.

"Mendez managed to break Dolman out of jail last night," Zane said. "They attacked the ranch this morning."

Ravyn cried out. "No, no, oh god. Harper? Addison and Jenna? Are they okay? What about Cassie and Marisol? Everyone?"

Deuce put his hands on her shoulders and gave her a reassuring squeeze.

"They're all safe and nobody is injured," Zane said. "My brothers, Mac, and Ben have the ranch secured. The ranch hands are on high alert. They're all ex-military."

Ravyn nodded. "Harper?"

Zane smiled. "He's fine. I just spoke to him on the phone. He loves talking on the phone, by the way." He chuckled. "He's doing fine and everyone's keeping him out of trouble."

"Okay, then I need to get him." Ravyn looked at McCabe. "You said something about a safe house. Could Harper and I go to one now?"

McCabe glanced at Zane then back at Ravyn. "We're taking both of you to the ranch as soon as the doctor makes the arrangements for Zane to be discharged. Jenna has everything set up for him at the ranch."

Before Ravyn could protest, McCabe added, "It will be more efficient and safer for all of you to be at the ranch. You're still in my custody but I've made arrangements for custody to be transferred to Zane an—"

"Oh, hell no." Ravyn stood up. "I know how the Ramseys work." She glared at Zane. "Somehow the woman always ends up stuck at the ranch and then the next thing you know, she's spending the rest of her life forgiving a series of bad decisions and bad behavior by one of you. That is not happening to me"—she crossed her arms over her chest—"and, that's final."

Thor chuckled. "She's got you there, Zane."

"Shut up, Thor," Zane said as he struggled to sit up then let out a groan of pain and dropped onto his back. He groped for his leg.

Ravyn rushed to his side and grabbed his hand. "See what you've done now? Why can't just one of you be sensible? You've probably torn your stitches." She looked at Thor. "Don't just stand there. Get help."

Thor sent her a you-can't-be-serious look, then shrugged and sauntered toward the door. "I'm going to check on the breakfast trays. If I see a nurse, I'll tell them the idiot in this room did something idiotic."

Ravyn ignored him as she turned back to Zane. "Are you all right? Does your leg hurt?"

Zane grimaced. "I just moved wrong." He adjusted his leg. "Could you adjust the pillow, princess?"

"Sure," Ravyn said then folded the sheet back, but was careful to keep most of him covered. She gently lifted his leg, then moved the pillow and let his leg rest on it. "Is that better?"

"Much better, thanks." Zane smiled at her, then patted the bed by his hip. "Sit here and let's try to have a conversation about what we need to do to keep you and Harper safe. Okay?"

Ravyn nodded, sat down, and couldn't keep herself from brushing his hair back from his forehead. Of the five brothers, Zane was the best looking, she decided. Cade and Jackson were masculine and tough looking, although Jackson was definitely calmer than Cade. Luc and Logan were gorgeous but puzzling, and she sometimes didn't know how Cassie coped with them. Zane, on the other hand, was sophisticated. Well groomed, comfortable, and sexy in suits. He was her idea of a hot, wet dream, if only he wasn't so, so…She glanced at him and saw the look of satisfaction in his eyes. *Damned arrogant and self-assured.* She smiled at him. If there was one thing she knew how to deal with, it was a man who thought he had her where he wanted her.

"So what do you think we should do?" she asked Zane.

"I think you should stay at the ranch. We have it secured and there are plenty of people to keep watch." Zane sent her an encouraging let's-be-rational look. "That way, McCabe and his brothers can look for Mendez and Dolman and we won't have to spread our assets so thin." He held up his hands. "But it's up to you."

Ravyn smiled again then patted his arm. "Well, of course, I'm going to stay at the ranch, silly." She giggled, then touched the collar around her neck. "I meant what do you think we should do about this?" She held out the medallion.

"What's wrong with it?" Zane asked.

"It needs to be removed."

"I lost the key when I was shot." Zane shrugged. "I guess we could get a locksmith to remove it, if that wouldn't embarrass you."

A silky brow drifted upward as he talked. She smiled then looked at the other men in the room. "I can't believe one of you can't pick a lock. Help a girl out here?"

"What do you need help with?" Thor asked from the door as he pushed a large cart with several dozen breakfast trays stacked on it into the room.

"Picking the lock on her collar. I lost the key when that guy was trying to kill me," Zane said.

"Poor baby," Ravyn said with another pat. "But, really, being a Ramsey, you should be used to people trying kill you by now, huh?"

"That's true," McCabe said.

"True can pick locks," Deuce said. "The rest of us are all thumbs."

Ravyn smiled and patted Zane again. "Then we'll have True do it when he has time. Until then, I'll just have to work around it." She slid off the bed and sat down in the wheelchair. "All of a sudden I'm really hungry." She licked her lips and watched the men in the room watch her tongue sweep from side to side. She heard a growl from Zane and looked down, smoothing her robe over her knees. Thor was right. It was fun fucking with a Ramsey.

* * * *

Three evenings later, Ravyn carried a tray up the stairs to Zane's room. When she pushed the door open with her foot, she heard Harper giggle, then say, "Oh, Papa," before he giggled again.

"There should be one more, son," Zane said.

Ravyn searched the room for Harper and saw his booted feet sticking out from beneath the bed. "What's he doing?" she asked.

Zane looked up, then grinned. "I dropped my cards and they scattered everywhere. He's getting the ones that went under the bed."

She frowned at the stacks of chips on the bed. "Are you teaching my little brother poker, Zane?"

"Well, er, sort of, but I'm really using the cards to teach him to count."

"Yeah, right." She set the tray down, then pulled Harper out from beneath the bed by his ankles. He giggled and she hugged him. "Its dinnertime and Aunt Addison is waiting for you downstairs, Harper. Be sure to wash your hands first, okay?" Harper whooped and ran out of the room. Ravyn smiled, then turned back to Zane. "Can you scoot up a little?"

"Sure." Zane adjusted the pillows behind him. He was bare-chested, and the muscles in his arms flexed as he pushed himself up, then leaned back.

Ravyn watched the sheets fall to Zane's lap. They draped over the interesting bits and she licked her lips as she wondered if he had something on under there. She missed his touch more than she'd ever thought possible.

The day they'd been discharged from the hospital, Addison had met them in the foyer and led the way up the stairs. Cade and Jackson had carried Zane to his room, dumped him on his bed, and then left. Addison had smiled at her and she'd known instantly that the little redhead had a plan and she was in trouble. Before she could run away, Addison had asked her to help take care of Zane because she wasn't feeling well, Jenna was helping with the cooking, Cassie was riding shotgun with Luc and Logan, and Marisol was hiding from Thor.

Ravyn had done the gracious thing and agreed to nurse him. What choice had she had, really? But then bedtime had come around and Zane had patted the bed next to him. She'd protested, but he'd acted shocked when she'd told him she didn't think it was a good idea for them to share a bed. Before he'd been able to say anything, Cade had knocked on the door and walked in with a pile of bedding in his arms. He'd dumped it on the couch. "For Harper," he'd said then left.

Zane had folded his arms behind his head and watched her, and she'd known he was waiting for her to throw a fit, so she hadn't. Instead, she'd smiled and fixed a bed for Harper, bathed him, and dressed him in his new pajamas. He'd refused to wear the shirt because his "Papa" didn't wear a shirt and she'd gritted her teeth and smiled through everything. Then, she'd showered and put on a gown and approached the bed. Zane had thrown the covers back, smiled and patted the bed. She'd grabbed the decorative pillows, arranged them in a line down the center of the bed, ignored his chuckle, and then claimed her side of the mattress.

Harper had truly become one of them when he'd said, "Night, Mama. Night, Papa."

Zane, the dirty rat, had said, "Night, son," then reached over the line of pillows and poked her. "Tell our son goodnight, Ravyn."

She'd sighed loud enough for Zane to hear, then said, "Night, sweetie. I love you, Harper."

Every morning since then, including this one, she'd woken up pressed back against Zane. His left leg had been thrown over her hip and his arm had been around her waist, holding her firmly against his chest. His hand had cupped her breast and as soon as she moved, it had tightened and he'd mumbled a complaint against the top of her head that had made her shiver with arousal. The fact that he knew exactly what he was doing to her and was enjoying it really got to her. This morning, as soon as she'd rose from the bed, he'd taken a deep breath, then said, "I love the scent of an aroused woman, princess." Then, he'd patted the bed and invited her to snuggle. She'd fled to the bathroom for a shower and a stern self-lecture with the sound of his chuckle following her.

Most of the day had been spent thinking she should just give in and let him have his way, and her, but some sixth sense forced her to stand against him. Zane wasn't the kind of man who wanted a woman who was easy to conquer, and she wasn't the kind of woman who wanted to be easily conquered.

Plus, the thrill of going up against him really turned her on. Resisting him was becoming the best game they'd played so far, she thought, as she opened the bedroom door. The sight that met her eyes froze her in her tracks. Zane stood by the bed, buck naked, with drops of water running down his back. They followed the muscular curve of his waist, then converged and slid down the crack of his butt. She licked her lips and shivered.

He turned and smiled at her. "Could you dry my back, pet?"

"Uh, sure." Ravyn closed the door, then took the towel he handed her. She dabbed at the water on his back, then stroked it down his spine and side to side. Her heart pounded in her chest as she concentrated on drying him. Without even thinking about it, she slid the cloth over the sharp angle of his waist then down both sides of his hips and over his buttocks. She went to her knees and paid extra attention to the drops that had disappeared between his toned ass cheeks.

Zane moved his feet farther apart and she leaned closer to him as she ran the towel down the back of his right leg. When it was dry, she buffed his skin on the way back up, then dried his left leg, being careful around the area of the healing wound. "Turn around, please, Sir."

When he did as she asked, she was on eye level with his erection. Ravyn stared at it, licked her lips, and then concentrated on drying his feet. She worked her way up his left leg, then over his belly and down his right leg. She moved the towel up to his belly and a drop of water ran down from his belly button. She dropped the towel and caught the drop on her tongue. Zane groaned and she rose up on her knees and kissed her way from one side of his flat belly to the other, deliberately avoiding his cock.

His cock rested against her cheek as she kissed him and slid her hands up his torso. The highest she could reach was his nipples, which suited her spur-of-the-moment plan. She strummed her fingers over them and felt them harden as he took a deep breath. She grinned against a hip bone, then licked her way across to the other one and his dick bumped her chin. His chest rose and fell with every stroke of her hands as she traced his muscles. They rippled when she stroked her fingers over them and then grasped his waist and urged him to step back. When his knees hit the edge of the bed, he lowered himself onto it, then lay back with his arms out to his sides, fists clenched.

"Where's Harper?" Zane asked, his voice desperate.

"Jackson and Jenna took him to see the colts."

Ravyn moved between his knees, then licked her way up to his cock. She licked him from his scrotum to the head, then back down. She loved the silky, smooth texture of his cock against her lips and tongue as she used the veins to navigate from the base to the head. Zane groaned when she closed her lips around the mushroom-shaped head and sucked, then whipped her tongue back and forth before tracing circles over the top.

His hands fisted in her hair. "God, Ravyn," he groaned. "Feels so good, pet. So good."

Ravyn pursed her lips around the head, then took more of his shaft into her mouth and pulled back. Each time, she took a little more as she flicked her tongue over him, until she took him to the back of her throat. She swallowed and hummed her pleasure, and he groaned and tightened his fists in her hair.

She pulled off him, then kissed the crease spot where his thigh met his pelvis, then flicked her tongue over his balls. He stilled as she kissed one, then the other, then sucked one into her mouth. She heard him mumble something about torture and almost smiled as she released him and moved to the other one. Her heart pounded out a fierce rhythm and she couldn't seem to pull in enough air as moisture slipped down the inside of her thighs. Ravyn pulled in a deep breath, then moved back to Zane's cock. She sucked the head into her mouth then worked her way down the shaft, flicking her tongue down the length over and over again. She felt him lengthen and harden and took him to the back of her throat and swallowed around the spongey head.

Zane hands pressed down on her head as his cum exploded from his cock and he yelled her name. She swallowed and lashed him with her tongue as he shook and groaned. She sucked on him, then slowly released him and blew her breath across his dick before she stood up and looked down at him. He looked totally wasted and she almost laughed.

"There. I think you're dry now." She smiled, swiveled around, and walked toward the door. "Lunch is ready."

"Ravyn, would it make a difference if I told you I love you?"

Ravyn leaned against the closed door and looked at Zane. He was up on his elbows, watching her. "I love you, too, but words are easy, Zane."

He nodded. "Would you agree that some words are more important than others?"

"Yes, I agree with that."

"I was wrong for not trusting you. When I heard you say you loved Harper, I felt like I'd had my heart torn out." Zane looked away for a moment. "You could marry me and make me grovel. I could get some tips from Logan."

Ravyn smiled. The groveling game Cassie had been playing with Logan had given her and the other royals some great laughs. It was a great game for Luc and Logan and Cassie, but not for her and Zane. She smiled as she felt a small spark of hope flare in her heart. "Are you proposing?"

"Yes. I love you and I want you to marry me." Zane narrowed his eyes at her. "I also want you to be my slave."

"What about your job?"

"I've resigned. I'm going to work with Cade, Thor, and McCabe on their new project."

"You had to resign because of me."

Zane shook his head. "No. I knew I'd have to give up my job when I found you." He smiled. "How would I explain to a judge why you were handcuffed to my side? And, besides I wanted to move back home."

Ravyn saw the sincerity in his eyes and her heart sped up. She was going to be another one of the Ramsey women. All happy fools for the men they loved. She smiled. "You and Harper are going to gang up on me, so my vote will count for two until I can get a daughter of my own."

"I see a lot of stalemates in our future." Zane grinned.

"That's what you get for waiting for the woman you earned."

"Come here and kiss me." Zane reached down and stroked his cock. "I've got something for you, pet."

Ravyn laughed, then shook her head. "Doc said no strenuous activity for you for a week."

"You can be on top, but I'm in charge."

Ravyn shook her head. "I'd die for you, but I won't let you take a risk that I can prevent. Get dressed and come down for lunch."

"I can see we're going to spend a lot of time in the playroom in the future."

"You wouldn't have me any other way." Ravyn smiled, then closed the door behind her. As soon as it closed, she fist-pumped the air and covered her mouth to keep from laughing with the sheer joy of being alive and in love and getting married. There was no doubt in her mind, or her heart, that she was going to be Mrs. Zane Ramsey, but she'd let him sweat for a few days before she gave him the answer he expected.

Epilogue

A week later, Ravyn sat on Zane's lap in Cade's den and wondered what was going on. She kissed his jaw and he glanced at her, then lifted her hand and kissed the three-carat pink diamond he'd place on her finger the night before.

All of the Ramsey brothers, as well as Addison, Jenna, and Cassie, were present. Thor and Marisol sat in the chairs by the window. McCabe sat across from her and Zane, with Deuce a few feet away from him. Trey and True leaned against the back of the couch while Cin and Ace leaned against the wall of bookshelves behind them.

McCabe had just arranged to build a small residential area on the Ramsey ranch for his family and friends he referred to as a clan. Ravyn figured by the time all of the building projects were completed, they'd have a small, populated town. Cade, Thor, and McCabe had agreed that the new buildings would be off the grid and self-sufficient, with plenty of land for animals, gardens and orchards. McCabe had said the females in his clan insisted on growing their own food as well as weaving their own cloth. Ravyn could see from the expressions on the other women's faces that she wasn't the only royal interested in meeting these mysterious women.

The McCabe's had shaved and it was startling to see them together. The only difference between them was the tattoos that circled their arms. The design was a tribal design with the outside line in black, then an inside line in red, but the center was filed in with different colors. McCabe's and Deuce's were black, while Trey and True's were amethyst, and Cin and Ace's were green. She wondered what they meant, then blushed when Cin caught her staring. He winked, then grinned when Zane growled, almost as if he'd heard the low sound.

Ravyn snuggled into Zane. "What are we waiting for now? I thought they'd settled it."

"We're waiting for the DEA to get here," Zane said, just as the door opened and Nate and Isabella walked in.

Ravyn felt Zane stiffen, then curse beneath his breath.

Nate pulled out a leather holder and flashed his badge. Isabella did the same.

"Well, I'll be damned," Cade said.

Nate didn't smile. In fact, Ravyn thought he appeared tense and as if he was being forced to be here.

Isabella stepped forward. "Nate and I were sent here two years ago to keep an eye on Earl Baume and Barbie Johnson. When I heard about the opening Luc and Logan had for a cook, I applied for the job and got it. Several weeks ago on the night Cassie escaped from Luc's and Logan's house, Mendez had sent three men after her. Nate and I managed to intersect them at the truck stop. They're in federal custody and being questioned. We brought the McCabe's in to help us with Ravyn and her little brother."

"You knew about Harper?" Ravyn asked McCabe.

"We found out about him recently and figured out he was the reason you were letting Mendez control you," McCabe said.

"You didn't think that was something we should have known?" Zane asked.

"Not at the time, no," Isabella said, drawing their attention back to her. "You were doing such a good job gathering intel, you made our job easy."

"Mendez will continue to come after all of you until we shut him down," Nate said.

"We're aware of that," Cade said. "We're prepared for it."

Nate nodded. "We were informed this morning that Mendez sent some men after Marisol's sister Valentina. They didn't get her, and now the convent is being guarded by your father's men, Marisol."

Marisol jumped to her feet. "He must not get his hands on her." She turned to Thor. "Please, you have the flash drive. Please help me get my sister out of Colombia."

Thor rose to his feet and slid his arm around her waist. He tugged her into him. "We'll get her, *skjebne*."

McCabe cleared his throat. "My jet is on standby. Cin and Ace are going with you."

Thor nodded. "I'll take Ben and Mac with me as well."

"And, me," Marisol said. "I'm going, and you can't stop me." Thor crowded her and she said, "I mean it. You take me with you or I'll follow you on my own."

Ravyn saw Addison smile as she cuddled closer to Cade and realized this had probably been her plan all along.

Cade grinned, then said, "Better tighten those reins, Thor."

Isabella laughed. "We're going to be sticking around until this is over, and because we're sticking around, there's something else you all need to know."

"Isabella," Nate said, his voice desperate. "Not now."

"Yes, Nate, now. You promised." Isabella looked from one Ramsey brother to the next. "They deserve to know the truth."

Zane stood and lowered Ravyn to her feet but kept his arm around her waist. She felt his hand dig into her as the other brothers rose to their feet.

"Zane?" Ravyn asked, trying to reassure him as the room buzzed with tension. "What's wrong?"

Zane patted her shoulder. "It's okay. Trust me."

Nate paled, then swallowed, and Ravyn swore she saw tears glaze his eyes.

"Go on, Nate. Tell them," Isabella said.

Nate stepped forward. "I go by Nate Grant but my name is Jonathan Grant McLeod. I'm your father."

THE END

WWW.MARDIMAXWELL.COM

ABOUT THE AUTHOR

I was born in Utah, but I've traveled throughout America and lived in sunny California, hot and dry West Texas, and the mountains of Colorado. I wrote my first erotic romance in the summer of 2013. It was accepted and published that same year. Since then, I've written three more books in The Doms of Club Mystique series. At this time, I'm busy writing the fifth and final book in the series. My heroes are tough cowboys with military backgrounds and my heroines are strong, sassy, and submissive. I like my readers to laugh, and cry, so I put a lot of emotion in my books as well as suspense and happy endings.

Other than writing, I love to read, travel, garden, swim with my family, and go to the local drive-in movie with a carload of friends and a huge container of homemade cheese popcorn.

www.facebook.com/MardiMaxwellRomance
www.twitter.com/MardiMaxwellRom

For all titles by Mardi Maxwell, please visit
www.bookstrand.com/mardi-maxwell

Siren Publishing, Inc.
www.SirenPublishing.com

Lightning Source UK Ltd.
Milton Keynes UK
UKOW07f1835190115

244748UK00011B/259/P